Poison is Always in the Prettiest Bottle

The Butcher and the Witch

Book 1

Cassandra Doon

Dedicated to everyone who understands that revenge, like wine, is best served in a gorgeous glass bottle.

A Heads-Up Before You Dive In...

Alright, let's talk triggers. Because apparently, not everyone's cup of tea is a vengeful witch poisoning her enemies with a smile. Shocking, I know. It is what it is.

So, consider this your official, legally-mandated (not really) warning that this book contains a few things that might make you clutch your pearls. Or at least, spill your tea.

Here's a taste of what's in this book:

•**A Touch of the Ol' Ultra-Violence:** There's a bit of a rough-and-tumble. And by 'a bit,' I mean someone probably should have invested in a good stain remover. Think less 'paper cut' and more 'artistic splatter pattern.'

•**Witchcraft, Obviously:** This book is powered by witchcraft, sarcasm, and an unhealthy amount of caffeine. Expect spells, curses, and a general disregard for the laws of both physics and man.

•**Spicy Scenes:** Things get a little... heated. Let's just say there's more than just potions being brewed. You might want to have a fan handy.

•**Salty Language:** Our characters have the vocabulary of a sailor who just stubbed their toe. On a lego. While on fire. You've been warned.

•**Creative Chemistry:** Features a loving homage to the lost art of creative poisoning. Don't try this at home. Seriously. The legal paperwork is a nightmare, and it's so hard to get good belladonna these days.

•**Surprise Protein Sources:** There may or may not be an incident involving someone being sold as wild boar mince. Accidentally, of course. Check your meat labels, folks.

•**Happily Never After:** We deal with some heavy stuff, including domestic violence and abusive relationships. But don't worry, our heroine has a... permanent solution for that.

•**The Great Beyond:** People die. Sometimes messily. It's a whole thing.

So, if you're a fan of morally grey heroines, questionable life choices, and a healthy dose of magical mayhem, you're in the right place. For everyone else... well, you can't say we didn't warn you.

Now, go on. Get reading.

Chapter 1
Face Cream & Fuckery
Genie

The Death card stared up at me from my worn tarot deck, its skeletal rider grinning like he knew something I didn't. Typical Tuesday morning bullshit.

"Not today, you bony bastard," I muttered, flipping the card face down and reaching for my coffee instead.

My name is Genevie Alden—Genie to the living, and a whole lot of other names to the dead. I'm a twenty-six-year-old witch running a skincare boutique in Lancaster, that specialises in natural beauty products with a little something extra. And by "extra", I mean magic; the kind that would make my ancestors proud and the local parish priest reach for his holy water.

I lit a bundle of rosemary and sage, waving it around the shop in lazy figure eights. The smoke curled through the air, sweet and sharp, coiling around the dried herbs hanging from the rafters. My fingers moved automatically—match, burn, wave—while my brain ping-ponged between existential dread and whether I'd remembered to label the new "Youth in a Jar" batch correctly.

Which I hadn't. Fuck.

The shop was my sanctuary—"Alden Alchemy," where the tagline "Transform Your Skin" had a double meaning only I understood. Dried herbs hung from the beams like sleepy witches and the shelves sparkled with amber and green glass jars in my signature sarcastic fonts:

Wrinkles Be Gone (But Your Trauma's Forever)
Witch Hazel, Not a Real Witch (Or Is She?)
and my personal favourite, *Love Potion #FuckOff*

No one outside these walls knew the real magic wasn't just the herbs or the packaging—it was me. Me, and the blood that whispered when I stirred potions in copper bowls. Me, and the tarot that had told me it was okay to kill the man who broke my ribs and tried to break my magic. Me, and the garden in the back where the roses bloomed a little too red over a spot I never talked about.

The bell above the front door jingled like it belonged in a cursed Christmas movie. Bernie, my favourite clumsy-chaos gremlin, stumbled in wearing mismatched boots and a cardigan that looked like it had been in a fight with a bramble bush, dragging a reusable bag full of candles, crushed biscuits, and regret behind him.

"Genie! The good news is I didn't burn the kitchen down," she chirped with the enthusiasm of someone who obviously had come close.

"That means there's bad news," I replied, already bracing myself.

"I tried lighting a candle with my boobs. For Reels."

I didn't even flinch. "That's the sentence that gets me locked up for accessory to idiocy."

She beamed like I'd given her a gold star, then promptly knocked over a display of *Glow Like a Virgin* night cream with her elbow while trying to remove a biscuit from her bag. The sound of glass clinking and a single jar rolling across the floor was my standard morning serenade.

"Bernie," I sighed, rubbing my temple. "This is why we can't have nice things. Or candles. Or Reels."

"Technically…" She fished around in her bag and pulled out what I think used to be a scone. "This is your fault. You left the good matches next to the cinnamon oil."

"Because obviously, the cinnamon oil was going to light itself on fire and give us all warm hugs."

Bernie was the sweetest soul I'd ever met—a twenty-five-year-old disaster who made candles for a living. What she didn't know was that she had an untapped magical ability that manifested in chaos. I'd seen her accidentally set a plant on fire by looking at it too intensely once, and since then I'd kept her close; partly because I adored her and partly because someone needed to ensure she didn't accidentally burn down half of Newchurch in Pendle.

The front door creaked again, this time heralding the entrance of my other roommate. Daisy strolled in like sin personified—wearing last night's crop top, a leather skirt that had definitely seen at least three laps around someone's waist, and sunglasses that cost more than my monthly rent. She carried her iced coffee as if it were a weapon.

If Bernie was a golden retriever with a death wish, Daisy was a lioness in heat who'd slept with the zookeeper, the park ranger, and probably the lion, too.

"If I don't get to drink this caffeine and apply a face mask in the next five minutes, I'm hexing a man," she said, flopping onto the velvet stool near the front counter.

"Line forms behind me," I said, tying my hair into a messy bun before spritzing rosewater onto my cheeks.

Daisy Elin Bjerke was twenty-seven, Norwegian, and had

the sexual appetite of a mythological goddess. Her great-grandmother had been a Sámi witch, although Daisy hadn't inherited any actual magic, she had the confidence of a woman who knew exactly how to use her body as a weapon.

"Is this the new eye serum?" Daisy asked, holding up a jar labelled *Bye-Bye Bags (And Maybe Your Husband)*.

"That's the one," I replied. "Soothes puffiness and delivers poetic justice."

She unscrewed the lid, dabbed some under each eye, and sighed; like I'd personally revived her from the depths of a tequila-induced coma.

"No offense," she said, "but I'd sacrifice a man to keep this in stock."

"Sweetheart." I leaned against the counter. "You've sacrificed a man for less."

"True," she said, and winked.

What Daisy didn't know was that the serum contained a touch of belladonna—not enough to harm, just enough to make her eyes dilate slightly; giving her that doe-eyed, innocent look that made men stupid. It was one of my more popular products among women who knew to ask for it specifically.

I moved to the workroom to check on my latest batch of "Midnight Glow" moisturiser, which contained crushed moonstone and a spell whispered in for protection. The workroom was my true domain—copper bowls and glass beakers lined the shelves, alongside jars of dried herbs labelled in my grandmother's spidery handwriting. A worn grimoire sat open on the workbench; the pages yellowed with age and dappled with various stains from generations of Alden women.

My fingers traced the recipe for a skin-brightening serum, but my mind wandered to the other book hidden beneath the floorboards—the one with recipes that had nothing to do with beauty and everything to do with justice. Or revenge, depending on who you asked.

I'd found it after my parents died, tucked away in a hidden compartment of my mother's vanity. The first page bore a single name in elegant script: Giulia Tofana. Inside was a detailed account of how to create Aqua Tofana, the infamous poison used by women in the 17th century to kill abusive husbands.

My mother had been experimenting with a modern version; one that left no trace for an autopsy. I'd perfected it after my ex-boyfriend decided my ribs looked better broken.

The bell jingled again and pulled me from my thoughts. I closed the grimoire and returned to the front of the shop.

Mrs. Beecham stood at the counter, her seventy-three-year-old frame somehow managing to look both frail and intimidating at the same time. As the self-appointed head of the town's historical society, she knew everything about everyone—or at least, she thought she did.

"Good morning, Genevie," she said, emphasizing my full name like she always did. "I've run out of that lovely hand cream you made me last month."

"The one with lavender and chamomile?" I asked, already reaching for a jar on the shelf behind me.

"Yes, that's the one. My arthritis has been much better since I started using it."

What Mrs. Beecham didn't know was that the cream contained more than just lavender and chamomile. There was a touch of magic in there, too—a simple spell for pain relief that my grandmother had taught me when I was twelve.

"I've added a bit of rosemary this time," I said, handing her the jar. "It should help with circulation."

She nodded approvingly, then leaned in conspiratorially. "Have you heard about the new butcher shop opening up in the old Harrington place? Three men from Ireland, they say. One of them is quite the looker."

I hadn't heard, but I wasn't surprised that Mrs. Beecham had.

"I haven't had the pleasure," I said, ringing up her purchase.

"Well, you might want to pop by. The dark-haired one has eyes that could melt butter." She winked at me, before she paid for her cream and shuffled out of the shop.

Daisy perked up immediately. "New men in town? And butchers? I do love a man who knows how to handle his meat."

Bernie snorted so hard that she knocked over another jar.

"For fuck's sake, Bernie," I sighed, grabbing a broom that was kept close by for this very reason. "That's the third one this week."

"Sorry," she mumbled, her face flushing red. "But Daisy's right. We should check out the new butcher shop. For... meat purposes."

"Meat purposes," I repeated flatly. "Sure."

The truth was, I didn't have time for men, no matter how butter-melting their eyes were. I had a business to run, potions to brew, and occasionally, justice to serve; with tiny bottles labelled *For Emergency Use Only.*

But as I swept up the broken glass, the Death card flashed in my mind again. Death didn't always mean literal death in tarot—sometimes it meant transformation, endings that led to beginnings. Change.

I glanced at the calendar on the wall. It was the first day of September, only one month from when the veil between worlds grew thinner and my magic grew stronger. Samhain was approaching, the most powerful time of the year for a witch with Pendle blood in her veins.

Perhaps it was time for a change. Or at least, time to buy some meat.

I dusted the counter with crushed lavender and smirked at my reflection in the gilded mirror by the register. I whispered to no one in particular, "Let the fuckery begin."

The bell jingled again. Customer.

Business was open.

Chapter 2
This Shit is Organic
Genie

I always knew when someone wasn't here for the skincare. It was noticeable in the twitchy fingers, the red-rimmed eyes, and the way they hovered near the display of *Glow Like a Virgin;* like they were trying to remember how it felt to be untouched by trauma—or a man's stupidity.

She came in around ten the next day, wrapped in a camel-coloured coat that exuded wealth, but with a nervous energy that clung to her almost like static. Early thirties, gold band still on her finger and foundation layered too thick to success-fully cover a fading bruise just beneath her right cheekbone.

Victim.

But not for long.

"Good morning," I said, as I smiled with just enough sweetness to be disarming. "Here for something gentle or something that bites back?"

She blinked, startled, then forced a smile. "I… I heard you have a night serum. Midnight something?" she asked hesitantly.

I leaned forward, resting my hands on the polished wood

counter. "Midnight Renewal Serum," I said smoothly. "Brightens the skin, softens fine lines... and offers certain enhancements if you know what to ask for."

The woman licked her lips, clearly trying to decide how far to trust me. Her gaze darted around the shop.

No one else was in sight. Daisy was upstairs doing a vibrator review for her subscribers. Bernie had gone down the road to pick up the herbs I'd ordered from the local greengrocer, which meant she'd probably return with the wrong herbs and a stray cat.

"You want fast or slow?" I asked, voice low.

Her shoulders tensed. "How... how fast is fast?" she whispered.

"Fast is 'he takes one bite of the pasta, and you're widowed by dessert.' Slow is 'he deteriorates mysteriously over the next two weeks, and everyone thinks he had a stroke,'" I explained.

She hesitated. "Slow," she decided.

Of course. The ones who'd been beaten didn't want blood. They wanted peace.

"Follow me," I said, slipping behind the counter and opening the panel that led to the side room.

She stepped inside as if she were entering a church. The room was warm, lit by low amber sconces and candles. Shelves lined with labelled jars—some neat, some scrawled like curses—covered every wall.

The air smelled like honey and smoke, with subtle hints of nettle and clove. I could feel the magic humming in the floorboards; the same magic that had flowed through generations of Alden women.

"This one's subtle," I say, moving to the shelf labelled *Quiet Vengeance*. "But effective."

I pulled down a dark amber bottle, sealed with wax and wrapped in black silk ribbon.

The label read: *Midnight Renewal–Night Use Only. Only for Arseholes.*

She gave a soft, strangled laugh. I handed it to her gently.

"Inside, you've got a very special blend," I began, my voice shifting into the tone I reserved for real magic. "At the base: foxglove, belladonna, and monkshood—small amounts, enough to build up in the system over time if used consistently."

Her eyes widened. "Won't they show up...?" she asked nervously.

I shook my head. "Not if you mix it with food or drinks. They degrade fast in high heat and metabolise cleanly. No one will suspect anything, unless they're specifically testing for poison. And most coroners in Lancashire haven't been trained to even look for monkshood since the 1970s" I assured her.

I turned the bottle in my hand. "I've also included yew bark extract—mildly cardiotoxic, enough to cause arrhythmia. Chamomile and valerian root to soothe the nervous system—makes him sleepy, calm, off guard," I continued.

A small, almost vicious spark lit in her eyes.

"Use three drops in his evening tea," I instructed. "Every night. It'll take effect slowly—fatigue, mood swings, tremors, insomnia, and hallucinations. By the second week, he'll be too exhausted to lift a hand. By week three, his heart won't remember how to beat right."

She swallowed hard, holding the bottle like it might shatter. "And no one will know?" she asked.

"Unless you tell them," I replied. "Or unless you overdose him. Then it's messy. And obvious."

She nodded. I could see her calculating, thinking of the

bruises, the fear, the silence. The way she probably looked over her shoulder every time she boiled the kettle.

"Seventy-five pounds," I said gently.

She dug into her handbag, counted the notes with trembling fingers, and handed them over.

As she turned to leave, I added, "One more thing."

She paused.

"If you change your mind and want fast, come back and ask for 'Aphrodite's Escape.' That one works in under twenty minutes," I told her.

Her eyes met mine. For a second, we were no longer shopkeeper and customer. We were women. We were survivors.

"I'll remember," she said quietly.

She left without another word.

I sat back down at the bench in my little room and opened my grimoire. My handwriting was neat, clinical:

Client #219.
Brunette.
Wedding ring.
Right cheek bruise.
Chose 'slow.'

I flipped my tarot deck.
Tower.
Lovers.
Of fucking course.

I blew out a sigh and scribbled that down too. Sometimes the cards were subtle. Sometimes they were drunk and screaming.

The Tower meant sudden change, upheaval. The Lovers could represent choices, and relationships. Together, they whispered of a relationship about to be violently transformed. Fitting for a woman about to poison her husband, but something about the combination made my skin prickle.

Daisy peeked her head in. "Did someone just buy the 'marry and bury' blend?" she asked, her eyes wide with curiosity.

"Yes," I replied as I looked up at her, "and she tipped."

"She's my hero," Daisy declared with genuine admiration.

"You said that about the lady who fake-applied it to her husband and left him for his chiropractor," I reminded her.

"Still a hero," Daisy insisted with a shrug, then disappeared back up the stairs again.

I rolled my eyes and stood to re-label a few of the more volatile jars. My fingers hovered over jars of crushed poppy, henbane, datura—each one labelled not just with their contents, but what they were best used for:

Datura–Confusion, hallucinations. Use for gaslighting.
Henbane–Excellent in meat sauces. Bitter aftertaste.
Yarrow–Stops bleeding. Keep on hand when Daisy shaves
drunk again.

I loved this room. It smelled like power. And rosemary. Also, a little bit like bleach, because Bernie had once tried to clean it with lavender bleach and nearly passed out.

I'd inherited my house and my magic from the family bloodline. The bodies of every member are in the pendle cemetery, in my family plot. The official report said they died in a car accident, but I'd always had my suspicions. My mother wasn't careless, and my father was the most cautious driver I'd ever known. My mother had helped women like the one I'd just served. Everything I did was for women like that one.

Quiet. Afraid. Desperate.

Until they weren't.

I walked back into the front of the shop just as Daisy stumbled back down the stairs, wearing a silk robe and one of my face masks.

"Is Bernie back?" she asked, adjusting her cleavage.

"Not yet," I answered.

She leaned over the counter and eyed the tarot deck. "Did you pull the Tower again?" she asked knowingly.

"I don't wanna talk about it," I muttered.

"Bet it's a sex omen," she suggested with a waggle of her eyebrows.

"You say that every time," I pointed out.

"And one day, I'll be right," Daisy insisted confidently.

She kissed my cheek, then snatched a serum off the shelf.

"Gonna go take a bath and flirt with ghosts. Yell if you need me," she announced.

"You know we have a bathtub at home, right?" I reminded her.

"Yeah, but the shop one has better acoustics for my Reels," she explained over her shoulder.

I didn't bother arguing. Daisy was a force of nature, and trying to redirect her was like trying to convince a hurricane to take a different route.

The bell over the door jingled again, and Bernie burst in, her arms full of paper bags that were already starting to tear at the bottom.

"I got the herbs!" she announced triumphantly, seconds before one of the bags gave way completely, spilling dried lavender, rosemary, and what suspiciously looked like catnip all over the floor.

"And apparently half the garden centre," I muttered, moving to help her.

"The guy at the shop gave me extra," she said, beaming. "He said I had a nice smile."

"Did he also say you had nice tits?" Daisy called from the staircase.

Bernie blushed furiously. "No! He was just being nice," she protested.

"Men aren't nice without an agenda," I said, gathering the scattered herbs. "Especially not to pretty girls who look like they'd believe anything."

"That's not true," Bernie argued. "Some men are genuinely kind."

Daisy and I exchanged a look as she comes back down the staircase. Bernie's unwavering belief in the goodness of people was both her most endearing quality and the reason we never let her go to bars alone.

"Speaking of men," Bernie continued, "I walked past that new butcher shop on my way back. It's opening tomorrow."

"And?" Daisy perked up.

"And there were three guys setting up. One of them was..." She paused as if searching for the right word. "Intense," she finally said.

"Intense how?" I asked, despite myself.

"Dark hair, blue eyes, tattoos. He was breaking down a side of beef with a cleaver, and he didn't even look like he was trying. Just—" She made a chopping motion. "Like it was nothing," Bernie explained, clearly impressed.

"Sounds like my type," Daisy said, grinning.

"He's everyone's type," Bernie replied. "But he wasn't the one who noticed me. The posh one did. Tall, fancy watch, looked like he'd rather be anywhere else." Bernie continued, "they're having a grand opening tomorrow. Free samples and everything."

"We should go," Daisy said immediately. "For research purposes."

"Research into what?" I asked sceptically. "The tensile strength of their meat?"

"Among other things," she replied with a wink.

I rolled my eyes, but I couldn't deny the flicker of curiosity. Mrs. Beecham's comment about the dark-haired one with eyes that could melt butter had planted the seed, and Bernie's description had watered it.

Not that I was interested. I didn't have time for men, especially not intense ones with blue eyes and tattoos, that could break down a side of beef without trying. Men were complications, and my life was complicated enough.

Chapter 3
Red Flags & Dead Men
Genie

Mondays were sacred.

No shop. No customers. No pretending that 'Miracle Youth Drops' weren't quietly laced with the smallest trace of something that would gently encourage a bastard's demise. Mondays were for me, and the house that still breathed with the ghosts of family members.

The Alden estate had been standing on the edge of Newchurch-in-Pendle for over three centuries. It had the look of something half alive and half wanting to crumble. Ivy crawled over the grey stone walls like it had a vendetta against the architecture. The windows creaked when the wind blew, and the pipes moaned like lonely banshees trapped within copper prisons. The floorboards remembered every secret whispered within the walls, and sometimes, in the dead of night, I swore they tried to tell me them.

But now, she was mine.

My home. My graveyard. My sanctuary.

I padded barefoot across the old wooden floors, the boards groaning under my weight like they were tired of keeping secrets. My robe trailed behind me; its dark green velvet catching bits of dust and fallen lavender heads that'd fallen from the dried bundles hanging from the rafters. The air smelled of smoke, and soil, with a subtle hint of decay kissed with roses; the perfume of my particular brand of justice.

I had a new potion brewing in the basement—one that required fresh rose petals from the garden. A special order for a woman whose husband had a wandering eyes and wandering hands; especially around their teenage daughter. This one needed to be perfectly balanced: slow enough to seem natural, fast enough to save the girl.

I hated going into the garden, but, the petals had to be cut at their peak—right before the sun had reached them; when their oils were the strongest and their magic most potent. I slipped on my boots, tied my hair up in a messy knot and I grabbed my silver-handled shears—the ones that had belonged to my grandmother, their handles worn smooth from generations of Alden women who'd harvested ingredients for spells; both benevolent and deadly.

My breath fogged as I stepped into the garden, the chill of early autumn seeping through my robe and settling against my skin. The morning was mist-wrapped, dew clinging to the grass like tears. The garden was wild and overgrown by design—herbs, flowers, and poisonous plants all intermingling in a chaotic tapestry that only I could read.

The roses were in full bloom. Deep crimson. Lush. Vicious. Their thorns gleamed like tiny daggers in the pale morning light.

Their scent hit me, ensnaring me in a memory.

And I was trapped back there.

He had a laugh like broken glass.

That was the first red flag. Not the bruises, no, they came later. Not the way he twisted my words or isolated me from study groups. No. It was the sound of him laughing—sharp and mocking; like something mean pretending to be charming.

James Whitmore. Top of our chemistry class. Smarter than everyone, and he knew it. He liked that I was clever, too —until he didn't. Until my grades edged past his, and suddenly my intelligence became a threat, rather than an attraction.

It started with words. Always does. A sharp comment about my grades. About my clothes. About how I didn't really need to ace the lab work, when he could "help me." Each criticism was delivered with that glass-shard laugh, as if cruelty was just a joke and I was too sensitive to understand.

Then came the hands.

The first time, he pushed me during an argument about a research paper. I'd tripped and fallen into the counter. The bruise bloomed across my hip like a poisonous flower. He apologised with roses, chocolate, and a poem he copied from some dead poet's website. I believed him because I wanted to. Because love makes you stupid sometimes.

The second time, it was a slap. Quick and shocking, leaving my cheek burning and my eyes wide with disbelief. He cried afterward, blamed his father, stress, and the pressures of finals. I forgave him, because I thought I understood broken things.

The third time, it was a punch. Deliberate. Calculated. Right to the ribs; where no one would see. I heard something crack inside me—not just my bones, but something fundamental. Something that had once believed in second chances.

By then, I wasn't Genie anymore. I was a ghost in my own skin. I wore foundation thick enough to coat a car. I smiled at professors and pretended I was just clumsy. I stopped calling *friends. Stopped going home on weekends. Stopped believing I deserved better.*

But I never stopped learning.

I knew the exact dose of digitalis that would make someone's heart forget its rhythm. I knew what belladonna tasted like when slipped into red wine—sweet and slightly bitter, with an aftertaste like copper pennies. I knew that lime, when poured over a body, could eat through flesh like fire through paper; leaving nothing but bones and secrets.

I waited. I planned. I brewed.

Then one night, he came home drunk. Reeking of whiskey and another woman's perfume, his eyes bloodshot and mean.

I was in the attic, making a tincture of valerian and yew bark. My tarot cards sat beside the steaming copper pot, as always. I pulled them, heart in my throat, hands trembling with a mixture of fear and something darker, something that tasted like revenge.

The Fool. The Wheel of Fortune.

A beginning. A turning point.

He found me upstairs and started screaming. Said I was a freak with my herbs and cards. Told me he was done playing house with a witch. That I was a waste of space, a burden, damaged goods. The way he called me a witch, like it was the worst thing a woman could be.

He was wrong.

The first punch came out of nowhere. Straight to the ribs, right where the old fracture was still healing. The pain exploded like fireworks behind my eyes. The second made my vision go white, stars bursting across a field of nothing. The third never landed.

Because I moved.

I grabbed the boiling pot and hurled it at him. The tincture hissed as it splashed across his chest, burning through his designer shirt and onto the skin beneath. He screamed. Stumbled backward. Slipped on the slick wood floor. His head hit the corner of my grandmother's antique trunk with a sickening crack that echoed through the attic like a gunshot.

I don't know if it was the potion, or the fall, or the rage in my bones that killed him. But he was dead. His eyes stared up at the ceiling, empty and accusing all at once.

I stared at his body for a long time. Watched as blood pooled beneath his head, dark and thick against the worn floorboards. Watched as his chest remained still, no breath, no movement. Watched as the man who had tried to break me, broke instead.

Then I cleaned.

Bleach. Gloves. Incense to mask the smell. More bleach. I scrubbed until my hands were raw and the floor was spotless. I burned the rug. Washed the pot seven times. Showered until the hot water ran out, then kept standing under the cold spray, watching as invisible blood circled the drain.

I wrapped his body in canvas from my painting stash and hauled him down to the garden with trembling arms; his weight almost too much for me to bear. Dug the hole with a rusted shovel as the moon watched, impassive and cold. My breath came in wet sobs. My hands bled from blisters. The soil clung to me like guilt.

I poured lime over him—buckets of it. Covered him with earth. Planted three rose bushes. I prayed they'd thrive.

They did.

They bloomed brighter than any others out here. Fed by death, justice, and the bones of a man who thought he could break a witch.

The memory faded like the morning mist; I came back to myself with shears hovering over a fresh bloom. My hands were steady now, no longer the trembling things they'd been that night. Time and practice had hardened me.

The ruby red petals were velvet-soft against my fingers. I snipped them gently, dropping them into my copper bowl one by one, whispering a small incantation with each cut. The roses seemed to sigh as I harvested them; as if they understood their purpose.

"Morning ritual?" Bernie's voice startled me from my trance as it floated from the kitchen window.

"Harvesting sacrifice flowers," I called back, keeping my tone light despite the heaviness in my chest.

"Oh, cute. Death by dewdrop vibes," she replied cheerfully.

I rolled my eyes, smiling despite myself. Bernie had a way of making even the darkest things seem somehow whimsical. It was why I kept her around—that and the fact her untapped magic needed supervision.

She poked her head out the window, her blonde hair wild around her face, a smudge of what looked like pancake batter on her cheek. "You sure you don't want to call that poison something prettier? Like... 'Twilight's Kiss' or 'Lover's Respite'?" she suggested.

"It's a slow death serum, Bernie. Not a rom com," I replied dryly.

"Fine. But if I ever kill a man, I want mine labelled 'Moonlight Murder,'" she declared with surprising conviction for someone who apologised to spiders before removing them from the house.

"Duly noted," I promised, gathering the last of the petals.

I headed back inside with the bowl, heart pounding, stomach churning. The roses' scent followed me, sweet and cloying, a reminder that the past never really stayed buried.

Especially when you plant roses over it.

The kitchen was warm and bright; a stark contrast to the misty garden and the even darker corners of my mind. Bernie had made coffee and pancakes, the latter slightly burned around the edges. Daisy sat at the island, scrolling through her phone, her hair wrapped in a towel.

"Morning, murder queen," Daisy greeted without looking up. "Nice harvest?"

"Bountiful," I replied, setting the bowl of petals on the counter. "The dead do make excellent fertiliser."

"Gross," Bernie commented, flipping another pancake with more enthusiasm than skill. "But also, kind of poetic."

"Speaking of poetic," Daisy said, finally looking up from her phone, "don't forget we're checking out the butcher shop today. Grand opening. Free meat. Hot men with knives."

I groaned. "I didn't forget. I was hoping you did."

"Not a chance," Daisy grinned, her eyes gleaming with mischief. "I've been practicing my 'I'm interested in your meat' face all morning."

"Please tell me that's not the face you were making in the bathroom mirror," Bernie said, sliding a plate of misshapen pancakes toward Daisy. "Because it looked more like constipation than seduction."

"You're just jealous because your flirting technique is to blush and knock things over," Daisy retorted, as she drowned her pancakes in syrup.

"It works!" Bernie protested, as she moved to the coffee machine. "Men find clumsiness endearing."

"Men find anything with a pulse endearing, especially if they think it might lead to sex," I muttered, taking the coffee Bernie offered me. "Which is why I'm not interested in meeting the new butchers."

"Liar," Daisy accused, pointing her fork at me. "You've

been curious ever since Mrs. Beecham mentioned the dark-haired one with the butter-melting eyes."

I hadn't. Much. Maybe a little. But only because it had been a while since anything new happened in Newchurch-in-Pendle, and a butcher shop run by three men from Ireland was practically headline news for our small town.

"I'm only going because you two will probably need supervision," I responded, sipping my coffee. "Bernie will accidentally set something on fire, and you'll try to seduce all three of them simultaneously."

"That's the plan," Daisy confirmed with a wink.

I shook my head, but there was no real annoyance behind it. These two chaotic women were the closest thing to family I had now. Daisy, with her unapologetic sexuality and surprising loyalty. Bernie with her clumsy sweetness and hidden power. They balanced me, ensuring I never sunk too deep into the darkness that sometimes threatened to swallow me whole.

"But I'm finishing this potion first. And I'm not dressing up." I responded.

"No one asked you to," Daisy said, then paused. "But maybe wear the green sweater? The one that makes your eyes look like you're about to either kiss someone or kill them?"

"That's all my sweaters," I pointed out.

"Exactly," she grinned.

I grabbed the coffee cup and my bowl of rose petals and headed toward the basement door. "Give me an hour. Then we can go meet your meat men."

"They're not my meat men, *yet*," Daisy called after me. "But by noon, at least one of them will be."

I descended into the cool darkness of the basement, my sanctuary within our sanctuary. Here, among the shelves of ingredients and ancient grimoires, I could breathe. Here, I could be exactly what James had accused me of being—a witch. A woman with power. A force to be reckoned with.

I set the rose petals beside the simmering cauldron and began to work; pushing thoughts of blue-eyed butchers and painful memories aside. I had a potion to brew, and justice to dispense.

The rest could wait.

Chapter 4
Meat and Greet
Ciarán

Blood. The smell of it, no matter how many times I washed them, clung to my hands. Not that I minded —blood had been my constant companion for longer than I cared to remember.

"Dia dhuit ar maidin daoibh go léir," I muttered to the empty shop as I flipped the sign from 'Closed' to 'Open.' *Good morning to you all*. Old habits from home died hard.

The butcher shop gleamed in the early morning light. We'd spent weeks getting the place ready, pristine white tiles, polished steel counters and glass display cases just waiting to be filled with the day's cuts; transforming the abandoned storefront into something that would have made even my da proud, God rest his soul.

"Oi, Ciarán! Stop admiring your reflection and help me with this bloody pig!" Fraser bellowed from the back room.

I rolled my eyes. "Coming, ya eejit," I called back, my Irish accent thickening as it always did when I was tired or annoyed—or both.

Fraser Boyd stood over a massive sow, cleaver in hand, his muscled forearms already spattered with blood despite the early hour. At thirty-four, the Scotsman was built like a brick shithouse and had the temperament of a bear with a hangover.

"About fuckin' time," he grumbled, wiping sweat from his brow with his sleeve. "Thought you were out there reciting poetry to the shop window."

"Póg mo thóin," I replied with a smirk. *Kiss my arse.*

"Speak English, you Irish bastard," Fraser said, but there was no heat in it. We'd been through too much together for any real anger.

I grabbed my cleaver and took position opposite him. The weight of the blade felt right in my hand—familiar, balanced, deadly. Not so different from other tools I'd wielded in my previous life. The life I'd left behind in Dublin; where things got too hot, too bloody, and far too complicated.

"Where's his lordship?" I asked, nodding toward the empty space where our third partner should have been.

Fraser snorted. "Theo's doing the books. Says his delicate hands aren't made for morning butchery."

"Posh wanker," I muttered, though there was some affection to it. Theo Winthrop III might be a trust fund escapee with the manners of royalty, but he'd saved our arses more than once with his financial wizardry.

We worked in companionable silence, breaking down the pig with practiced efficiency. My hands moved automatically—slice, separate, trim—while my mind wandered. This shop was supposed to be our fresh start. A legitimate business far from the shadows of Dublin and Glasgow. A place where the only blood on our hands would be from animals, not men.

At least that was the plan.

"Nervous about the grand opening?" Fraser asked, interrupting my thoughts.

I shrugged. "It's just meat, lad. Not rocket science."

"It's a small town," he reminded me. "Everyone will be watching. Judging."

"Let them," I said, perhaps more sharply than intended. "We've faced worse than gossiping villagers."

Fraser raised an eyebrow but said nothing. He knew my history—or parts of it, anyway. Knew I'd done things for certain people in Dublin that couldn't be undone. I still woke up sweating, reaching for a weapon that wasn't there.

"Speaking of gossiping villagers," Theo's crisp voice cut through the silence as he appeared in the doorway looking immaculate in a button-down shirt, despite the early hour. "Mrs. Beecham has been peering through the window for the last five minutes. I think she's our first customer."

"Christ on a bike," I muttered. "That woman could talk the hind legs off a donkey."

"Be nice," Theo warned. "She's the town gossip. Get her on our side, and half our marketing is done for us."

I wiped my hands on my apron and headed to the front, plastering on what I hoped was a welcoming smile. "Good morning, ma'am. Welcome to Boyd, Winthrop, and Ó Duinn Butchers."

Mrs. Beecham was exactly as advertised—seventy-something, sharp-eyed, and came with the air of someone who collected secrets like some collected stamps. "Oh my," she tittered, looking me up and down. "You must be the Irish one."

"Guilty as charged," I replied, leaning slightly on the accent. Women of a certain age seemed to love it, and I wasn't above using that to my advantage.

"I'll take a pound of your best sausages," she said, "and any gossip you might have about why three handsome young men, like yourselves, have chosen our little town to set up shop."

I chuckled. "The sausages I can provide. The gossip will cost extra."

She cackled at that, the sound like rusty hinges. "Cheeky! I like you. You know, there's a lovely young woman who runs the skincare shop down the street. Single, too."

"Is that right?" I replied noncommittally, wrapping her sausages in paper.

"Genevie Alden. Comes from old Pendle stock. Bit odd, but pretty as a picture. Those eyes of hers—as green as poison, my Harold used to say."

Something in her tone made me pause. "Poison, eh?"

Mrs. Beecham leaned in conspiratorially. "The Alden's have always had a reputation. Some say witchcraft, though not to their faces. Her parents died in a car crash a few years back. Very sad. Left her the old family estate out in Newchurch and enough money to buy that shop in town."

I nodded, filing away the information. Witchcraft. Old family. Parents dead. Interesting.

"Well, I'll have to stop by and introduce myself," I said, handing her the wrapped package. "Neighbourly courtesy and all that."

"You do that," she replied with a knowing smile. "Just mind those eyes of hers. They see more than most."

After Mrs. Beecham left, the floodgates opened. Word had spread about the new butcher shop, and it seemed every resident of Newchurch-in-Pendle and the surrounding area needed meat that day. Fraser manned the back, breaking down carcasses and preparing cuts. Theo handled the register with his private school charm. And I worked the counter, wrapping packages while making small talk; playing the stereotypical role of friendly Irish butcher.

By noon, my cheeks hurt from smiling, and my brain was numb from answering the same questions over and over. Yes,

I was from Ireland. Dingle, originally. No, I didn't know their cousin in Cork—Ireland wasn't that small. Yes, the accent was real. No, I didn't have a lucky charm.

"I need a smoke," I announced during a rare lull. "Back in five."

"Don't get lost," Theo called after me. "The next rush will start soon."

I stepped outside, the cool autumn air a blessed relief after the warmth of working the shop. I leaned against the brick wall, lit a cigarette, and took a deep drag, letting the smoke fill my lungs. The nicotine hit my bloodstream, and I felt my shoulders relax slightly.

That's when I saw them.

Three women were walking up the street toward the shop, laughing and talking animatedly. Even from a distance they commanded attention—like a force of nature, wrapped in human forms.

The first was tall and Nordic-looking, with platinum blonde hair that cascaded down her back. She moved like sex on legs, all swaying hips and knowing smiles. Her outfit—tight jeans and a crop top despite the autumn chill—left little to the imagination, and from the way she carried herself, that was entirely intentional.

Beside her walked a shorter woman with a riot of curls and the wide-eyed look of someone perpetually surprised by life. She practically bounced as she walked, gesturing wildly while she spoke, and nearly tripped on a crack in the pavement. There was something endearing about her clumsiness, like a puppy that hadn't grown into its paws.

And then there was the third woman.

"Mo Dhia," I whispered. *My God.*

She walked slightly behind the other two, her posture straight and confident. Dark hair pulled back in a messy knot, revealing the elegant line of her neck. She wore a green sweater that hugged her curves and made her eyes—visible even from this distance—gleam like emeralds. There was something almost predatory in her gaze as it swept the street, something that spoke of secrets and power.

This, I instinctively knew was, Genevie Alden; the witch with poison-green eyes.

As if she heard my thoughts, her gaze snapped to mine. For a moment, the world seemed to still. The cigarette burned away; forgotten between my fingers. Something electric passed between us—recognition, challenge, desire—I couldn't name it, but it felt like a physical blow.

She stumbled slightly, clearly caught off guard. The blonde reached out to steady her, before following her gaze to where I stood. A slow, knowing smile spread across the blonde's face as she leaned in and whispered something in the dark-haired woman's ear. Whatever she said made Genevie's cheeks flush and her eyes narrow.

"Tá sí go hálainn," I murmured to myself. *She is beautiful.*

The three women continued toward the shop, the blonde now openly staring at me with appreciation, the curly-haired one trying to appear to not look while stealing glances, and Genevie—Genevie was pointedly not looking at all, her jaw set in a stubborn line.

I took one last drag of my cigarette, crushed it under my boot, and headed back inside. I had a feeling the day was about to get a lot more interesting.

The bell above the door jingled as the three women entered the shop. Fraser, the lucky bastard, was already at the counter, turning on the charm for the blonde.

"Welcome to Boyd, Winthrop, and Ó Duinn," he greeted them, his Scottish accent thickening as it always did around attractive women. "What can I get for you lovely ladies today?"

The blonde leaned on the counter, giving Fraser an excellent view of her cleavage. "I've heard you have the best meat in town," she purred, the innuendo impossible to miss.

"Jesus, Mary, and Joseph," I muttered under my breath, moving to the back counter to prepare some cuts for display.

"I thought you were from Ireland?" the blonde asked, turning her attention to Fraser. "I mean, that was the word around town..."

Theo stepped forward, his English accent crisp and proper. "Oh no, just that idiot over there," he said, pointing at me with a smirk.

I flipped him off without looking up, which made the blonde laugh.

"I'm Daisy," she introduced herself, extending a hand to Fraser, who took it and held it perhaps a second too long. "This is Bernie," she added, nodding to the curly-haired woman who was now examining the display case with intense concentration. "And this is Genie."

Genie. Not Genevie. The nickname suited her somehow —magical, powerful, contained in a deceptively delicate vessel.

"Fraser Boyd," the Scotsman replied, still holding Daisy's hand. "The posh one is Theo Winthrop, and the surly one with the knife is Ciarán Ó Duinn."

I looked up then, meeting Genie's eyes directly for the first time. "Dia dhuit," I said, the Gaelic slipping out before I could stop it.

She raised an eyebrow. "English, please. Some of us don't speak 'brooding Irishman.'"

"It means hello," I translated, a smile tugging at the

corner of my mouth. "Though, I could teach you some more interesting phrases if you'd like."

"I'll pass," she replied coolly, though there was a spark in her eyes that belied her tone. "I'm just here for the meat."

"Aren't we all," Daisy murmured, still gazing at Fraser.

Bernie, who'd been quiet until now, suddenly spoke up. "Do you have any lamb? I'm making a stew tonight."

Theo stepped forward, seemingly relieved to have a normal customer question. "We have some excellent shoulder cuts. Perfect for slow cooking."

As Theo helped Bernie, and Fraser continued his flirtation with Daisy, I found myself face to face with Genie from across the counter.

"What can I get you?" I asked, keeping my voice professional despite the way my pulse had picked up.

She studied the display case, her expression unreadable. "Two ribeye steaks. Thick cut."

I selected two perfect steaks and began wrapping them. "Special occasion?"

"Does dinner need to be a special occasion?" she countered.

"It does when you're buying the best steaks in the case," I replied. "Most people save these for birthdays or anniversaries."

She shrugged. "Maybe, I just appreciate quality."

"In meat, or men?" The words slipped out before I could stop them.

Her eyes narrowed. "Excuse me?"

"Ah, shite," I muttered. "That came out wrong."

"Did it?" she challenged. "Or did you just say exactly what you were thinking?"

I met her gaze steadily. "I think you know the answer to that, Genevie Alden."

Her eyes widened slightly at the use of her full name. "How do you—"

"Small town," I interrupted with a shrug. "People talk."

"About me?" she asked, a dangerous edge to her voice.

"About everyone," I clarified. "But especially about the beautiful witch who runs the skincare shop."

For a moment, she looked genuinely startled, then her expression hardened. "I'm not a witch," she stated, but there was something in her tone—a hesitation, with careful precision—that told me she was lying.

"No?" I leaned in slightly, lowering my voice. "Then why do I feel like I've been hexed since the moment I saw you walking up the street?"

Her cheeks flushed, but her gaze remained steady. "That's not witchcraft, Mr. Ó Duinn. That's just your ego talking."

I laughed, genuinely amused by her sharpness. "Maybe so. But I'd still like to find out."

"Find out what?" she asked warily.

"If you're as magical as they say," I replied, holding out the wrapped steaks.

As she reached for them, our fingers brushed. A jolt of something—electricity, awareness, desire—passed between us. She pulled back quickly, almost dropping the package.

"Careful there," I said softly. "Wouldn't want to waste good meat."

"I never waste anything," she replied, her voice equally soft, with an undercurrent of steel. "Especially not on men who aren't worth it."

"Ouch," I pressed a hand to my chest in mock hurt. "You wound me, and we've only just met."

"You'll survive," she said dryly. "Though if you don't, I know several excellent places to hide a body."

I grinned, delighted by her darkness. "I bet you do."

She opened her mouth to reply, but Daisy interrupted, linking arms with her. "Come on, Genie. We've got that thing to get to."

"What thing?" Genie asked, confusion evident on her face.

"You know," Daisy insisted, giving her a meaningful look. "That very important thing we discussed this morning."

Bernie joined them, clutching her wrapped lamb. "Oh, are we leaving? But I was just asking Theo about his marinade recipe."

"We'll come back another time," Daisy promised, already steering them toward the door. "Thanks for the meat, boys. It was... enlightening."

Fraser watched them go with undisguised appreciation. "Christ on a crutch," he breathed once the door closed behind them. "That blonde is something else."

"Daisy," Theo supplied. "And the curly-haired one is Bernie. She's quite sweet, actually."

"And the dark-haired one is Genevie Alden," I added. "Though she goes by Genie."

Both men turned to look at me.

"How do you know that?" Theo asked suspiciously.

I shrugged. "Mrs. Beecham mentioned her this morning. Said she runs the skincare shop down the street."

"Alden Alchemy," Fraser nodded. "Heard about it from one of the customers. Apparently, she makes all the products herself. Organic, herbal stuff. Women in town swear by it."

"Interesting," I murmured, my mind already turning over the possibilities. A woman with an old name, with a reputation for witchcraft, that made potions and creams in a shop called 'Alchemy.' It was almost too perfect.

"Don't even think about it," Theo warned, reading my

expression. "We're here to keep a low profile, remember? Not to get tangled up with the local women."

"I'm not thinking anything," I protested innocently.

"Bullshite," Fraser coughed into his hand.

I grinned. "Alright, maybe I'm thinking something. But it's nothing sinister."

"With you, it never starts sinister," Theo sighed. "It just ends that way."

The rest of the day passed in a blur of customers, meat, and more small talk. By closing time, my feet ached and my shoulders were tight from hours of cutting and wrapping. But the till was full, and we'd made a good impression on the town. All in all, was a successful first day.

"Pint?" Fraser suggested as we locked up the shop. "There's a pub just down the road. The Pendle Witch, coincidentally enough."

"God, yes," Theo agreed. "I need alcohol after dealing with the public all day."

I nodded, though my mind was still on Genie and her 'poison-green' eyes. "Lead the way."

The Pendle Witch was exactly what you'd expect from a small-town English pub—low-beamed ceilings, and worn wooden floors, with a bar polished by generations of elbows. It was busy but not overly crowded; the after-work mob settling in for an evening pint.

And there they were, the three women from earlier, seated at a corner table. Daisy spotted us first and begun waving enthusiastically.

"Look who it is!" she called. "The meat men!"

" Dia a shábháil sinn," I muttered. *God save us.*

Fraser made a beeline for their table, sliding into the seat next to Daisy with a grin. "Ladies. Fancy meeting you here."

Theo hesitated, then shrugged and joined them, taking the

seat beside Bernie, who immediately knocked over her glass of water in surprise.

"Oh! I'm so sorry!" she exclaimed, frantically mopping up the spill with napkins.

"No harm done," Theo assured her, his usual aristocratic reserve softening slightly.

I stood at the bar, watching the scene unfold. Genie sat stiffly, her back to the wall, her eyes darting between her friends and the door. When she caught me looking, she glared; a clear warning to stay away.

Naturally, I did the opposite.

I ordered a round of drinks and carried them to the table, setting one deliberately in front of Genie. "Peace offering," I said, sliding into the last available seat—directly across from her.

"I don't recall us being at war," she replied, though she didn't push the drink away.

"Not yet," I agreed with a smile. "But the night is young."

She rolled her eyes, but I caught the slight twitch of her lips. Not quite a smile, but close.

"So," Daisy said, leaning forward eagerly. "Tell us everything. What brings three gorgeous men to our little town? And please don't say it was the meat market."

Fraser laughed. "Change of scenery. Got tired of Glasgow."

"London was becoming tedious," Theo added with practiced casualness.

All eyes turned to me. I took a sip of my Guinness, considering my answer. "Let's just say Dublin and I needed some time apart."

"Mysterious," Daisy commented approvingly. "I like it."

"You like anything with a pulse and a penis," Genie muttered into her drink.

Daisy grinned, unashamed. "Not true. I have standards."

"Since when?" Bernie asked innocently, then clapped a hand over her mouth. "Oh God, I said that out loud, didn't I?"

The table erupted in laughter, even Genie cracked a reluctant smile. I found myself watching her, the way her eyes crinkled at the corners and the slight dimple that appeared in her left cheek when she was amused.

"So, Ciarán," she said suddenly, catching me staring. "What did you do in Dublin that made you need to leave?"

The table quieted, the question hung in the air like smoke. I met her gaze steadily, recognising the challenge for what it was.

"I worked in protection," I said finally, the half-truth rolled easily off my tongue.

"Bouncer?" Daisy guessed.

I smiled thinly. "Something like that."

"And now you're a butcher," Genie pressed. "Quite a career change."

"Not really," I replied, holding her gaze. "Both jobs involve knowing where to cut to cause the most damage."

A flicker of something—recognition, wariness, interest—passed across her face. "Efficient," she commented.

"I've always thought so," I agreed.

The conversation moved on, but the tension between us remained; a living thing that crackled and sparked across the table. I found myself both irritated and intrigued by her—from her sharp tongue to her guarded eyes, and the way she seemed to see right through my carefully constructed facade.

As the night wore on, Fraser and Daisy grew increasingly tactile, their flirtation obvious to everyone. Theo and Bernie had fallen into a surprisingly deep conversation about classical literature, of all things. And Genie and I continued our verbal sparring, each exchange revealing a little more about the other.

"You're not what I expected," she admitted after her second drink, her guard lowering slightly.

"What did you expect?" I asked, genuinely curious.

She shrugged. "From an Irish butcher? I don't know. Less..."

"Less what?"

"Less observant," she said finally. "Most men don't really see what's in front of them."

I leaned forward, lowering my voice. "I see you, Genevie Alden. I see the way you watch the door. The way you keep your back to the wall. The way you've been nursing that same drink for an hour now, because you don't like to lose control."

Her eyes widened slightly. "And what does that tell you?"

"That you're running from something," I replied honestly. "Or someone."

"Aren't we all?" she countered.

I raised my glass in acknowledgment. "Fair point."

"What are you running from, Ciarán?" she asked, her voice soft but penetrating.

I met her gaze, allowing her to see a glimpse of the darkness I usually kept hidden. "The same thing as you, I suspect."

"And what's that?"

"The consequences of our actions," I said simply.

She didn't respond, but I saw the recognition in her eyes, the understanding that passed between us. Whatever her secrets were—and I was increasingly certain they were significant—she recognised a kindred spirit in me. Someone else who had blood on their hands. Someone else who had done things that couldn't be undone.

"Another round?" Fraser called, breaking the moment.

Genie stood abruptly. "Not for me. I should get home. Early start tomorrow."

"Party pooper," Daisy pouted, though she made no move to leave Fraser's side.

"I'll walk with you," Bernie offered, gathering her things.

"No need," Genie assured her. "Stay, enjoy your conversation. The house is just down the street."

"At least let someone walk you," Daisy insisted. "It's dark out."

Before I could think better of it, I stood. "I'll go. I could use some air anyway."

Genie's eyes narrowed. "I don't need an escort."

"Never said you did," I replied easily. "But I'm heading that way regardless."

She looked like she wanted to argue, but after a moment she simply shrugged. "Fine. But keep your hands to yourself."

"Wouldn't dream of doing otherwise," I assured her, though the thought had certainly crossed my mind.

Chapter 5
Whiskey & Bad Decisions
Genie

I blame the whiskey.

That's what I told myself, as Ciarán followed me up the winding path to the Alden estate, his presence mixed with the heat radiating from him and his scent—leather, sandalwood and something metallic that reminded me of the copper bowls I used for brewing potions, trailed behind me like a physical weight..

"Quite the place," he commented as we approached the ancient stone house, its ivy-covered walls looming against the night sky.

I fumbled with my keys, suddenly aware of how my hands were shaking. "It's just a house."

"It's your house," he replied, his voice dropping to that low, gravelly register that had been doing things to my insides all evening. "That makes it interesting."

I rolled my eyes, though he couldn't see my face. "Are you always this full of shit, or is it just for my benefit?"

He laughed, the sound rich and warm in the cool night air. "I save my premium bullshit for special occasions."

The lock finally gave way, and I pushed the door open,

flicking on the lights as we entered. The entryway was grand in an old-world way—wooden floors worn smooth by generations of Alden's, walls lined with botanical prints and family photographs, the air perpetually scented with herbs and something older; something that spoke of history and secrets.

"Drink?" I asked, moving toward the sitting room to hide my nervousness. What the hell was I doing? I didn't bring men home, ever. Especially not men with eyes that seemed to see right through me and accents that made my knees weak.

"Please," he replied, wandering over to examine the bookshelves that lined one wall. "Whatever you're having."

I pulled out the good whiskey—the one I saved for special occasions or particularly bad days—and poured two generous drams. When I turned around, he was studying my tarot deck I'd left on the side table after my morning reading.

"You read cards," he said. It wasn't a question.

"Sometimes," I replied, handing him a glass. "When I need clarity."

He took the whiskey, his fingers brushing mine in a way that felt deliberate. "And do they give you answers?"

I shrugged, taking a sip of my drink and letting the burn steady me. "They give me perspective. The answers are usually already inside me."

"Philosophical for a skincare shop owner," he remarked, his eyes never leaving mine as he drank.

"And you're awfully observant for a butcher," I countered.

A smile played at the corners of his mouth. "Touché."

We stood there for a moment, the air between us charged with something I couldn't—or wouldn't—name.

"Why did you let me in, Genie?" he asked finally, setting his glass down.

The directness of the question caught me off guard. "I… I don't know," I admitted. "I don't usually do this."

"Do what?" he pressed, taking a step closer.

"Invite strange men into my home," I said, standing my ground, despite the flutter in my stomach. "Especially not ones who ask too many questions."

He was close enough now that I could see the flecks of darker blue in his eyes, the slight stubble along his jaw. "I'm not asking questions about your secrets," he said softly. "Just about this. About why I'm standing in your house at midnight, looking at you like I want to devour you whole."

My breath caught. "And do you?" I asked, my voice barely above a whisper.

"What do you think?" he replied, his gaze dropping to my lips.

I set my glass down with a decisive click. "I think you talk too much."

And then I was kissing him, or he was kissing me—I couldn't tell who moved first, only that his mouth was on mine, hot and demanding, his hands tangled in my hair. I gasped against his lips, and he took the opportunity to deepen the kiss, his tongue sliding against mine in a way that made heat pool low in my belly.

"Christ," he muttered, breaking away to trail kisses down my neck. "I've been wanting to do that since I first saw you."

"Shut up," I breathed, tugging at his shirt. "Less talking, more—"

"More what?" he asked, his voice rough as he nipped at my earlobe.

"More everything," I demanded, pulling him toward the bedroom.

We stumbled through the house, shedding clothes as we went. His shirt hit the floor, revealing a torso sculpted by hard work, rather than a gym—broad shoulders, defined chest, and a scattering of scars that told stories I wasn't ready to ask about. My sweater followed, then my bra, his hands immediately cupping my breasts like he couldn't wait another second to touch me.

"Beautiful," he murmured, thumbs brushing over my nipples, making me arch into his touch.

"Bed," I managed, already working on his belt. "Now."

He grinned, wolfish and hungry. "Bossy. I like it."

We fell onto the mattress in a tangle of limbs and half-removed clothing. His jeans joined the trail on the floor, followed by my own. His mouth was everywhere—my neck, breasts, stomach—leaving a line of fire in its wake. I ran my hands over his shoulders, down his back, feeling the play of muscles beneath my fingertips.

"Wait," I gasped as his fingers hooked into the waistband of my underwear. "Protection."

He paused, looking up at me with those impossibly blue eyes. "I've got it covered," he said, reaching for his discarded jeans and pulling a condom from his wallet.

"Presumptuous," I commented, raising an eyebrow.

He shrugged, a half-smile playing on his lips. "Boy Scout motto: Be prepared."

"You were never a Boy Scout," I scoffed.

"No," he agreed, his smile turning wicked. "But I was an altar boy, and that taught me all sorts of things about sin."

I laughed despite myself, the sound morphed into a moan as his hand slipped between my legs, finding me already wet and wanting. "Fuck," I breathed.

"That's the general idea," he murmured against my skin, his fingers working magic that had nothing to do with the kind I practiced.

I arched into his touch, my head falling back against the pillows. It had been so long since I'd been with anyone—not since James, not since that ended with blood on my hands and a body in my garden. I'd closed that part of myself off; locked it away with all the other vulnerabilities I couldn't afford.

But now, with Ciarán's hands and mouth on me, I felt something breaking open, something dangerous and exhilarating.

"Stop thinking," he commanded softly, as if he could read my mind. "Just feel."

And I did. I felt his fingers inside me, curling just right, his mouth on my breast, teeth grazing my nipple, the weight of him, solid and real, anchoring me to the present and driving away the ghosts.

When I came, it was with a cry that surprised even me; my body clenched around his fingers as waves of pleasure crashed over me. He watched me with an intensity that should have been unnerving, but instead only stoked the fire higher.

"Condom," I gasped when I could speak again. "Now."

He complied with a grin, tearing the packet open with his teeth and rolling it on with practiced ease. Then he was hovering over me, his arms braced on either side of my head, his eyes locked on mine.

"Sure about this?" he asked in a final check.

Answering, I wrapped my legs around his waist and pulled him down to me. He entered me in one smooth thrust, both of us groaning at the sensation. For a moment, we stayed like that, connected and still, adjusting to the feel of each other.

Once he began to move, all coherent thoughts fled. There was only the rhythm our bodies in motion, with the sound of skin against skin, and mingled gasps and moans that filled the room. He whispered things in my ear—filthy promises in English, tender endearments in Gaelic—as his pace increased.

I dug my nails into his back, urging him on, meeting him thrust for thrust. The ancient bed frame creaked beneath us;

the sound echoed throughout the high-ceilinged room. Ciarán shifted his angle and hit a spot that made me see stars.

"There," I gasped. "Right there."

He obliged, driving into me with renewed purpose as one hand slipped between us to circle my clit. "Come for me again," he urged, his voice strained with the effort of holding back. "Let me feel you."

The combination of his words, his touch, and the relentless rhythm of his hips pushed me over the edge. I came with his name on my lips, my body clenching around him in waves. He followed moments later, his rhythm faltering as he buried his face in my neck and groaned something that might have been my name or might have been Gaelic—I was too far gone to tell.

We collapsed in a sweaty, satisfied heap, his weight pressing me into the mattress in a way that should have been uncomfortable, but somehow wasn't. For a few minutes, we just breathed, coming down from the high; neither of us speaking.

Finally, he rolled off me, disposing of the condom in the wastebasket beside the bed before flopping back down. "Jesus, Mary, and Joseph," he muttered, throwing an arm over his eyes. "That was…"

"Yeah," I agreed, staring at the ceiling. My body felt boneless, satisfied in a way it hadn't been in years. But my mind was already racing ahead, calculating the risks of what I'd just done.

I'd slept with a man I barely knew. A man who asked too many questions and noticed too much. One who might be dangerous—not only to my body, but to my secrets, to the careful life I'd built.

"I can hear you thinking from here," he said, turning his head to look at me. "It's deafening."

I snorted. "Sorry to disturb your post-coital bliss."

"Apology accepted," he replied with a grin. "Though I'd rather you join me in said bliss, instead of whatever mental gymnastics you're performing."

I sat up, pulling the sheet around me in a belated gesture of modesty. "I need to check something."

He raised an eyebrow but didn't stop me as I reached for my tarot deck on the nightstand. I shuffled quickly, my hands still trembling slightly from exertion, and drew a single card.

The Devil stared back at me, his leering face illuminated by the bedside lamp.

"Seems appropriate," I muttered, setting the card down with a sigh.

Ciarán propped himself up on one elbow, studying the card. "The Devil, eh? Should I be flattered or concerned?"

"Both, probably," I replied. The Devil represented temptation, addiction, materialism—being chained to physical desires. It was a warning about being trapped or bound by one's own choices. Given what had just happened between us, it felt a little on the nose.

"What does it mean?" he asked, genuinely curious.

I hesitated, then decided on a simplified version. "It's about temptation. Giving in to desires that might not be good for you in the long run."

"Ah," he nodded, a slow smile spreading across his face. "Definitely flattered, then."

I rolled my eyes but I couldn't help the small smile that tugged at my lips. "You need to leave," I said, though with less conviction than I'd intended.

His smile faltered slightly. "Not one for cuddling, then?"

"Not one for sleepovers," I corrected, though the truth was I desperately wanted to curl up against his warmth and sleep with his arms around me. But that was a vulnerability I couldn't afford. "I have an early morning tomorrow."

He studied me for a moment, those blue eyes seeing far too much. "Alright," he said finally, sitting up. "But for the record, I'm an excellent cuddler. Top marks in spooning."

"I'll take your word for it," I replied dryly.

He began gathering his clothes, pulling on his boxers and jeans with an effortless grace that made my mouth go dry all over again. As he reached for the rest, his phone buzzed from the floor closest to me, it must have fallen from his jeans when he pulled them off.

"Your phone," I said, picking it up from the floor and handing it to him.

The screen lit up with a notification, the name "Rose 🌹 🌹" clearly visible above a text message I couldn't read.

My stomach dropped. Of course. Of fucking course.

"Thanks," he said, taking the phone and glancing at it before silencing it and shoving it in his pocket.

"Girlfriend?" I asked, trying to keep my voice casual and failing miserably.

He looked confused for a moment, then understanding dawned. "No, not a girlfriend."

"Wife, then?" I pressed, anger beginning to simmer beneath my skin. "Because the rose emojis suggest a certain level of intimacy."

"It's not like that," he insisted, running a hand through his tousled hair. "Rose is… complicated."

"Isn't it always?" I said coldly, pulling the sheet tighter around me. "You should go."

He sighed, frustration evident in the set of his shoulders. "Genie, it's not what you think."

"What I think," I said, standing up with as much dignity

as one can muster while wrapped in a bedsheet, "is that you should leave. Now."

He looked like he wanted to argue, but something in my expression must have warned him against it. "Fine," he said, pulling on his shirt. "But this conversation isn't over."

"Yes, it is," I replied, exiting the bedroom door. "This was fun, but let's not pretend it was anything more than a one-night stand."

He followed me to the front door, his expression unreadable. "Is that what you want it to be?"

The question caught me off guard. Did I want it to be just a one-night stand? The sex had been incredible, and there was something about him that called to the darkest parts of me. But he was clearly hiding something—or someone—and I had enough complications in my life.

"What I want," I said carefully, "is for you to go home to whoever Rose is and leave me to my early morning."

He sighed, a sound of genuine frustration. "It's not—" he began, then stopped himself. "Fine. Have it your way. But don't think this is over, Genevie Alden."

"Goodnight, Mr. Ó Duinn," I said firmly, opening the door.

He paused on the threshold, his eyes searching mine one last time. Then, without warning, he leaned in and kissed me —a brief, fierce press of his lips that left me breathless.

"Oíche mhaith, a stór," he murmured against my mouth before pulling away and heading down the path.

I closed the door behind him, leaning against it as my legs threatened to give way.

What the hell had I just done?

. . .

"I BANGED THE BUTCHER," I announced the next morning, dropping into a chair at the kitchen table where Daisy and Bernie were having breakfast. Daisy had taken Fraser back to the shop apartment for a romp in the sheets; she had a thing about bringing men to the main house and always used the shop apartment instead. I was secretly happy about the idea. To be honest, the last thing I needed was to be kept awake at night with moans and groans from her room.

Daisy looked up from her phone, a slow grin spreading across her face. "Sweetheart, from the noises I heard when I got home, you butchered the butcher."

I groaned, burying my face in my hands. "You heard?"

"I'm pretty sure more than just the ghosts in the house heard," Bernie said, pushing a mug of coffee toward me. "Mrs. Finch next door probably needs smelling salts."

"Kill me now," I muttered into my palms.

"After you give us details," Daisy insisted, leaning forward eagerly. "On a scale of 'meh' to 'religious experience,' how was it?"

I peeked at her through my fingers. "I'm not discussing this."

"That good, huh?" she smirked. "I knew it. He has that look about him."

"What look?" Bernie asked, genuinely curious.

"The 'I'll ruin you for all other men' look," Daisy explained. "It's in the eyes. And the hands. Men with big hands never disappoint."

"Can we please talk about something else?" I begged, reaching for the coffee. "Like how I'm a complete idiot who sleeps with men who have girlfriends?"

That got their attention. Daisy's eyebrows shot up. "Girlfriend? The Irish hottie is taken?"

I nodded miserably. "His phone rang right after… you

know. The name 'Rose' with rose emojis popped up on the screen."

"What a loser," Daisy said, as her expression darkened. "I hate cheaters."

"It could have been anyone," Bernie suggested hopefully. "A sister? A cousin?"

"With rose emojis?" I asked sceptically. "And when I confronted him, he didn't deny it. Just said it was 'complicated.'"

"Ugh, the classic 'it's complicated' defence," Daisy rolled her eyes. "Translation: 'I'm a cheating scumbag but don't want to admit it.'"

"Maybe there's an explanation," Bernie protested, ever the optimist. "Maybe they're separated, or in an open relationship."

"Or maybe, he's just another man who thinks with his dick," I said bitterly, taking a long sip of coffee. "Either way, it was a mistake. One that won't be repeated."

"His loss," Daisy shrugged. "Though if you don't mind, I'm gonna keep Fraser for a while; I have a thing for that accent of his."

"Be my guest," I replied.

Bernie giggled, then quickly sobered when I glared at her. "Sorry, it's just… you have to admit it's a little funny. Our first night out with new men in town, and you end up in bed with one of them, this never happens to you."

"Hilarious," I deadpanned. "I'm dying of laughter."

"Look on the bright side," Daisy offered. "At least you got laid. When was the last time that happened? When Elisabeth was crowned?"

I threw a napkin at her, which she dodged easily. "I hate you."

"No, you don't," she sang. "You love me because I'm

going to help you avoid Sexy McButcher today by picking up the meat that Bernie special ordered."

I groaned again. "I forgot about that. Someone's going to have to pick it up."

"I'll go, I mean I did order it after all," Bernie volunteered immediately.

Daisy and I exchanged a look. "No offence, Bern," Daisy said gently, "but you're a terrible liar. One look at those blue Irish eyes and you'll tell him exactly how upset Genie is about it all."

"I will not!" Bernie protested, then wilted under our sceptical stares. "Okay, maybe I would. But I don't see why we need to lie. Can't we just be adults about this?"

"Adults?" I repeated incredulously. "Bernie, I slept with a man I barely know, who probably has a girlfriend, and then kicked him out of my house at one in the morning. There's nothing adult about this situation."

"I'll go," Daisy decided. "I can handle Irish McCheaterson. And I wanted to see Fraser anyway."

"Fine," I agreed, relieved. "Just… don't mention last night, okay?"

"My lips are sealed," Daisy promised, making a zipping motion across her mouth. "Though I can't promise I won't give him the stink eye."

"Fair enough," I conceded.

As they continued chatting, my mind drifted back to the night before. The way Ciarán had looked at me, touched me, and made me feel things I'd thought were long dead. The connection had been intense, almost frightening in its immediacy.

And then there was Rose. Whoever she was—girlfriend, wife, complicated situation—she was a reminder of why I didn't do relationships. Why I kept people at arm's length. Why I trusted my tarot cards more than I trusted men.

The Devil card had been right. I'd given in to temptation, and now I was paying the price.

But as I sipped my coffee and half-listened to Daisy and Bernie's chatter, a small, traitorous part of me wondered if it had been worth it. If one night of feeling alive, of being wanted, of feeling something other than the constant vigilance that defined my life, had been worth the morning-after regret.

The answer, much to my dismay, was yes.

Chapter 6
Meat Market Mayhem
Ciarán

I knew I was fucked the moment Daisy walked through the door instead of Genie.

"Morning, butcher boy," she called out, her voice sweet as honey but her eyes were cold as ice. "I'm here for our order."

Fraser perked up immediately, wiping his hands on his apron and flashing that charming Scottish smile that had women dropping their knickers from Glasgow to London. "Daisy! Wasn't expecting you. Thought Genie might come by."

"Genie's busy," Daisy replied, her gaze sliding to me with all the subtlety of a knife to the ribs. "Very, very busy. With important things."

"Ah, shite," I muttered under my breath. "Dia ár sábháil." *God save us.*

Fraser looked between us, confusion evident on his face. "Did I miss something?"

"Nothing important," I said quickly, turning back to the lamb chops I was preparing. "Just a misunderstanding."

"Is that what we're calling it?" Daisy asked, leaning

against the counter. "Because from where I'm standing, it looks like you shagged my best friend and then got a booty call while still in her bed."

Fraser's eyebrows shot up. "You and Genie? Last night?"

"Jesus Christ," I groaned, setting down my knife before I was tempted to use it. "It's not what it looks like."

"It never is," Daisy replied with a saccharine smile. "Now, about that meat order?"

Fraser, the traitorous bastard, was grinning like he'd just won the lottery. "Coming right up," he said, disappearing into the back room.

Left alone with Daisy, I tried again. "Look, Rose isn't—"

"Save it for someone who cares," she interrupted, examining her perfectly manicured nails. "I'm just here for the meat. The actual meat, not whatever you're packing in those jeans."

I bit back a retort. Getting into an argument with Genie's best friend wasn't going to help my case. Instead, I focused on wrapping the lamb chops, keeping my movements precise and controlled.

"She deserves better, you know," Daisy said after a moment, her voice softer but no less pointed. "She's been through enough shit without adding cheating butchers to the list."

I looked up at that, curiosity piqued despite myself. "Been through what?"

Daisy's eyes narrowed. "None of your business. Just know that if you hurt her again, they'll never find your body. And I know people who know people."

"I believe you," I replied honestly. There was something in her eyes—a hardness, a certainty—that told me she wasn't bluffing.

Fraser returned with a large package wrapped in butcher

paper. "Here we go. Everything you ordered, plus a little extra."

"Aren't you sweet," Daisy said, her demeanour changing instantly as she flashed him a dazzling smile. "Any chance you're free tonight?"

"For you? I'll make myself free," Fraser replied, his accent thickening as it always did when he was flirting.

"Perfect. Meet me at the shop apartment at eight?" She purred.

"I'll be there."

I watched this exchange with a mixture of amusement and disbelief. One minute she was threatening to dispose of my body, the next she was making plans with Fraser for a date; women were a mystery, I'd never fully solve.

"Well, I'm off," Daisy announced, taking the package and throwing some cash at Fraser. "Thanks for the meat. And Ciarán?"

"Yes?"

"If I were you, I'd check my car tires before leaving today." With a wink and a wave, she sauntered out of the shop, leaving behind the scent of expensive perfume and thinly veiled threats.

The moment the door closed, Fraser turned to me. "Alright, spill. What the fuck happened with you and the witch?"

I sighed, running a hand through my hair. "When I walked her home, one thing led to another…"

"And you shagged her," Fraser finished, looking impressed. "Didn't think you had it in you, mate. She seemed like a tough nut to crack."

"It wasn't like that," I protested, though it absolutely had been like that. "There was… I don't know. A connection."

Fraser snorted. "A connection. Right. And where does Rose fit into this 'connection'?"

I groaned. "That's the problem. Rose called and texted while I was there, and Genie saw the name on my phone. Now she thinks I've got a girlfriend."

"And you don't?" He said with a smile, he knew precisely who Rose was.

"Of course I don't, you eejit," I said, throwing my hands in the air.

Fraser stared at me for a beat, then burst out laughing—great, heaving guffaws that had him clutching the counter for support. "Oh, this is fucking brilliant," he wheezed. "She has no idea who Rose is, does she?"

"None," I reply.

"Well, you're in for a fun time wiggling out of this one," Fraser said, wiping tears from his eyes. "That blonde looked ready to castrate you with a dull spoon."

"Tell me something I don't know," I muttered, returning to my lamb chops with perhaps more force than necessary.

"Why don't you just tell Genie the truth?" Theo asked, appearing from the office with his usual impeccably timed eavesdropping ability..

"Because she won't talk to me," I replied. "And something tells me showing up at her door, saying 'Hey, by the way, Rose is my sister' isn't going to go over well."

"Women do appreciate honesty," Theo pointed out.

"Women appreciate not being lied to in the first place," I countered. "And technically, I didn't lie. I just didn't explain fully."

"Semantics," Theo said with a dismissive wave. "Either way, you're in the doghouse."

"Thanks for the insight, relationship guru," I said sarcastically. "Any other pearls of wisdom?"

"Yes, actually. Don't shit where you eat. We're new in town, trying to establish a business. Getting into drama with the local witch isn't exactly good for our cover."

I bristled at that. "This isn't about our 'cover.' This is about—"

"About what?" Theo challenged. "Your feelings? Since when do you have those for anyone outside this operation?"

"Fuck off," I growled, the words coming out harsher than intended.

Theo raised his hands in surrender. "Just saying. We're here for a reason, remember? And it's not to play 'house' with the local potion-maker."

I knew he was right, which only made it more infuriating. We weren't in Newchurch-in-Pendle by accident. We had a job to do—a job that had nothing to do with Genie Alden and her poison-green eyes.

But something about her had gotten under my skin. The way she looked at me was like she could see right through my carefully constructed facade. The way her body had felt against mine, like we were two pieces of a puzzle finally clicking into place. The darkness I sensed in her, matched my own.

"Just fix it," Theo advised, heading back to the office. "Before it becomes a problem we can't contain."

DAISY HADN'T BEEN BLUFFING about the tires.

I discovered this at the end of the day when I went to drive home and found all four tires on my car, flat as pancakes. Not slashed—that would have been too obvious.

"Clever witch," I muttered, kneeling to inspect the damage.

It was petty but effective. I'd have to call a tow truck or

spend the next hour with a portable air compressor. Either way, I wasn't getting home quickly. Fraser and Theo had already left, but I'd stayed to put the last of the lamb I was cutting up into the fridge for tomorrow.

I opted for the air compressor, using the time to think about how to approach Genie. Direct confrontation seemed unwise—she clearly had a vindictive streak. Flowers were out of the question, given the Rose misunderstanding. I needed something that would get her attention without escalating the situation.

By the time I got home to the small cottage I shared with Fraser and Theo on the outskirts of town, I still hadn't come up with a plan. Fraser was already gone, presumably on his date with Daisy, and Theo was holed up in his room with his laptop, doing whatever mysterious financial wizardry kept our operation funded.

I grabbed a beer from the fridge and stepped out onto the back porch, staring up at the stars. The night was clear and cold, the kind of autumn evening that reminded me of home, of Dingle; with its wild coastline and ancient myths. I missed it sometimes, the simplicity of life before I'd gotten tangled up with the wrong people, before blood and secrets became my stock-in-trade.

My phone buzzed in my pocket. For a brief, hopeful moment, I thought it might be Genie. But it was Rose, checking in as she did every few days.

> How's small-town life treating you? Bored out of your skull yet?

I smiled despite myself. Rose had never understood why I'd chosen this path—why I'd left Dublin for a life of uncertainty and danger. She thought I was simply running a butcher shop with friends, taking a break from city life. She had no idea what I really did, what I was capable of. And I intended to keep it that way.

> It's growing on me

> Met someone interesting

Her response was immediate.

> Female someone? Details please.

I hesitated, then typed.

> Complicated. She thinks you're my girlfriend.

> WHAT?? Why would she think that??

> She saw your name on my phone, with the rose emojis.

> OMG, that's hilarious! Did you tell her I'm your sister?

> I called it complicated.

> She kicked me out.

> Sounds feisty. I like her already.

I snorted. Rose would like Genie—they shared the same sharp tongue and take-no-prisoners attitude. In another life, they might have been friends.

> Fix it!

> I refuse to be the reason my brother isn't getting laid.

> Thanks for the support.

I replied dryly.

> Always here for you, bro. Love you. Don't
> fuck this up.

I put my phone away, smiling faintly. Rose had always been my conscience, my anchor to normalcy in a life that had veered far from it. She was the reason I was trying to get out, trying to build something resembling a normal life after this last job.

The question was whether Genie Alden could be part of that life. Or whether she had too many secrets of her own.

I shouldn't have called Rose complicated, but she was. I should have just said she was my sister. Rose had changed her contact details in my phone before we had left, thinking the rose emojis were a great touch; except now they were just cock blockers.

THE NEXT MORNING, I arrived at the shop early to find the front window covered in some kind of oily substance that distorted the view from outside. It clung to the glass like a film, and no amount of scrubbing seemed to affect it.

"What the actual fuck?" Fraser muttered, his breath fogging in the cold morning air as we stood outside, staring at our ruined display. "Is that… oil?"

"Something like that," I replied, running a finger along the edge of the window. The substance was slick, but not quite like any oil I'd encountered. It had a faint herbal scent, almost like rosemary but with something sharper underneath.

"This is going to cost a fortune to fix," Theo complained,

no doubt already calculating the expense in his head. "We'll need to replace the entire front window."

"No, we won't," I said, an idea forming. "I know exactly who did this."

"Your witch?" Fraser guessed, looking more amused than concerned.

"She's not *my* witch," I corrected automatically. "But yes, I'd bet my left bollock this is Genie's handiwork."

"So what do we do?" Theo asked. "Call the police? File a vandalism report?"

I shook my head. "No. Open as usual. And I pay a visit to Alden Alchemy."

"Bad idea," Fraser warned. "Those women will skin you alive if you show up there."

"I'll take my chances," I replied, already heading down the street.

Alden Alchemy was just opening, the lights flickered on inside as I approached. Through the window, I could see Genie moving around, setting up displays and arranging bottles on the shelves. She looked beautiful in the morning light, her dark hair pulled back in a messy bun, her green sweater bringing out the colour of her eyes.

I steeled myself and pushed open the door, the bell jingling cheerfully to announce my presence.

Genie looked up, her expression shifting from professional welcome to cold disdain in an instant. "We're not open yet," she said flatly.

"I'm not here to shop," I replied, letting the door close behind me. "I'm here about my window."

"Your window?" she repeated, all innocence. "What about it?"

"It's covered in some kind of oil that won't come off," I

said, watching her carefully. "Interesting timing, don't you think? Right after you decided I was a cheating bastard."

She shrugged, turning back to her display. "Sounds like bad luck. Maybe you should check your karma."

"My karma is fine," I said, stepping closer. "My tires, on the other hand, were mysteriously flat yesterday. And now my window is ruined. Quite the coincidence."

"This town is full of strange coincidences," she replied, still not looking at me. "Mrs. Beecham says it's built on ley lines. Creates unusual energy."

"Is that what she says?" I moved closer until I was standing right behind her. "And what do you say, Genevie Alden? What kind of energy are you creating?"

She turned then, her eyes flashing with something that might have been anger or might have been something else entirely. "I say you should leave. Now."

"Not until you fix my window," I said, holding my ground.

"I don't know what you're talking about," she insisted, but there was a slight twitch at the corner of her mouth—almost a smile.

"Fine," I said, stepping back. "Have it your way. But just so you know, Rose is my sister."

That caught her off guard. "What?"

"Rose. The woman who texted me that night. She's my sister. Not my girlfriend, not my wife. My little sister, who uses too many fucking emojis and has terrible timing."

Genie stared at me, clearly trying to decide if I was lying. "Your sister," she repeated slowly.

"Yes. My sister. Who I love dearly, but who is not, nor has ever been, romantically involved with me because that would be disgusting and illegal."

A faint blush coloured her cheeks. "You could have said something that night."

"I tried," I pointed out. "You were too busy kicking me out to listen."

She had the grace to look slightly abashed. "Well, you should have tried harder."

I laughed at that, the tension breaking slightly. "Noted for future reference. Now, about my window…"

"I still don't know what you're talking about," she said primly, but her eyes were dancing with mischief now.

"Right. And I suppose you don't know anything about my tires either?"

"Not a thing," she replied, turning back to her display.

"Now, if you'll excuse me, I have a shop to open," Genie said, a small smile playing at the corners of her mouth.

I knew when I was being dismissed. "Fine. But this isn't over, a stór."

"It never is with you, is it?" she replied, but there was less ice in her tone now.

I left feeling slightly more optimistic than when I'd arrived. She hadn't admitted to anything, but she hadn't denied it either. And she'd listened about Rose, which was a start.

Now I just needed to figure out how to get that damn oil off my window.

THE OIL MYSTERIOUSLY DISAPPEARED OVERNIGHT, but our troubles weren't over. The next day, the refrigerated display case kept shorting out, turning off at random intervals and threatening to spoil thousands of pounds worth of meat. The day after that, every piece of chalk I tried to use to write the daily specials on the board outside crumbled to dust in my fingers.

It was petty, annoying, and increasingly difficult to explain to Theo, who was growing more suspicious by the day.

"This isn't normal," he insisted as we closed up shop after another day of mysterious malfunctions. "First the window, then the fridge, now the chalk. Someone's targeting us."

"It's just bad luck," I said, not entirely convincingly.

"Bullshit," Theo replied. "This is about you and that woman, isn't it? The one from the skincare shop."

I sighed. There was no point denying it. "It's a misunderstanding. I'm handling it."

"Handling it?" Theo repeated incredulously. "Our business is being sabotaged, and you're 'handling it'? What's next, Ciarán? The gas lines? The electrical system? Are we going to burn down because you couldn't keep it in your pants?"

"It's not like that," I protested, though I wasn't entirely sure what it was like. "She's just… making a point."

"Well, make her stop," Theo said firmly. "Or I will."

The threat in his voice was unmistakable, and it sent a chill down my spine. Theo might look like a posh banker, but I'd seen what he was capable of when pushed. We all had our demons, our dark sides. It was why we worked so well together—and why we were so dangerous as a team.

"I'll handle it," I repeated, more firmly this time. "Just give me a day or two."

Theo studied me for a long moment, then nodded curtly. "Two days. Then we do it my way."

I waited until he left before letting out the breath I'd been holding. This was getting out of hand. What had started as a petty revenge prank was escalating into something that could blow our cover—or worse, put Genie in Theo's crosshairs.

I needed to end this, one way or another.

The answer came to me the next morning as I was walking to work; just as I had walked every day since she flattened my tires. The bus stop directly outside Alden Alchemy had an advertising panel that was currently displaying a poster for a local festival. A quick inquiry to the advertising company and a not-insignificant amount of cash later, and I'd secured the space for the next week.

"What are you grinning about?" Fraser asked as I entered the shop, whistling cheerfully.

"Just had a brilliant idea," I replied, heading straight for the office to draft my masterpiece.

It took most of the morning to get it right, but by lunchtime, I'd created what I considered to be a work of art. The new bus stop advertisement was installed that afternoon, just in time for the after-work rush.

I positioned myself across the street, pretending to check my phone while actually waiting for Genie to notice. It didn't take long.

She emerged from her shop around five, locking up for the day, when her eyes fell on the bus stop. I watched as she did a double-take, then stood frozen, staring at my handiwork.

The advertisement featured a close-up image of roses surrounding our signature meatballs that were glistening with sauce, alongside the text:

FORGET THE ROSES. GRAB THE BALLS.

Roses are red. Our meatballs are better.
Hand-rolled. Slow-cooked. Drippin' in saucy goodness.
The perfect gift for anyone who prefers meat over
meaningless gestures.

Comes with optional garlic bread. (Because we're not
savages.)

It was crude, juvenile, and exactly the kind of thing that
would get under her skin. I watched as her expression shifted
from shock to outrage to—was that a smile? She quickly
suppressed it, but I was certain I'd seen the corner of her
mouth twitch upward before she schooled her features back
into a scowl.

She turned, scanning the street, and her eyes locked with
mine. I raised an eyebrow, challenging her. For a moment, we
just stared at each other across the distance, the air between
us practically crackling with tension.

Then she did something unexpected. She laughed—a
genuine, head-thrown-back laugh that transformed her face
and sent a jolt of something warm and dangerous through my
chest.

She shook her head, still smiling, and mouthed what
looked like "Touché" before turning and walking away.

I stood there for a moment, watching her go, feeling like
I'd both won and lost at the same time. The petty war might
be over, but something else was just beginning.

OVER THE NEXT FEW DAYS, things settled into an uneasy
truce. The mysterious malfunctions at the butcher shop
stopped. The bus stop advertisement remained, drawing equal
parts amusement and outrage from the townspeople. Genie
and I maintained a careful distance, acknowledging each
other with nods when we passed on the street, but nothing
more.

It was during this time that I began to notice something
odd about Alden Alchemy. The shop had a steady stream of

customers, as expected for a successful business, but there was a pattern to some of the visitors that caught my attention.

They were almost exclusively women, which made sense for a skincare shop. But a certain type came in looking distinctly nervous; glancing over their shoulders, wearing sunglasses indoors, or sporting long sleeves even on warmer days. They would speak with Genie, who would then lead them to a back room. When they emerged, sometimes as much as an hour later, their demeanour had changed completely. They stood straighter, walked with more confidence, and often left with small, unmarked packages tucked under their arms.

At first, I thought little of it. Private consultations weren't unusual in specialty shops. But the frequency and the pattern began to nag at me. Especially when I overheard Mrs. Beecham commenting on it one afternoon as I was struggling with yet another piece of crumbling chalk.

"Having trouble there, dear?" she asked, watching me with amusement as I tried to write "Sirloin Special" on the board outside the shop.

"Just a bit," I replied, forcing a smile. "Seems the chalk doesn't like me today."

She chuckled, a knowing gleam in her eye. "Did you upset our Genie? Word on the street is if you cross the witch, strange things happen for a week after."

I paused, chalk dust coating my fingers. "What are you implying?"

"The Alden's have always had a reputation," Mrs. Beecham said, lowering her voice conspiratorially. "Her grandmother could curse a man with impotence just by looking at him sideways. And her mother—well, let's say there's a reason the women of this town go to see an Alden when they have… problems."

"What kind of problems?" I asked, my interest piqued.

Mrs. Beecham tapped the side of her nose. "The kind that come with wedding rings and bruises, if you catch my meaning. Evelyn Alden had quite the knack of aiding in divorces, and our Genie inherited the same traits."

A chill ran down my spine that had nothing to do with the autumn air. "Are you saying she—"

"I'm not saying anything," Mrs. Beecham interrupted firmly. "Just that some men in this town have died very convenient deaths over the years; Heart attacks, strokes, mysterious wasting illnesses. And their widows always seemed to have lovely complexions afterward."

She patted my arm, her bony fingers surprisingly strong. "Just a bit of local culture for you, dear. Nothing to worry about if you're a good man." Her eyes twinkled mischievously. "You are a good man, aren't you, Mr. Ó Duinn?"

Before I could answer, she'd tottered away, leaving me standing on the sidewalk with chalk dust on my hands and a growing suspicion in my mind.

Genie Alden wasn't just a witch who could make my tires go flat and my chalk crumble. She was something far more dangerous.

She was a poisoner.

And God help me, that only made me want her more.

Chapter 7
Dinner with Ghosts
Genie

"If you add any more rosemary to that stew, we'll all be communing with the dead by midnight," I said, watching Bernie hover over the pot with a handful of herbs.

She froze, hand suspended mid-sprinkle. "Too much?"

"Unless your goal is to poison us all, yes," I replied, gently taking the rosemary from her. "A pinch, Bernie. A pinch."

"Sorry," she said sheepishly. "I got excited. The recipe said it pairs well with lamb."

"So does arsenic, technically, but we don't dump that in by the fistful," I muttered, stirring the stew to distribute the already excessive herbs.

It was Wednesday night—our traditional midweek dinner at the Alden estate. No matter how busy we got with the shop or our own lives, we always made time for this ritual. Tonight, Bernie was attempting a lamb stew with the meat Daisy had picked up from the butcher shop—from Fraser, specifically, which explained why she'd gotten twice what we'd ordered for "the same price."

"Speaking of poison," Daisy said, perched on the kitchen counter despite my numerous requests that she use an actual chair like a civilised human, "how's your war with the sexy Irish butcher going?"

I shot her a look. "There is no war."

"Really?" She raised a perfectly sculpted eyebrow. "So his chalk just spontaneously disintegrates on its own, every time he tries to write the daily specials? And that oily substance on his window was, what, an act of God?"

"I have no idea what you're talking about," I replied primly, focusing on rescuing the stew.

"Uh-huh." Daisy's tone dripped with scepticism. "And I suppose you also know nothing about his flat tires or the refrigerator that keeps shorting out?"

I allowed myself a small smile. "Karma's a bitch."

"So are you, apparently," Daisy laughed. "Though I have to admit, his retaliation was pretty brilliant."

The bus stop advertisement. I'd nearly choked when I saw it—"FORGET THE ROSES. GRAB THE BALLS." It was crude, juvenile, and embarrassingly effective at making me laugh, despite myself. The man had a sense of humour; I'd give him that.

"It was… creative," I conceded.

"It was hilarious," Bernie chimed in, chopping carrots with alarming enthusiasm. "Mrs. Beecham was scandalised. She told everyone at her bridge club."

"Great," I groaned. "Now the entire geriatric population of Newchurch-in-Pendle thinks I'm in some kind of sexual feud with the new butcher."

"Aren't you?" Daisy asked innocently.

I threw a dish towel at her, which she caught with irritating grace. "No. I slept with him once, discovered he was potentially involved with someone else, and now I'm expressing my displeasure in creative ways."

"By cursing his chalk," Bernie nodded sagely.

"I didn't curse his chalk," I protested. "I infused it with a mild crumbling charm."

"And the window?" Daisy pressed.

"A simple oil-based hex. It dissolved the same night."

"And the tires?"

I shrugged. "Physics. Air tends to escape when valve stems are loosened."

"You're evil," Daisy said admiringly. "I love it."

"It's not evil, it's justice," I corrected. "He slept with me, whilst having a girlfriend named Rose."

"Allegedly," Bernie pointed out, dumping the carrots into the stew. "He did say she was his sister."

"Men lie," I said flatly. "Especially when they're caught."

"True," Daisy agreed. "But what if he's telling the truth?"

I stirred the stew with more force than necessary. "Whose side are you on?"

"Yours, always," Daisy assured me. "I'm just saying, maybe verify before you escalate to full-on witch warfare. Because at the rate you're going, his shop's going to mysteriously burn down next, and then we'll have the police asking questions."

She had a point, though I loathed to admit it. My 'creative expressions of displeasure' had been escalating, partly because each one gave me a little thrill of satisfaction, and partly because... well, because I couldn't stop thinking about him. About his hands, his mouth, the way he'd looked at me like he could see all my darkness and wasn't afraid of it.

"Fine," I sighed. "I'll ease up on the hexes. But I'm not apologising."

"Of course not," Daisy agreed. "That would be mature and reasonable."

"Exactly," I nodded, ignoring her sarcasm. "Now, is this stew actually edible, or are we ordering pizza again?"

Bernie lifted the lid and peered inside. "It looks… stew-like?"

"High praise," I muttered.

"It'll be fine," Daisy assured us, hopping off the counter. "And if not, we've got wine. Lots of wine."

"Speaking of which," I said, reaching for the bottle of red I'd opened earlier so it could breathe, "shall we take this show on the road? The sun's setting, and I want to get there before it's completely dark."

"Are we really doing this?" Bernie asked, a hint of nervousness in her voice. "Eating dinner in a cemetery?"

"It's tradition," I reminded her. "First full moon of autumn. We eat with the dead, we honour our ancestors, we drink too much wine and we tell inappropriate stories. Same as every year."

"I know, but…" Bernie glanced out the window at the darkening sky. "It's creepy."

"You're friends with a witch who makes poisons in her basement," Daisy pointed out. "Creepy is kind of our brand."

"Besides," I added, ladling the stew into a large thermos, "the Newchurch Cemetery is practically my backyard. Those ghosts have watched me grow up. They're like family."

"Except dead," Bernie muttered.

"Details," I waved dismissively. "Now, grab the bread and the wine. It's time to dine with the departed."

THE NEWCHURCH CEMETERY was a five-minute walk from the Alden estate, a picturesque graveyard that had been in use since the 1600s. Ancient headstones had tilted at odd angles and worn smooth in places by centuries of rain and wind. Newer graves stood in neat rows toward the back, their marble and granite monuments gleaming in the moonlight.

We spread our blanket out in our usual spot near the oldest section; where my ancestors were buried. A large stone angel marked the Alden plot, its features eroded but still recognisable, wings spread as if in protection over the graves below.

"To the Alden's," I said, raising my wine glass in a toast. "May they continue to rest in peace and occasionally offer useful advice from beyond the veil."

"To the Alden's," Daisy and Bernie echoed, clinking their glasses against mine.

We dug into the stew, which had turned out surprisingly edible despite Bernie's heavy hand with the herbs. The night was cooler but not cold, the full moon bathed everything in silver light. It was peaceful here among the dead—more peaceful than I'd often felt among the living.

"So," I said, breaking the comfortable silence, "are we going to talk about the fact that Daisy has seen Fraser three times now? A new personal record."

Daisy nearly choked on her wine. "How did you—"

"Bernie told me," I grinned.

"Traitor," Daisy glared at Bernie, who shrugged apologetically.

"It just slipped out," Bernie defended herself. "Besides, it's a big deal! You never see anyone more than twice. It's like your cardinal rule."

"It's not a big deal," Daisy insisted, though the faint blush on her cheeks suggested otherwise. "He's just… interesting."

"Interesting?" I pressed. "Or are you just a sucker for that Scottish accent?"

"The accent helps," she admitted. "But it's not just that. He's… I don't know. Different."

"Different how?" Bernie asked, leaning forward eagerly.

Daisy took a long sip of wine, clearly stalling. "He doesn't try to impress me," she said finally. "Most men put on this whole show. They brag about their jobs or their cars or how many women they've slept with. Fraser is just. He's comfortable in his skin."

"Plus, those arms," I added helpfully.

"God, those arms," Daisy agreed with a dreamy sigh. "Like tree trunks. And his hands are so big, they make mine look like a child's."

"And we all know what they say about men with big hands," Bernie giggled.

"In Fraser's case, it's absolutely true," Daisy confirmed with a wicked grin.

"TMI," I groaned, though I was secretly pleased to see Daisy genuinely interested in someone. For all her flirtation and casual hookups, she kept her heart carefully guarded. If Fraser had managed to slip past those defences, he must be special indeed.

"What about you, Bernie?" Daisy asked, clearly eager to shift the spotlight. "Any progress with Theo the Posh?"

Bernie blushed furiously. "We're just friends. We talk about books."

"Sexy books?" Daisy waggled her eyebrows.

"No! Well, not specifically. Though we did discuss 'Pride and Prejudice' last time, and there's definitely sexual tension in that."

"Ah, yes, nothing gets the blood pumping like Regency-era repression," I teased.

"It's not like that," Bernie insisted. "He's nice to talk to.

He listens when I ramble about nineteenth-century literature, whereas most men's eyes glaze over."

"Most men are idiots," Daisy declared. "Present company's potential boyfriends excluded, of course."

"He's not my boyfriend!" Bernie protested.

"Yet," Daisy and I said in unison, causing Bernie to bury her face in her hands.

I was about to press for more details when I noticed movement from the corner of my eye—a shimmer in the air near one of the older gravestones. I turned to look directly at it, and the shimmer solidified slightly into the translucent form of a man in Victorian-era clothing.

"We've got company," I murmured, nodding toward the ghost.

Daisy squinted in that direction. "Oh yeah, I see him. Nice top hat."

"And great jawline," Bernie added, peering through the darkness. "Very distinguished."

"For someone missing half his face, sure," I replied dryly.

They both turned to stare at me, then back at the ghost, who indeed was missing the right side of his face—a detail visible only to those with the Sight; which I'd inherited from my mother's side.

"He looks whole to me," Daisy said slowly.

"That's because you can't see how he died," I explained. "Shotgun to the face, if I had to guess. Victorian-era suicide, probably over a business failure or a woman."

"That's… disturbing," Bernie said, wrapping her cardigan tighter around herself.

"That's death," I shrugged. "Rarely pretty, often violent, always final. Except for the whole lingering-as-a-ghost part."

As if hearing us, the ghost turned in our direction, tipped his hat politely, then faded back into the ether.

"At least he has manners," Daisy commented, refilling our wine glasses. "Unlike some of the living men in this town."

"Speaking of which," Bernie said, accepting her refilled glass, "when *are* you going to stop your war on Ciarán?"

"Who said I needed to?" I replied innocently.

Daisy snorted. "Please. I see the poor man struggling daily with the chalk. It's actually kind of hilarious. He looks like he wants to murder it."

"It would be nice not to see a bus stop 'Ball's' advertisement," Bernie added.

"That's true." I conceded.

"So you're not mad about it?" Bernie asked, surprised.

I considered the question. Was I mad? The advertisement was meant to get under my skin, to respond to my petty hexes with equally petty humour. But there was something almost playful about it. Like we were engaged in a game, rather than a war.

"No," I said finally. "I'm not mad. It was a good move in our… whatever this is."

"Sexual chess?" Daisy suggested.

"Flirtatious feuding?" Bernie offered.

"Foreplay," Daisy decided with a definitive nod. "This is definitely foreplay."

I rolled my eyes but didn't contradict her. Because the truth was, there was something exciting about the back-and-forth with Ciarán. Something that made my pulse quicken and my magic tingle beneath my skin.

"It doesn't matter what it is," I said instead. "It's ending. I've made my point."

"And what point is that, exactly?" Daisy asked. "That you're a petty witch who holds grudges?"

"That I'm not to be trifled with," I corrected. "That actions have consequences."

"Mmm-hmm," Daisy hummed sceptically. "And it has nothing to do with the fact that you're still attracted to him, and this is your way of keeping his attention?"

I glared at her. "I am not still attracted to him."

"Liar," she chirped. "Your pupils dilate every time someone mentions his name. It's science, honey. You can't fake that."

"My pupils do not—" I began, then stopped as both Daisy and Bernie burst into laughter. "You're the worst friends ever."

"We're the best friends ever," Daisy corrected. "And we're telling you to stop hexing the hot Irish butcher and start having conversations with him. Like an adult."

"Adult conversations are overrated," I muttered, taking a large gulp of wine.

"So is being alone," Bernie said quietly.

That brought me up short. Bernie rarely pushed on personal matters, preferring to let Daisy play bad cop. The fact that she was speaking up now meant she was genuinely concerned.

"I'm not alone," I protested. "I have you two. I have the shop. I have my craft."

"You know what she means," Daisy said, her tone gentler now. "When was the last time you let someone in? Really let them in?"

I stared into my wine glass, watching the dark liquid catch the moonlight. "You know why I can't."

"Because of James?" Bernie asked. "Genie, that was years ago. And he was—"

"A mistake," I finished for her. "A mistake that ended with me burying a body in my garden."

"A mistake that was trying to kill you," Daisy corrected firmly. "What happened with James was self-defence."

"Try explaining that to the police," I said bitterly. "'Sorry, officer, I didn't mean to kill him. I just threw a boiling pot of poisonous herbs at him, and then he fell and cracked his skull open. Totally an accident.'"

"It was an accident," Bernie insisted. "You didn't mean for him to die."

I wasn't so sure about that anymore. In my darkest moments, I wondered if some part of me—the part that had been learning about poisons and studying my grandmother's grimoires—had known exactly what would happen when I threw that pot.

"It doesn't matter what I meant," I said finally. "What matters is that I can't risk letting someone get that close again. I can't risk them finding out what I am, what I do."

"What you do helps people," Daisy reminded me. "Those women who come to you—you're saving lives."

"By taking others," I pointed out. "Not exactly the kind of thing you put on a dating profile. 'Enjoys long walks on the beach, reading by the fire, and helping abused women poison their husbands.'"

"You don't have to tell him everything right away," Bernie suggested. "Just give him a chance to explain about Rose. If she really is his sister—"

"Then I've been hexing an innocent man," I finished. "Which makes me the villain in this story."

"No one's the villain," Daisy said firmly. "Just two stubborn people with trust issues and enough sexual tension to power a small city."

I couldn't help but laugh at that. "When did you get so wise?"

"I've always been wise," Daisy sniffed. "You just never listen to me because you're too busy being a dramatic witch."

"Fair point," I conceded, raising my glass in a mock toast. "To being less dramatic."

"And more communicative," Bernie added.

"And getting laid regularly," Daisy finished with a wink.

We clinked glasses, the sound echoing slightly throughout the quiet cemetery. Around us, the night had deepened, stars appearing one by one in the velvet sky. The moon cast long shadows across the graves, and in the distance, an owl hooted softly.

"Do you ever wonder what they think of us?" Bernie asked suddenly, gesturing to the graves surrounding us. "The dead, I mean. Do they judge us for our choices?"

I considered this, looking around at the silent stones. "I think they understand better than most that life is short and often brutal. I think they'd tell us to grab happiness where we can find it."

"Even if that happiness is a potentially complicated Irish butcher?" Daisy asked pointedly.

I sighed, defeated. "Fine. I'll talk to him."

"Baby steps," Daisy grinned. "Now, who wants more wine? I think we need to toast to Genie's imminent return to the land of the sexually active."

"I hate you both," I groaned, but held out my glass anyway.

As Daisy poured, I caught movement again from the corner of my eye—not the Victorian gentleman this time, but a woman in a long dress, her hair piled high on her head in an elaborate style that hadn't been fashionable for at least a century. She stood near the Alden family plot, watching us with what looked like approval.

I raised my glass slightly in her direction, a silent

acknowledgment. She nodded once, then faded away like mist in morning sun.

"What are you looking at?" Bernie asked, following my gaze.

"Just saying hello to Great-Great-Grandmother Alden," I replied. "She always shows up for these dinners."

"What does she think of your butcher situation?" Daisy asked, only half-joking.

I smiled, remembering the approving nod. "I think she's Team Ciarán."

"Smart woman," Daisy declared. "Now, let's finish this wine and head back. I'm starting to lose feeling in my arse from sitting on this cold ground."

"So romantic," I teased. "Fraser is a lucky man."

"Damn right he is," Daisy agreed without a hint of modesty. "And soon, Ciarán will be a lucky man too. If you stop hexing him long enough to have a conversation."

"No promises," I said, but I was smiling as I said it.

As we packed up our picnic and headed back toward the house, I found myself thinking about Ciarán—about his blue eyes and his scarred hands and the way he'd looked at me like he understood my darkness. Maybe, just maybe, it was time to give him a chance to explain properly.

Chapter 8
I Smell a Snitch
Ciarán

Our plans were coming together nicely. I was nearly out of the game, just this last job.

I stared at the file on my laptop, the blue light casting shadows across my face in the darkened cottage. Outside, rain pattered against the windows in a steady rhythm that matched the pounding in my head. Three in the morning was a shite time to be awake, but sleep had been elusive lately. Ever since I'd realised what Genie Alden might be.

My boss had given me an out, one that seemed so easy. Find out what happened to Cameron Smith. Simple, right? He had died of a heart attack about six months ago. Nothing suspicious on the surface—a middle-aged man with high cholesterol and a stressful job. Happens every day.

Except my boss didn't believe in coincidences. And neither did I.

The last place Cameron and his wife had visited was Newchurch-in-Pendle. They'd stayed for a weekend, supposedly for the "charming countryside atmosphere." Two weeks later, Cameron was dead, and his wife, Melissa, had inherited his considerable fortune.

I scrolled through the photos in the file—Cameron alive, smiling with his arm around a blonde woman who looked at least fifteen years his junior. Cameron dead, his face frozen in what the coroner had described as "consistent with cardiac arrest." Melissa at the funeral, appropriately devastated in designer black.

And then there was the receipt—the one piece of evidence that had brought me to this town. A credit card charge from Alden Alchemy for a "Personalised Skincare Consultation." Two hundred pounds for what was presumably face cream.

Very expensive face cream.

I closed the laptop, rubbing my eyes. We had originally had the idea of the butcher shop as a front, but that idea had become permanent. Fraser had gotten out of his work with the Glasgow outfit, and Theo's side gig was entirely online, so when we decided to move here, we chose here because we thought when it was done, we could settle down and run the butchers as a retirement job. Even though Theo talked about upping the side gig to a more permanent style of work, which I didn't mind. I knew I would never be able to run from the darkness, and this way I could free it when the itch happened and not have a boss.

It was a good plan. A clean exit from a dirty business. One last job, then freedom.

Then I'd met Genie Alden, with her poison-green eyes and her secrets that seemed to match my own. And everything had gotten complicated.

"Still up?" Theo's voice came from the doorway, making me jump slightly.

"Jesus Christ," I muttered. "Make some noise when you move, would you?"

He smiled thinly, the expression never reaching his eyes. Theo had that quality about him—like he was always calculating, always three steps ahead. It made him excellent at what he did, but it also made him dangerous.

"Thinking about our witch?" he asked, moving into the room with silent grace.

I closed the file on my laptop. "Working."

"Same thing, these days." He sat across from me, his posture perfect even at this ungodly hour. "I've been doing some digging."

"And?"

"Not much on the surface. The Alden's have been in Newchurch for generations. Old money, old property, old reputation for alternative practices."

"Witchcraft," I translated.

"If you believe in that sort of thing," Theo shrugged. "What's more interesting is the pattern of deaths associated with women who've visited Alden Alchemy."

My stomach tightened. "What pattern?"

Theo pulled out his phone, scrolling through notes with practiced efficiency. "In the past five years, there have been seven deaths of men whose wives or girlfriends were regular customers at Alden's shop. All natural causes—heart attacks, strokes, and one case of liver failure. All with perfectly reasonable medical explanations."

"That doesn't prove anything," I pointed out, though the coincidence was damning.

"No," Theo agreed. "But it's enough to warrant further investigation. Especially given what happened with Cameron Smith."

I leaned back in my chair, processing this information. "What about the other two? Daisy and Bernie?"

"Less interesting. Daisy was a barmaid until moving in with Genie. Now she works in the shop and makes those ridiculous Reels videos. Quite popular, actually—over a hundred thousand followers."

"And Bernie?"

"Makes candles that Genie sells in the shop. Seems harmless enough, though I'd avoid them if I were you. No telling what might be in the wax."

I frowned at that. "Bernie wouldn't hurt a fly."

"Perhaps not intentionally," Theo conceded. "But she lives with a woman who I'm increasingly convinced is a poisoner for battered women. Proximity to darkness tends to stain even the purest souls."

I thought of Bernie's sunny smile and her clumsy enthusiasm; the way she knocked over her water glass when Theo sat next to her at the pub. It was hard to imagine her involved in anything sinister. But then again, I'd learned long ago that appearances were often deceiving.

"So, what's the plan?" I asked, though I already knew the answer.

"We continue as we have been. Build trust. Gather evidence. Find out if Genie Alden helped Melissa Smith murder her husband, and if so, how."

"And then?"

Theo's eyes met mine, cold and clear. "Then we complete the job we were hired to do."

The implication hung in the air between us. Complete the job. Eliminate the threat. Tie up loose ends.

Kill Genie Alden.

"There might be another explanation," I said carefully. "The deaths could be coincidental. Or—"

"Or what?" Theo challenged. "She's actually a witch who casts death spells? Don't tell me you're buying into the local superstition."

I wasn't, not exactly. But I'd seen enough in this world to

know that there were things that defied rational explanation. There was something about Genie—something in the way she moved, the way she spoke, and the way she looked at me like she could see right through to my soul; that made me believe she was capable of things beyond ordinary understanding.

"I'm just saying, we should be certain before we act," I replied. "If we're wrong—"

"We're not wrong," Theo cut me off. "But by all means, continue your... research. Just remember why we're here, Ciarán. Remember who you work for."

As if I could forget. The man who'd plucked me from the streets of Dublin, who'd seen my potential for violence and honed it into a weapon. The man who made me what I was today—a killer with a conscience that only occasionally kept me awake at night.

"I remember," I said quietly.

Theo nodded, satisfied. "Good. Get some sleep. You look like shite."

He left as silently as he'd arrived, leaving me alone with my thoughts and the rain tapping against the window like impatient fingers.

Sleep wasn't going to come, not with my mind racing like it was. I pulled on a jacket and stepped outside onto the small porch, lighting a cigarette and inhaling it deeply. The night was cool and damp, the kind of weather that seeped into your bones and made old injuries ache. My shoulder—the one that had taken a bullet three years ago in Belfast—throbbed in agreement.

I thought about Genie, about the women I'd seen entering her shop with fear in their eyes and leaving with something that looked like hope. I thought about the bruises I'd glimpsed on their wrists, their necks, their souls. I thought about what it might mean to help such women, to give them a way out when all legal avenues had failed.

Was it murder? Technically, yes. Was it wrong? That was a more complicated question, one that I—with my own blood-soaked hands—was hardly qualified to answer.

"You're up late," Fraser's voice came from behind me, as the door opened then closed, followed by the man himself, wrapped in a ridiculous tartan dressing gown that had seen better days.

"Could say the same to you," I replied, offering him a cigarette.

He took it, leaning in as I held out my lighter. "Couldn't sleep. Kept thinking about that blonde."

"Daisy," I supplied.

"Aye, Daisy." He smiled, the expression softening his usually hard features. "She's something else."

"That she is," I agreed. "You seein her again?"

"Tomorrow night. Taking her to that fancy new restaurant in Lancaster." He puffed on the cigarette, looking uncharacteristically nervous. "Think I might be in trouble here, mate."

"What kind of trouble?"

"The kind where I actually give a shite what she thinks of me," he admitted. "Haven't felt that way about a woman in… well, ever."

I chuckled. "Welcome to the club."

Fraser raised an eyebrow. "So, you admit it, aye? You've got feelings for the witch?"

I took a long drag of my cigarette, considering my answer. "It's complicated."

"It always is with you," he snorted. "But I've seen the way you look at her. Like she's a puzzle you're dying to solve."

"She might be a murderer," I said bluntly.

Fraser didn't even blink. "Aren't we all?"

He had a point. Between the three of us—Fraser, Theo, and myself—we had enough blood on our hands to fill a small lake. Who were we to judge?

"You ever fall for someone who might be a murderer?" I asked, only half-joking.

"Constantly," Fraser replied with a grin. "It's my type. Dangerous women with secrets and the ability to kill me in my sleep. What can I say? I like to live on the edge."

I laughed despite myself. Fraser had always had that effect on me—the ability to make light of even the darkest situations. It was why we'd remained friends long after our professional paths should have separated.

"Seriously, though," he continued, his tone sobering slightly. "If you like her, and she likes you—which she obviously does, or she wouldn't be wasting her witchy powers on making your chalk crumble—then what's the problem? So, she might have helped a few abusive bastards shuffle off this mortal coil. Can't say they didn't deserve it."

"The problem," I said carefully, "is that we were hired to find out who killed Cameron Smith. And to deal with the situation."

Fraser's expression darkened. "By 'deal with,' you mean—"

"You know exactly what I mean."

He was quiet for a moment, the only sound the sizzle of his cigarette as he took another drag. "And if she did do it? What then?"

"Then I have a decision to make," I replied, the weight of it settling on my shoulders like a physical burden.

"Between the job and the girl," Fraser nodded. "Classic dilemma. Very Romeo and Juliet, except with more murder and less teenage angst."

"Thanks for the literary analysis," I said dryly.

"Any time," he grinned, then grew serious again. "Look, I know you've always been the loyal soldier. Following orders, doing what needs to be done. But maybe it's time to ask yourself, what do you want, not what does your boss wants."

What I wanted. It had been so long since I'd allowed myself to consider such a luxury that the concept felt almost foreign. What did I want? Freedom from the life I'd built? Peace from the nightmares that plagued me? Redemption for the sins I'd committed?

Or did I want something simpler—a woman with green eyes who saw my darkness and didn't flinch?

"It's not that simple," I said finally.

"It never is," Fraser agreed. "But for what it's worth, I think you deserve a shot at happiness. Even if it's with a woman who might occasionally poison people."

I laughed, the sound harsh in the quiet night. "You're a terrible influence."

"The worst," he agreed cheerfully. "Now, I'm going back to bed to dream about my blonde bombshell. You should get some sleep, too. You look like shite."

"So I've been told," I muttered.

After Fraser left, I stayed on the porch, smoking another cigarette and watching the rain. The logical part of my brain—the part that had kept me alive in this business for over a decade—was screaming warnings. Genie Alden was a complication, a potential target, and a danger to the clean exit I'd been planning.

But another part of me, a part I'd thought long dead, was whispering something else entirely. Something about second chances and the possibility of a life beyond blood and shadows.

I crushed out my cigarette, decision made. I needed to know the truth about Genie Alden. Not for my boss, not for the job, but for myself. I needed to know if the connection I felt with her was real or just another illusion in a life built on deception.

And there was only one way to find out.

THE NEXT MORNING, I was at Alden Alchemy before it opened, a peace offering in hand. Not flowers—that would have been too on the nose given the Rose misunderstanding. Instead, I'd brought coffee from the café down the street, the good stuff that cost twice as much as regular coffee but tasted like it had been brewed by angels.

I watched through the window as Genie moved around inside, setting up displays and checking inventory. She wore a dark green sweater that matched her eyes, her hair pulled back in a messy bun that somehow looked both effortless and elegant. Even from a distance, she was magnetic.

Taking a deep breath, I knocked on the door.

She looked up, surprise flashing across her face when she saw me. For a moment, I thought she might ignore me, but then she approached the door, unlocking it but not opening it fully.

"We're not open yet," she said, her voice cool, but not hostile.

"I know," I replied, holding up the coffee cups. "Peace offering?"

She eyed the cups suspiciously. "Is this your way of apologising for that bus stop advertisement?"

"No," I grinned. "That was brilliant, and I stand by it. This is my way of asking for five minutes of your time."

A small smile tugged at the corner of her mouth. "At least you're trying to be honest."

"I try to be," I said, the irony of the statement not lost on me. "So, five minutes?"

She hesitated, then opened the door wider. "Fine. But only because it's cold out and that coffee smells amazing."

I stepped inside, the shop's herbal scent enveloping me immediately—lavender, rosemary, something deeper and earthier that I couldn't identify. The space was warm and inviting, with wooden shelves lined with bottles and jars; each meticulously labelled in elegant script.

"It smells amazing in here," I commented, handing her one of the coffees.

"Thanks," she replied, taking a cautious sip. Her eyes widened slightly. "This is good."

"I know," I said, perhaps a bit smugly. "I do occasionally get things right."

She leaned against the counter, studying me over the rim of her cup. "So, what did you want to talk about that couldn't wait until normal business hours?"

I took a breath, deciding on directness. "Rose really is my sister."

"So you've said," she nodded.

"And I can prove it," I continued, pulling out my phone and opening my photos. I scrolled to a picture of Rose and me at Christmas last year, her arm around my shoulders, both of us wearing ridiculous paper crowns from crackers. "See? Sister. Not girlfriend, not wife. Just my annoying little sister who uses too many emojis and has terrible timing."

Genie took the phone, examining the photo. "You have the same eyes," she observed.

"And the same temper, according to our mother," I added.

She handed the phone back, her expression softening slightly. "Okay, I believe you. Your sister has terrible timing."

"The worst," I agreed. "So, now that we've established

that I'm not a cheating bastard, can we call a truce on the hexes?"

"Hexes?" she repeated innocently. "I have no idea what you're talking about."

"Right," I drawled. "My chalk just spontaneously disintegrates every time I try to write the daily specials. And that oil on our window was just… what? An act of God?"

A smile played at the corners of her mouth. "This town is full of strange coincidences. Mrs. Beecham says…"

"Ley lines, yes, you mentioned it," I said sceptically. "I suppose my flat tires and the refrigerator that keeps shorting out are also due to these… ley lines?"

"Probably," she shrugged, but her eyes were dancing with mischief now. "Or maybe it's karma."

"My karma is just fine, thank you," I replied, taking a step closer to her. "Though I'm curious about one thing."

"What's that?" she asked, not backing away despite my proximity.

"Why go to all that trouble? If you thought I was a cheating bastard, why not just tell me to fuck off and be done with it? Why the elaborate revenge?"

She considered this, her head tilting slightly. "I don't like being lied to," she said finally. "And I don't like feeling… vulnerable."

The admission seemed to cost her something, a small crack in her carefully constructed armour. I understood that feeling all too well—the need to protect oneself; to strike first, before being struck.

"Fair enough," I nodded. "For what it's worth, I'm sorry about the misunderstanding. And I'm sorry if I made you feel vulnerable."

She looked surprised by the apology. "Thank you," she said softly, then seemed to catch herself, straightening up and adopting a more businesslike tone. "So, truce?"

"Truce," I agreed, extending my hand.

She hesitated for a moment before taking it. The contact sent a jolt of awareness through me, a reminder of the night we'd spent together and all the ways we'd touched each other. From the slight widening of her eyes, I knew she felt it too.

"Well," she said, withdrawing her hand perhaps a bit too quickly. "Your five minutes are up, and I have a shop to open."

"Right," I nodded, taking a step back. "Thanks for the audience. And for believing me about Rose."

"Thanks for the coffee," she replied, gesturing toward the door in a clear dismissal.

I turned to leave, then paused. "One more thing," I said, looking back at her. "Would you have dinner with me? A proper date, not just a drunken stumble back to your place after the pub."

She blinked, clearly caught off guard by the invitation. "I… don't think that's a good idea."

"Why not?" I pressed. "We're both single, we're both attracted to each other—unless I've been reading things very wrong—and now that we've established that I don't have a secret girlfriend, there's no reason not to."

"There are plenty of reasons," she said, though she didn't sound entirely convinced.

"Name one," I challenged.

She crossed her arms, a defensive posture that told me more than her words. "I don't know you."

"That's what dates are for," I pointed out. "Getting to know each other."

"You're persistent," she observed.

"When I see something I want," I agreed. "So, dinner? Tomorrow night? I promise to be a perfect gentleman."

A smile tugged at her lips. "That would be disappointing."

I grinned, recognising the opening. "Alright, I promise to be mostly a gentleman, with occasional lapses into scoundrel territory if the mood strikes."

She laughed then, a genuine sound that transformed her face and sent a wave of warmth through my chest. "Fine," she conceded. "Dinner. Tomorrow night. But I'm not making any promises about what happens afterward."

"I wouldn't dream of presuming," I assured her, though my mind was already racing with possibilities. "I'll pick you up at seven?"

"Seven works," she nodded. "Now, seriously, I need to open the shop."

"I'm going, I'm going," I said, backing toward the door. "See you tomorrow, Genevie Alden."

"See you tomorrow, Ciarán Ó Duinn," she replied, a small smile playing on her lips.

I left feeling lighter than I had in days, despite the complications this development added to an already complex situation. I was supposed to be investigating Genie, not dating her. I was supposed to be gathering evidence, not falling deeper under her spell.

But as I walked back to the butcher shop, I couldn't bring myself to regret the invitation. For better or worse, I was drawn to Genie Alden. And I needed to know if she was what Theo suspected—a poisoner who helped women eliminate abusive men.

Because if she were, I had a decision to make. A decision that would cost me everything I'd worked for or would cost her life.

And neither option was one I was prepared to accept.

Chapter 9
Wine, Dine, and Hidden Agendas
Genie

"So, you're going on a date with the Irish butcher tonight?" Daisy's voice carried across the shop the next day, loud enough that Mrs. Finch—who was browsing our facial toners—looked up with undisguised interest.

I shot Daisy a glare that should have turned her to stone. "Could you say that a little louder? I don't think they heard you in Lancaster."

She grinned, completely unrepentant. "Just making sure I heard correctly. You, Genie Alden, scourge of cheating men everywhere, are voluntarily going on a date with the man whose chalk you hexed into oblivion."

"He explained about Rose," I muttered, rearranging a display of lavender-infused moisturisers with more force than necessary. "She's his sister."

"And you believed him?" Daisy raised a perfectly sculpted eyebrow.

"He showed me a picture," I said defensively. "They have the same eyes."

"Hmm." Daisy tapped her chin thoughtfully. "So, the hex

war is officially over, and now you're moving on to… what exactly? The kissing phase? The shagging-again-but-sober phase?"

Mrs. Finch was now openly staring, the bottle of toner in her hand long forgotten.

"Can we discuss this later?" I hissed, nodding pointedly toward our audience.

"Oh, don't mind me, dear," Mrs. Finch called cheerfully. "I think it's wonderful you're seeing that handsome Irish fellow. Those eyes! And those hands! My Harold had big hands, too, God rest his soul. Always said it was a sign of—"

"Thank you, Mrs. Finch," I interrupted hastily. "Did you find everything you were looking for today?"

She winked at me. "Not as much as you're going to find tonight, I'd wager."

Daisy burst into laughter, while I felt my face heat to approximately the temperature of the sun. This was exactly why I shouldn't have told the girls about agreeing to dinner with Ciarán. In a town this size, news travelled faster than light, and apparently, my love life—or lack thereof—was prime entertainment.

The rest of the day continued in much the same vein. Every customer who came in seemed to know about my date. Mrs. Beecham stopped by specifically to tell me that her second cousin had married an Irishman, and it had been "quite the education." Bernie, who was supposed to be on my side, kept giving me these soppy, encouraging smiles and had even brought in a special candle she'd made "for romance and protection."

By closing time, I was seriously considering hexing the entire town into silence.

"Don't forget these," Daisy said as I was locking up, handing me a small paper bag.

I peered inside and immediately closed it again. "Condoms? Really?"

"Better safe than sorry," she shrugged. "And the ribbed ones are for his pleasure, which means they're actually for your pleasure, if you know what I mean."

"I'm familiar with the concept," I said dryly. "But this is just dinner. At his place. Which is probably a terrible idea, now that I think about it."

"It's a great idea," Daisy countered. "Private, intimate, and you get to see where he lives. Plus, if he's a good cook, that's bonus points right there."

"And if he's a serial killer, I'll be conveniently at his murder house," I pointed out.

Daisy rolled her eyes. "Please. You're a witch who knows seventeen different ways to poison a man without leaving a trace. I think you can handle one Irish butcher."

She had a point, though I wasn't about to admit it. "Fine. But I'm not taking these," I said, trying to hand back the condoms.

"Yes, you are," she insisted, pushing my hand away. "Consider it my investment in your orgasm future."

"You're the worst friend ever," I grumbled, shoving the bag into my purse.

"I'm the best friend ever, and you know it," she corrected, giving me a quick hug. "Now go home and make yourself pretty. Not that you need much help in that department."

I walked home to the Alden estate alone. Bernie had book club, and Daisy was seeing Fraser, my mind racing with second thoughts. What was I doing, agreeing to have dinner with Ciarán? Yes, he'd proven Rose was his sister. Yes, the chemistry between us was undeniable. But there was something about him—something dark and hidden—that both attracted and alarmed me.

Then again, I was hardly in a position to judge someone for having secrets.

At home, I spent an embarrassing amount of time deciding what to wear. Too fancy would seem like I was trying too hard; too casual would look like I didn't care. I finally settled on a dark green wrap dress that brought out my eyes and hugged my curves without being overtly sexual. Paired with ankle boots and minimal jewellery, it struck the right balance between effort and nonchalance.

I was applying a final touch of lipstick when the doorbell rang at precisely seven o'clock. Punctuality—another point in his favour.

Taking a deep breath, I opened the door to find Ciarán standing on my porch, looking unfairly attractive in dark jeans and a blue button-down that made his eyes even more striking. He'd made an effort to tame his usually unruly dark hair, though a few rebellious strands had already escaped.

"Wow," he said, his gaze traveling from my face down to my boots and back up again. "You look… breathtaking."

"Thanks," I replied, fighting the urge to fidget under his intense scrutiny. "You clean up pretty well yourself."

"I try," he grinned, then held out a small, potted plant. Not flowers—which would have been the obvious choice—but a tiny, thriving rosemary bush. "For you. Seemed more appropriate than roses, given the circumstances."

I took it, genuinely touched by the thoughtfulness. "It's perfect. Rosemary for remembrance and protection."

"And for cooking," he added with a wink. "I'm a practical man."

"So I've noticed," I said, setting the plant on the entryway table. "Let me grab my purse, and we can go."

The drive to his place was surprisingly comfortable. He had good taste in music—a mix of indie folk and classic rock

—and didn't feel the need to fill every silence with chatter. When we did talk, it was easy, natural, like we'd known each other for years instead of weeks.

I'd expected him to live in town, perhaps in an apartment above the butcher shop. Instead, he drove us to the outskirts of Newchurch, where a small, stone cottage stood nestled among trees; its windows glowing warmly against the darkening sky.

"This is… not what I pictured," I admitted as he parked.

"What did you picture?" he asked, curious.

"I don't know. Something more temporary? You three don't seem like the cottage-in-the-woods types."

He laughed. "Fraser wanted to be closer to town, but Theo insisted on privacy. I just wanted a place with a decent kitchen and no neighbours to complain about my music."

The cottage was charming from the outside and surprisingly spacious within. The décor was minimal but tasteful—comfortable furniture, a few carefully chosen art pieces, bookshelves filled with an eclectic mix of titles. It felt lived-in but not cluttered, masculine but not aggressively so.

"Make yourself at home," Ciarán said, taking my coat. "Wine? I've got red or white."

"Red, please," I replied, wandering over to examine the bookshelves. The collection was interesting—crime novels, historical biographies, a surprising number of poetry books, and a well-worn copy of "The Táin," an Irish epic I recognised from my studies of Celtic mythology.

"You like Irish literature?" I asked as he returned with two glasses of wine.

"I like stories about warriors and cattle raids," he replied with a smile, handing me a glass. "Reminds me of home."

"Lots of cattle raids in Dingle, are there?"

"You'd be surprised," he said, his eyes twinkling. "The

dinner's almost ready. I thought we could eat on the balcony, if that's alright with you?"

"Sounds perfect," I agreed, following him through the kitchen—which was indeed impressive, with professional-grade equipment and a massive butcher block island—and out onto a small balcony that overlooked a wild, overgrown garden and the woods beyond.

He'd set up a small table with candles and a simple but elegant place setting. String lights hung overhead, casting a warm glow that made everything look magical. It was romantic without being cliché, intimate without trying too hard.

"This is lovely," I said, genuinely impressed. "You didn't have to go to all this trouble."

"It's no trouble," he assured me, pulling out my chair. "I enjoy cooking, and it's not often I get to cook for someone who might appreciate it."

"Fraser and Theo aren't culinary enthusiasts?"

"Fraser eats like he's still in the army—fast and without tasting. And Theo subsists primarily on tea and disdain."

I laughed at that. "Speaking of Theo, is he here? I noticed his car outside."

"He's hiding in his room," Ciarán confirmed, disappearing into the kitchen and returning with two plates. "Said he had work to do, but I think he's just avoiding social interaction."

"So, you only brought me here to wine and dine me in private?" I teased, taking a sip of my wine.

He set a plate in front of me—lamb with rosemary and garlic, roasted vegetables, and something that looked like a potato gratin. It smelled divine.

"Well, yes and no," he replied, taking his seat across from me. "I mean, I'm happy to do that, but I did it because I wanted a private dinner, not surrounded by noise and people and other stuff."

I smiled, oddly touched by his honesty. "I love quiet too," I admitted. "I sit at the cemetery for hours just to get some peace."

"The cemetery?" he raised an eyebrow. "That's… unique."

"Well, as much as I'm allowed," I laughed. "I get a lot of visitors."

"Living or dead?" he asked, only half-joking.

I took a bite of the lamb—which was perfectly cooked, tender, and flavourful—before answering. "Both, actually. The dead are usually more polite, though."

He paused, his fork halfway to his mouth. "You're serious."

"About the lamb being delicious? Absolutely. This is amazing."

"About seeing the dead," he clarified, though he looked pleased at the compliment.

I considered how to answer. This was usually the point where people either decided I was crazy or became uncomfortably fascinated. But something about Ciarán made me want to be honest.

"I see things others don't," I said carefully. "It's a family trait. My mother had it, and her mother before her."

"The Sight," he nodded, surprising me. "My grandmother talked about it. Said some people were born with a foot in both worlds."

"That's a good way of putting it," I agreed, relieved he wasn't immediately dismissing me as insane. "It's not always ghosts in the traditional sense. Sometimes it's just… impressions. Echoes of what happened in a place."

"Must be noisy in your head," he observed, refilling our wine glasses.

"Hence the cemetery visits," I smiled. "It's peaceful there. The dead don't want much, just to be remembered sometimes."

We ate in comfortable silence for a moment, the only sounds the distant hooting of an owl and the soft clinking of cutlery against plates.

"So," he said finally, "are you really a witch?"

I laughed. "Are you asking if I can turn you into a toad?"

"Can you?" he countered, eyes twinkling.

"Anything is real if you believe it," I replied enigmatically.

He chuckled. "Well, my mum was a believer, so I guess that makes me one too."

"Was?" I asked gently, noting the past tense.

A shadow crossed his face. "She died when I was sixteen. Cancer."

"I'm sorry," I said, meaning it. "My parents died in a car crash five years ago."

He nodded, understanding in his eyes. "It changes you, doesn't it? Losing them."

"It does," I agreed softly. "Makes you realise how fragile everything is. How quickly it can all be taken away."

"To those we've lost," he said, raising his glass in a toast.

"And to finding our way without them," I added, clinking my glass against his.

The conversation shifted to lighter topics after that. He told me about growing up in Dingle, about his sister Rose and her terrible taste in men, about his first job at a local butcher shop when he was fourteen. I shared stories about Bernie's disastrous attempts at cooking, Daisy's viral Reels fame, and the time Mrs. Beecham caught me skinny-dipping in the lake at midnight during a full moon ritual.

"In my defence, I thought the area was deserted," I explained as he laughed. "How was I supposed to know she walked her corgi there at that hour?"

"The real question is, did the ritual work?" he asked, eyes dancing with mischief.

"Wouldn't you like to know?" I teased.

"I would, actually," he said, his voice dropping to that low, gravelly register that sent shivers down my spine. "I find myself very interested in your… rituals."

The air between us suddenly felt charged, the easy conversation gave way to something more primal. His eyes held mine, dark and intent, and I found myself leaning toward him almost unconsciously.

"Ciarán," I began, not entirely sure what I was going to say.

"Genie," he replied, reaching across the table to brush a strand of hair from my face. The simple touch sent electricity racing across my skin.

The moment was shattered by the sound of a door opening inside, followed by Theo's crisp voice. "Ciarán? Have you seen my—oh, sorry. Didn't realise you were still out here."

Theo stood in the doorway, looking as polished as ever despite the late hour. His gaze flicked between us, calculating and cool.

"It's fine," Ciarán said, though his tone suggested it was anything but. "What do you need?"

"My laptop charger," Theo replied. "Thought I might have left it in the kitchen."

"Haven't seen it," Ciarán said shortly.

"Right. Well, don't let me interrupt." Theo's smile didn't

reach his eyes as he nodded to me. "Ms. Alden. Lovely to see you again."

"Likewise," I lied, feeling a strange chill despite the warm evening.

After he left, the mood had shifted. Ciarán looked annoyed, his jaw tight as he stared after his friend.

"Everything okay?" I asked.

He sighed, running a hand through his hair. "Yeah, sorry about that. Theo can be… intense."

"I've noticed," I said dryly. "He doesn't seem to like me much."

"He doesn't like anyone much," Ciarán assured me. "It's not personal."

"If you say so," I shrugged, unconvinced. "So, what brought you three to Newchurch anyway? It's not exactly a hotspot for ambitious butchers."

He hesitated, just long enough for me to notice. "Change of scenery," he said finally. "Dublin was getting… complicated. And Fraser was tired of Glasgow. Theo goes wherever the money is good."

It was a vague answer, carefully constructed to sound reasonable while revealing almost nothing. I recognised the technique because I used it myself when customers asked too many questions about my "special" products.

"Complicated how?" I pressed, curious despite myself.

"Just… personal stuff," he said, his expression closing slightly. "Nothing interesting."

He was lying. Or at least, not telling the whole truth. But then again, so was I. We all had our secrets, our hidden agendas. Who was I to demand complete honesty when I was keeping so much from him?

"Fair enough," I conceded, deciding not to push. "We all have our reasons for ending up in strange places."

Relief flickered across his face, quickly replaced by curiosity. "And what's yours? Why stay in Newchurch when you could take your business somewhere bigger? London, maybe, or Manchester?"

"This is home," I said simply. "The Alden's have been here for generations. The land knows us, and we know it. There's power in that kind of connection."

"Power," he repeated thoughtfully. "Is that what you're after?"

I laughed. "God, no. Power brings nothing but trouble. I'm after peace, if anything. A quiet life where I can help people and be left alone to do my work."

"Your skincare business," he said, watching me carefully.

"Among other things," I replied, holding his gaze steadily.

Something passed between us then—an understanding, perhaps, or at least an acknowledgment that we were both dancing around certain truths. Neither of us was ready to lay all our cards on the table, but we recognised the game the other was playing.

"Dessert?" he offered, breaking the tension. "I made chocolate mousse. Nothing fancy, but it's edible."

"I'd love some," I smiled, grateful for the shift back to safer territory.

He cleared our plates and returned with two small bowls of mousse, topped with fresh berries. It was, like everything else he'd prepared, delicious.

"You're wasted as a butcher," I told him after the first heavenly bite. "You should be running a restaurant."

"Ah, but then I'd have to deal with customers," he grimaced. "Dead animals are much less demanding."

"Fair point," I laughed. "Though I'd argue that some customers are indistinguishable from dead animals, just louder."

"Speaking from experience?" he grinned.

"Let's just say that Mrs. Hargrove's weekly complaints about our 'overpriced snake oil' would test the patience of a saint," I said dryly. "Which I am decidedly not."

"No," he agreed, his eyes warm as they met mine. "You're something much more interesting than a saint."

The way he looked at me made my heart race and my skin flush. There was appreciation there, certainly, but also curiosity, fascination, and something darker that I couldn't quite name.

"Flatterer," I accused lightly.

"Just observant," he countered. "Tá tú álainn agus contúirteach." *You are beautiful and dangerous.*

I raised an eyebrow. "Your Gaelic is showing."

"Happens when I'm… affected," he admitted, not looking particularly sorry about it.

"And what does it mean?" I asked, though I had a feeling I knew.

He smiled, slow and deliberate. "That's for me to know and you to find out."

"Tease," I accused.

"Absolutely," he agreed cheerfully. "It's more fun that way."

After dessert, we moved inside to the living room with the remainder of the wine. The conversation flowed easily again, touching on books we'd read, places we'd travelled, and music we loved. It was the kind of date I'd almost forgotten could exist—comfortable yet exciting, familiar yet full of discovery.

As the night grew later, I found myself reluctant to leave. There was something about Ciarán Ó Duinn that pulled at me, despite all my reservations. Maybe it was the way he listened, like really listened when I spoke. Or how he didn't flinch when I mentioned my more unusual abilities. Or perhaps it was simply the way he looked at me, like he saw all of me—the light and the dark—and wasn't afraid of either.

"I should probably go," I said finally, glancing at the clock. "It's getting late."

"I'll drive you home," he offered, standing and offering me his hand.

I took it, allowing him to pull me to my feet. We stood close, too close, his warmth radiating through the small space between us. His eyes dropped to my lips, and for a moment, I thought he might kiss me. Part of me—a larger part than I'd cared to admit—hoped he would.

Instead, he stepped back slightly, his hand still holding mine. "Thank you for coming tonight," he said softly. "I enjoyed this."

"So did I," I admitted. "You're a surprisingly good date, Ciarán Ó Duinn."

"Surprisingly?" he repeated, mock offended. "Were your expectations that low?"

"Let's just say my dating history hasn't set a high bar," I replied dryly.

"Well, I'm honoured to have exceeded your rock-bottom expectations," he grinned, grabbing his keys from a hook by the door.

The drive back to my place was quiet but comfortable, the kind of silence that doesn't need to be filled. When we arrived, he insisted on walking me to the door, a gentlemanly gesture that seemed at odds with the dangerous edge I sensed in him.

At my doorstep, under the soft glow of the porch light, he finally did what I'd been both dreading and anticipating all evening. He kissed me.

It wasn't the frantic, desperate kiss of our first night

together, fuelled by whiskey and poor decisions. This was slower, more deliberate, his lips moved against mine with a patience that was somehow more devastating than if it was urgent His hand cupped my face, thumb stroking my cheek as his mouth explored mine with exquisite care.

When we finally broke apart, I was breathless, my heart hammering against my ribs like it was trying to escape.

"Oíche mhaith, a stór," he murmured, his voice rough. Goodnight, my treasure.

"Goodnight, Ciarán," I replied, my voice not entirely steady.

He waited until I was safely inside before leaving, a small courtesy that shouldn't have affected me as much as it did. I leaned against the closed door and listened to his car drive away, my lips still tingled from our kiss.

I was in trouble. Deep, complicated trouble. Because despite all my reservations; despite the secrets I could sense he was keeping; despite the voice in my head warning me to be careful… I was falling for Ciarán Ó Duinn.

And that might be the most dangerous potion I'd ever brewed.

Chapter 10
Midnight Confessions
Ciarán

That date was exactly not what I had planned. I wanted to take her to my bed and fuck her until she screamed, but it just didn't feel right. I had already fucked her, and my dick, that had been hard since I picked her up, was down for the idea, but I wanted to do this right. Why, I wasn't sure.

One thing I was sure of was that Genie was most definitely who and what I thought she was, but she was also beautiful, kind, and sweet—and in my twisted book of life, was doing the right thing. I wouldn't touch a hair on her head, unless I was wrapping it around my fist and pulling her body into mine, while I fucked her.

God, the thoughts alone were going to make me cum on the spot.

I pulled into the cottages driveway and climbed from my car. The stars were still shining up above. It really was pretty out here. Made you feel like you were all alone in the world, just the way I liked it.

The cottage was quiet and dark when I entered, just a sliver of light visible under Theo's door. Good. I wasn't in the mood for questions about my evening with Genie. The way he'd interrupted during dinner had been no accident—the man never did anything without calculation. He was suspicious of her, and by extension, of my interest in her.

Let him be, I had other things on my mind.

I headed inside my room, where I got into the shower and fisted my dick to images of the first time I fucked her, just like I had every single night since I had felt her pussy. The water cascaded down my body as I closed my eyes, remembering every detail of that night.

The way she'd looked at me across the pub; the challenge in her eyes. Then walking back to her place, tension crackling between us like lightning. The moment we'd crossed her threshold, all pretences had fallen away.

I stroked myself harder, recalling how she'd felt beneath me—all soft curves and sharp edges. How she'd dug her nails into my back when I'd entered her, leaving marks I admired in the mirror the next morning. The sounds she'd made—half moans, half curses—when I'd found that spot inside her that made her arch off the bed.

"Fuck," I groaned, my hand moving faster now. In my mind, she was on her knees before me, those green eyes looking up as she took me in her mouth; then bent over the kitchen counter, her arse in the air as I pounded into her from behind. And finally, straddling me with her head thrown back in ecstasy as she rode me to completion.

The hot water beat down on my shoulders as I worked my cock, my breath grew ragged. I was hooked on her—her taste, her smell, the way she moved, the sounds she made when she came. I couldn't get enough.

My hand moved faster, gripping tighter as I felt my release building. Images of Genie flashed through my mind— her lips parted in pleasure, her eyes dark with desire, her body writhing beneath mine. I was obsessed, and I didn't want to change it.

I came with a shudder, her name on my lips, my release washed away down the drain. For a moment, I just stood there, letting the water beat down on me, my breath gradually returning to normal.

This had become a nightly ritual—shower, wank, sleep, repeat. I was obsessed with her, and it was getting worse, not better. Tonight's date had only intensified it. Seeing her in my space, eating food I'd prepared, laughing at my jokes… it had awakened something in me I'd thought long dead. Something that went beyond lust, beyond the physical need that had driven me to her bed the first night.

I wanted her—all of her. Not just her body, but her mind, her secrets, her darkness. I wanted to know what made her help those women; what drove her to risk everything to dispense her own brand of justice. I wanted to tell her about my own darkness; about the blood on my hands, the night-mares that kept me awake.

And that was dangerous.

For both of us.

THE NEXT MORNING, I was at the butcher shop early, my hands steady as I broke down a side of beef. There was some-thing soothing about the work—precise, methodical, requiring just enough concentration to quiet the chaos in my mind. The rhythmic sound of my knife against the cutting board filled the empty shop.

Fraser wouldn't be in for another hour, and Theo was handling deliveries, which meant I had the place to myself. Just me, my knives, and the meat. Simple. Uncomplicated. Unlike everything else in my life right now.

The bell above the door chimed, interrupting my thoughts. I looked up, surprised to have a customer this early.

He was tall—taller than me by a few inches, which was saying something—with broad shoulders and black hair cut close to his scalp. His face was all hard angles, with deep-set eyes that took in everything at once. He moved with the careful precision of someone who was always aware of his surroundings, always ready for trouble.

I recognised the type immediately. This man was dangerous.

"Morning," I said, setting down my knife and wiping my hands on a towel. "You're up early."

"So are you," he replied, his accent American but with something else underneath it. Eastern European, maybe. His gaze scanned the shop, taking in the layout, the exits, and the potential weapons. Not a typically casual assessment— More professional. "Names Jack."

"What can I help you with, Jack?" I asked, keeping my tone casual while my instincts screamed warning.

He approached the counter, his movements fluid and controlled. "Just passing through," he said. "Thought I'd pick up something. How long have you been open here?"

"Few weeks," I replied, watching him carefully. "Shop's new, but I've been a butcher for years."

"Irish, right?" he asked, though he clearly already knew the answer.

I nodded. "Sure am."

"Long way from home," he observed. "What brought you to this little town?"

"Change of scenery," I said, the same vague answer I gave everyone. "Dublin was getting crowded."

He nodded, as if this made perfect sense, though his eyes remained calculating. "What's the town like? Quiet?"

"Very," I confirmed. "Not much happens here."

"Other shops any good?" he asked, gesturing vaguely toward the street. "I noticed a few on my way in."

My guard went up even further. These weren't the questions of someone just passing through. "Depends what you're looking for," I said carefully. "Bakeries decent. Pub serves a good pint."

"What about that skincare place?" he asked, his tone deliberately casual. "Alden something?"

And there it was. The real reason for his visit.

"Alden Alchemy," I supplied, keeping my expression neutral even as alarm bells rang in my head. "Popular with the locals. Owner makes everything herself."

"That right?" he said, his interest sharpening. "She any good?"

"Wouldn't know," I lied. "Not one for face creams myself."

He smiled, a cold expression that didn't reach his eyes. "Of course. Man like you probably doesn't need that stuff."

I returned the smile with equal insincerity. "Was there something specific you wanted to order?"

"Two steaks," he decided. "Thick cut."

I selected two ribeye's from the case, wrapping them efficiently while keeping one eye on him. He continued to study the shop, his gaze lingering on the knife block, the heavy cleavers, before drifting to the back door.

"You planning to stay in town long?" I asked as I handed him the package.

"Just passing through," he repeated, handing me cash. "But you never know. Might find a reason to stick around."

The threat was subtle, but unmistakable. This man wasn't here by accident, and his interest in Genie's shop wasn't casual curiosity.

"Well, enjoy your stay," I said, handing him his change. "Not much excitement around here, but the scenery's nice."

"I'm sure it is," he agreed, pocketing the money. "Thanks for the steaks."

"Anytime," I replied, though I hoped I'd never see him again.

He left as silently as he'd arrived, the bell above the door the only indication he'd been there at all. I watched through the window as he walked down the street, noting the slight bulge under his jacket that suggested he was armed.

My mind raced with possibilities, none of them good. Was he connected to Cameron Smith? To my employer? Or was he here for something else entirely, something to do with Genie that I knew nothing about?

I considered calling her, warning her about the stranger asking questions, but what would I say? That a dangerous-looking man had asked about her shop? That wasn't exactly unusual—Genie was beautiful and ran a successful business. People talked about her all the time.

But this had felt different. Deliberate. Threatening.

Chapter 11
Chemistry Lessons
Genie

Today was a good day. I had seven customers before lunch had even hit, and I smiled every time my eye caught sight of the stupid bus stop advertisement. "FORGET THE ROSES. GRAB THE BALLS." It was so immature.

I wasn't one to get attached, not since He-Who-We-Don't-Talk-About, but here I was, hooked on an Irish man with secrets. At least he wasn't a cheater, I thought with a shrug, and begun refilling a shelving unit I'd just emptied to wipe down.

The shop smelled of lavender and rosemary today, with undertones of the new batch of facial toner I'd brewed last night. It was a comforting scent, familiar and grounding. I needed grounding these days, with my thoughts constantly drifting to blue eyes and scarred hands and a voice that did things to my insides.

Mrs. Beecham had been my first customer of the day, ostensibly to buy her usual moisturizer but really to fish for information about my date with Ciarán. The town gossip network was operating at peak efficiency, as usual.

"I hear the Irish butcher made you dinner at his place," she'd said, eyes gleaming with barely contained curiosity. "Was he any good?"

"He's not bad," I'd replied noncommittally, which was like throwing gasoline on her curiosity fire.

"Not bad?" she'd repeated, leaning in conspiratorially. "My dear, a man who can cook is worth his weight in gold. My Harold couldn't boil water without burning it, God rest his soul."

I'd smiled politely, ringing up her purchase. "Will there be anything else today, Mrs. Beecham?"

She'd left disappointed by my lack of juicy details, but I knew it was only a temporary reprieve. In a town this size, privacy was a theoretical concept at best.

The bell above the door jingled, pulling me from my thoughts. Daisy breezed in, looking suspiciously well-rested and cheerful for someone who should have been exhausted from her late night with Fraser.

"Morning, witch bitch," she greeted, dropping a kiss on my cheek as she passed. "Gods, I had the best orgasm last night. Fraser really knows what he's doing."

She perched on the stool behind the counter, a self-satisfied smile playing on her lips. Her blonde hair was pulled into a messy bun, and she wore one of her signature crop tops, despite the cool autumn weather.

"Good morning to you, too," I replied dryly. "So glad you could join us, mere mortals, after your night of transcendent pleasure."

"Don't be jealous," she grinned, stealing a sip from my coffee mug. "It's not attractive on you."

"I'm not jealous," I protested, rescuing my coffee. "I'm just tired."

"The perils of small-town retail," Daisy nodded sagely. "So, speaking of orgasms…"

"We're not speaking of orgasms," I cut her off, turning back to the shelving.

"We're always speaking of orgasms," she countered. "It's practically our love language. And don't change the subject. Did the hot Irish butcher give you a good slicing last night?"

I snorted at that, despite myself. "That's terrible, even for you."

"Did he tenderise your meat? Stuff your sausage? Polish your—"

"I will hex your eyebrows off," I threatened, pointing a bottle of facial cleanser at her. "Don't think I won't."

She held up her hands in surrender, though her eyes still danced with mischief. "Fine, fine. But seriously, how was it? You've been smiling at that ridiculous bus stop ad since I walked in."

"I have not," I lied, arranging bottles with unnecessary precision.

"You have," she insisted. "Every time you look out the window. It's adorable; in a pathetic sort of way."

I sighed, giving up the pretence. "Well, I hope you're using those condoms you tried to give me, because you need every single one by the sounds of it."

Daisy's expression shifted from teasing to concerned. "Oh no, did he not fuck your brains out last night?"

I just laughed and shook my head. "There is more to life than sex, Daisy."

"No, there isn't," came Bernie's voice as she walked through the door, catching the end of our conversation. "I mean, fuck, I masturbate every night. It's so good for your body, you know. It releases chemicals that make you feel good. It's like taking an antidepressant pill without having to take one. I highly recommend."

Daisy and I burst out laughing, the unexpected frankness from our usually shy Bernie catching us off guard.

"What?" Bernie asked, looking between us with genuine confusion. "It's science. Orgasms reduce stress, improve sleep, boost your immune system—"

"We're not questioning the science," I assured her, wiping tears of laughter from my eyes. "Just surprised to hear you extolling the virtues of regular masturbation at—" I checked my watch, "—10:17 in the morning."

"Oh," Bernie blushed slightly. "Well, it came up in my research for the new pleasure candle line. Did you know that the scent of vanilla can increase arousal by up to 30%?"

"I did not," I replied, exchanging an amused glance with Daisy. "But I'm sure our customers will be thrilled to learn that while buying face cream."

Bernie set down her bag and hung up her coat, still in full educational mode. "It's not just vanilla. Sandalwood, jasmine, lavender in certain combinations—they all have properties that can enhance sexual experience. It's fascinating, really."

"You're fascinating," Daisy said fondly. "Never change, Bernie."

Bernie beamed, pleased by the compliment. "So, what were you two talking about before I came in? Besides orgasms, I mean."

"Genie's date with the hot Irish butcher," Daisy supplied helpfully. "Which apparently didn't end in mind-blowing sex, much to my disappointment."

"It was just dinner," I said, though the memory of Ciarán's goodnight kiss sent a pleasant shiver down my spine. "At his place. Nothing special."

"Liar," Daisy accused. "Your pupils dilate every time

someone mentions his name. It's science, honey. You can't fake that."

"My pupils do not—" I began, then stopped as both Daisy and Bernie burst into laughter. "You're the worst friends ever."

"We're the best friends ever," Daisy corrected. "And we're invested in your happiness. And your orgasms. Which, according to Bernie's scientific research, are basically the same thing."

"I hate you both," I muttered, though there was no heat in it.

"No, you don't," Bernie said confidently, moving to help me with the reshelving. "You love us. Almost as much as you love a certain blue-eyed Irishman."

"I don't love—" I started, then caught myself. "I barely know him."

"But you want to know him," Daisy pressed. "Biblically and otherwise."

I couldn't deny it, so I changed the subject. "Don't you have work to do? Those Reels won't film themselves."

"Actually, I'm taking a day off from content creation," Daisy announced. "My followers can survive without seeing me apply lip gloss for twenty-four hours."

"The horror," I deadpanned. "However will they cope?"

"With difficulty, I'm sure," she agreed solemnly. "But I thought I'd help out in the shop today. We've been busy lately."

She wasn't wrong. The past few weeks had seen an uptick in customers, both for the regular skincare products and for my more... specialised consultations. Word of mouth was powerful in a small town, and apparently, word had spread that Alden Alchemy was the place to go when conventional solutions failed.

"Thanks," I said, genuinely appreciative. "I could use the help. New batch of toner needs to be bottled, and I've got a consultation at two."

Daisy's expression softened slightly at the mention of a consultation. She knew what that meant—another woman in trouble, another desperate situation requiring my particular skills.

"Anyone I know?" she asked quietly.

I shook my head. "New client. Friend of Mrs. Hargrove's niece."

"Ah," she nodded, understanding. Mrs. Hargrove's niece had come to me six months ago with bruises around her throat and fear in her eyes. She'd left with a small vial and a new chance at life. "Need me to run interference?"

"If you could," I agreed. "Bernie, can you handle the front while Daisy manages any walk-ins during my consultation?"

"Of course," Bernie nodded, her expression serious. For all her awkwardness and occasional social missteps, Bernie was fiercely protective of what we did. "I'll make sure you're not disturbed."

"Thanks," I said, feeling a rush of gratitude for these two women who had become my family. They knew my darkness and my secrets, but loved me anyway. More than that, they helped, each in their own way. Bernie, with her uncanny ability to sense which customers needed more than just skincare, and Daisy, with her talent for distraction and misdirection when necessary.

"So," Daisy said, returning to her favourite subject, "back to the hot butcher. When are you seeing him again?"

"I don't know that I am," I replied, though the thought made something twist uncomfortably in my chest.

"Bullshit," Daisy declared. "The way you two look at

each other? It's happening. The only question is when, and how many orgasms will be involved."

"There's something complicated about him," I said carefully. "Something he's not telling me."

"Honey, we all have secrets," Daisy pointed out. "You more than most."

"This feels different," I insisted. "Like he's here for a reason. A specific reason."

Bernie looked up from the display she was arranging. "You think he's dangerous?"

I considered this. Was Ciarán dangerous? Absolutely. I sensed it the moment I met him—the controlled power in his movements, the watchfulness in his eyes, the scars on his hands that hadn't come from butchering meat.

"Yes," I said finally. "But not to me, I don't think."

"Well, that's reassuring," Daisy said sarcastically. "He's dangerous, but don't worry, he probably won't murder you specifically."

"You know what I mean," I sighed. "He has darkness in him. I can feel it. But it's familiar. Like recognising a part of yourself in someone else."

"The part that killed your abusive ex-boyfriend and buried him in the garden?" Daisy asked bluntly.

"Daisy!" Bernie gasped, looking around frantically, though the shop was empty.

"What? It's not like it's a secret between us," Daisy shrugged. "And it's relevant. If Genie senses that Ciarán has the same capacity for violence that she does, that's significant."

"It's more than that," I said slowly, trying to articulate what I'd felt during our dinner. "It's like... he understands. Not just what I did, but why. The necessity of it. The justice in it."

"Has he said something?" Bernie asked, her brow furrowed in concern.

"No," I admitted. "Nothing specific. It's just a feeling I get when we're together. Like he sees all of me—the light and the dark—and isn't afraid of either."

"Well, that's either incredibly romantic or the beginning of a true crime documentary," Daisy observed. "Possibly both."

I threw a cleaning cloth at her, which she caught with irritating grace. "Thanks for that helpful analysis."

"Anytime," she grinned. "So, when are you seeing him again?"

"I don't know," I repeated. "We didn't make specific plans."

"But you want to see him again," Bernie stated rather than asked.

I hesitated, then nodded. "Yes. Despite my better judgement."

"The heart wants what it wants," Bernie said wisely. "Or in Daisy's case, the vagina wants what it wants."

"Bernie!" Daisy and I exclaimed in unison, before dissolving into laughter.

"What?" she asked innocently. "More science. The chemical cocktail of attraction is powerful stuff. Dopamine, serotonin, oxytocin—"

"Please stop, before you turn my love life into a chemistry lesson," I begged, still laughing.

"But it is chemistry," Bernie insisted. "Literal chemistry. Your brain on attraction is basically your brain on drugs."

"That explains so much about my dating history," Daisy mused. "I'm not boy crazy, I'm just a dopamine addict."

"Exactly!" Bernie nodded enthusiastically. "And the good news is, the more you have sex with someone, the stronger the chemical bonds become. So really, Genie, you should sleep with Ciarán again. For science."

I nearly choked on my coffee. "I'm not making life decisions based on your amateur neuroscience knowledge, Bernie."

"It's not amateur," she protested. "I've been reading peer-reviewed journals."

"Of course you have," I said fondly. "But I think I'll base my decisions on slightly more than just brain chemicals, thanks."

"Your loss," she shrugged. "The research is very compelling."

The bell above the door jingled, signalling a customer and effectively ending our conversation about my sex life, much to my relief. The day continued in a pleasant rhythm of customers, inventory, and gentle teasing from my friends. By afternoon, we'd had a steady stream of business, and I was feeling more centred than I had in days.

Until I looked out the window and saw him.

Not Ciarán—though my heart did a ridiculous little skip at the thought—but a stranger. Tall, broad-shouldered, with close-cropped black hair and the kind of face that had seen things. Hard things. He stood across the street, partially obscured by a parked car, but I could feel his gaze on the shop. On me.

"Daisy," I said quietly, not taking my eyes off the man. "Do you see that guy across the street? By the blue car?"

She looked up from the register, following my gaze. "The tall drink of danger? Hard to miss."

"Has he been there long?"

She shrugged. "Noticed him about twenty minutes ago. Thought he might be waiting for someone."

But he wasn't waiting. He was watching. I could feel it; a

prickling sensation on the back of my neck that I'd learnt long ago to trust.

"I don't like it," I murmured, more to myself than to Daisy.

"Want me to go ask if he's lost?" she offered. "I can turn on the charm, see what he's about."

"No," I said quickly, perhaps too quickly. "No, let's just… keep an eye on him."

Something about the man set off warning bells. He wasn't just a stranger; he was a threat. I could sense it as surely as I could sense the energy in my herbs or the intentions of my clients.

As if feeling my scrutiny, he turned his head, his eyes meeting mine through the window. He didn't smile, didn't nod, didn't give any acknowledgment of the contact. He just stared, his gaze cold and assessing.

Then he turned and walked away, his movements fluid and controlled. Professional. The kind of man who knew how to hurt people and had done so often enough that it no longer troubled him.

"Well, that was creepy," Daisy remarked, watching him disappear around a corner. "Friend of yours?"

"Definitely not," I replied, a chill settling in my bones despite the warmth of the shop.

"Maybe he's just a tourist," Bernie suggested, ever the optimist. "Newchurch gets them sometimes, for the witch trial history."

"Maybe," I agreed, though I didn't believe it for a second. Tourists didn't watch shops with that kind of focused intensity and tourists didn't move like predators.

"Or maybe he's a secret admirer," Daisy teased, trying to lighten the mood. "You do have a certain witchy sex appeal, you know."

I forced a smile, pushing down the unease. "Yes, that's definitely it. He's probably composing love sonnets as we speak."

"Terrible ones," Daisy nodded. "'Roses are red, violets are blue, I'm standing outside, watching you.'"

"Stop," I laughed, despite the unease. "You're going to give me nightmares."

"That's what you have your hot Irish butcher for," she winked. "Protection from creepy stalkers and bad poetry."

I rolled my eyes, but the mention of Ciarán brought another thought. What if the stranger wasn't here for me? What if he was here for Ciarán? The man had secrets and darkness in his past. It wasn't a stretch to think that the darkness might have followed him to Newchurch.

The thought should have reinforced my decision to keep my distance, to protect myself from whatever complications Ciarán brought with him. Instead, I found myself worrying about him; wondering if he was in danger.

"Earth to Genie," Daisy's voice broke through my thoughts. "You're doing it again. The thousand-yard stare of lust."

"I was not," I protested. "I was thinking."

"About Ciarán," she said confidently.

"Not everything is about sex, Daisy," I sighed.

"No, but the fun things usually are," she grinned. "Come on, admit it. You're into him."

I was saved from responding by the arrival of another customer, an elderly man looking for something to help with his wife's arthritis. As I helped him select a salve infused with arnica and willow bark, my mind kept returning to the stranger outside and the sense of foreboding his presence had triggered.

Something was coming. Something dangerous. I could

feel it in the air, in the energy around me, in the cards I'd drawn during my morning reading—The Tower, harbinger of sudden change and disruption, and The Moon, signifying illusion, deception, and hidden enemies.

I'd been a witch long enough to know when the universe was sending warnings. The question was, what exactly was I being warned about? And was Ciarán part of the danger—or in danger himself?

Either way, I had a feeling our paths were about to become even more entangled. Despite all my instincts for self-preservation, despite the voice in my head urging caution, I couldn't bring myself to regret it.

Chapter 12
The Fall Guy
Ciarán

I was working on a new ad to put at the bus stop, something to follow up on my "FORGET THE ROSES. GRAB THE BALLS" masterpiece. This one featured a cartoon steak with bedroom eyes saying, "MEAT ME TONIGHT." Juvenile? Absolutely. But the thought of Genie rolling her eyes every time she walked past it made it worth every penny.

"Why do you keep wasting money on these ads?" Fraser asked, leaning against the counter and watching me sketch. "We've got plenty of business already."

I just smiled, not looking up from my work. "Oh, it's not wasted."

Fraser's laughter filled the back room of the butcher shop. "Ohhhh, my poor Ciarán. You're pussy drunk."

I shook my head, finally glancing up at him. "You need to be getting pussy, to be drunk on it."

His eyebrows shot up in surprise. "Oh no, it's worse than I thought. You actually like this woman, don't you?"

I frowned, the truth of it hitting me like a physical blow.

"Yep," I admitted, the word feeling strange in my mouth. "Fuck."

"Fuck indeed," Fraser agreed, pulling up a stool and sitting across from me. "So, what are we gonna do? You can't get out unless you remove the one who killed Cameron, and after all the research we've done, it all points to Genie."

"I know," I said, setting down my pencil and running a hand through my hair. The irony wasn't lost on me. I'd come to Newchurch to investigate a murder, only to fall for the prime suspect. The universe had a twisted sense of humour.

"Which means we need a fall guy," I continued, the words tasting bitter.

Theo chose that moment to walk in, his timing impeccable as always. "Well, if we're being technical, the wife killed him," he said, making both Fraser and I jump. The man moved like a fucking ghost. "The scenario was more like someone bought rat bait from the grocer. Genie is the grocer."

"That might be the case," I acknowledged, "but we need a fall guy."

I leaned back in the chair, mind racing through possibilities. Our employer wanted someone to blame for Cameron Smith's death. They didn't care about justice—they cared about closure; about a neat package they could tie up with a bow and present to whoever had hired them. And if that package couldn't be Genie Alden…

"I need to start some recon," I said finally. "Find a fall guy."

Theo's expression remained impassive, but I could sense his disapproval. "I don't know, why don't we just do the job you're meant to do?"

I met his gaze steadily. "One, I don't kill women. I don't know about you, Theo, but that's a line I've always refused to cross."

He just shrugged, his face a mask of indifference. "Well then, you better find someone good enough to pass as a fall guy. Some random from the street won't do."

He was right, and I knew it. This wasn't just about finding a scapegoat; it was about creating a convincing narrative, one that would satisfy our employer and, more importantly, keep Genie safe.

"It needs to be someone with a motive," I mused, thinking aloud. "Someone who might have wanted Cameron Smith dead."

"Besides his wife, you mean?" Fraser asked.

"Exactly," I nodded. "Someone with a connection to him, but not so obvious that it raises questions."

"Business partner?" Theo suggested. "Rival? Jilted lover?"

I considered these options. Cameron Smith had been a successful businessman with interests in real estate development. He'd had partners, competitors, probably enemies. Finding someone with a motive wouldn't be the hard part. Finding someone who could believably have helped Melissa Smith poison her husband—that was the challenge.

"I need to dig deeper into Smith's background," I decided. "Find out who he pissed off, who might have had reason to want him gone."

"And then what?" Fraser asked, his expression concerned. "Frame some poor bastard for murder?"

The question hung in the air between us, heavy with implication. Was that what I was willing to do? Frame an innocent person to protect Genie?

"Not necessarily," I said carefully. "Maybe there's someone who's not so innocent. Someone who deserves what's coming to them."

"Ah, vigilante justice," Theo remarked dryly. "How noble."

I shot him a look. "Like you're one to talk about nobility, Theo. We all know what you did in Prague."

His eyes narrowed slightly, the only indication that my barb had landed. "Ancient history," he dismissed. "And irrelevant to our current situation."

"The point is," I continued, "we find someone who's already dirty. Someone who won't be missed if they take the fall for this."

"And if there isn't anyone?" Fraser pressed. "If all you find are decent people who just happened to cross paths with Cameron Smith?"

It was a fair question, and one I didn't have a good answer for. How far was I willing to go to protect Genie? Would I sacrifice an innocent person? Would I betray everything I thought I stood for?

"I'll cross that bridge when I come to it," I said finally, avoiding Fraser's gaze.

"Just be careful," he warned. "This isn't just about the job anymore. This is personal for you. And personal gets messy."

He wasn't wrong. I'd broken the first rule of our profession: never get emotionally involved. And now I was scrambling to find a way out, a solution that would satisfy our employer without sacrificing the woman I was falling for.

"I know what I'm doing," I insisted, though I wasn't entirely convinced myself.

"Do you?" Theo asked, his voice quiet but cutting. "Because from where I'm standing, it looks like you're compromising a job, for a woman you barely know."

"I know enough," I replied, thinking of Genie's green eyes, the way they seemed to see right through me. The way she'd talked about helping people, about justice that the law couldn't provide. The darkness in her that called to my own.

"You know what she wants you to know," Theo countered. "We all wear masks, Ciarán. Some are just better at it than others."

His words hit uncomfortably close to home. Wasn't I wearing a mask with Genie? Pretending to be just a butcher, hiding my true purpose in Newchurch? Who was I to judge her for keeping secrets?

"Look," Fraser interjected, ever the peacemaker, "we've got time to figure this out. Our deadline isn't for another two weeks. Let's gather more information before we make any decisions."

"Agreed," I nodded, grateful for the reprieve. "I'll start digging into Smith's background tonight. See if I can find anyone with both motive and opportunity."

"And I'll keep an eye on the wife," Theo offered. "See if she leads us anywhere useful."

"What about me?" Fraser asked.

I grinned, some of the tension easing. "You keep shagging Daisy and see if she lets anything slip about Genie's business."

Fraser's expression was comically offended. "I would never use sex to extract information!"

"No?" I raised an eyebrow. "Then what was that job in Edinburgh? The one with the banker's wife?"

"That was different," he protested. "I genuinely liked her."

"And you genuinely like Daisy," I pointed out. "I'm not asking you to seduce her for information. Just keep your ears open."

He considered this, then nodded reluctantly. "Fine. But for the record, I'm not doing it for the job. I'm doing it for you; you bloody lovesick eejit."

"Appreciated," I said dryly.

"If we're done with this touching display of brotherhood," Theo interrupted, "we have actual work to do. You know, the kind that pays the bills?"

Finding a fall guy was the obvious solution, but it felt wrong. Not just morally, but practically. Our employer wasn't stupid. They'd want evidence, a convincing narrative that explained how this person had helped Melissa Smith poison her husband. Creating that kind of false trail would be challenging, to say the least.

Then there was Genie. What would she think if she knew what I was planning? Would she be grateful for my protection, or disgusted by my willingness to frame someone else? Would she see it as justice, or just another form of the violence she was trying to fight against?

I didn't have answers to these questions, only a growing certainty that I was in too deep to back out now. Whatever happened, I would protect Genie Alden. Even if it meant crossing lines, I'd promised myself I never would.

The irony wasn't lost on me. I'd spent years as a hired gun, eliminating problems for people with enough money to pay. I'd justified it by telling myself I only targeted those who deserved it—the corrupt, the cruel, the predators. But now, faced with the possibility of framing an innocent person to protect someone I cared about, I wasn't hesitating.

Maybe I wasn't as morally flexible as I'd thought. Or maybe Genie Alden had awakened something inside me that I'd thought long dead—a conscience.

Either way, I was fucked.

LATER THAT AFTERNOON, I was alone in the shop, Fraser had left for a delivery and Theo was off doing whatever mysterious things Theo did in his free time. The bell above the door jingled, and I looked up from the counter I was cleaning to see Genie herself walk in.

My heart did that ridiculous little skip it always did when I saw her. Today she wore a dark blue sweater, her hair pulled back in a messy bun that somehow looked both effortless and elegant. She carried a small paper bag and wore an expression I couldn't quite read—somewhere between determined and nervous.

"Hi," she said, approaching the counter.

"Hi yourself," I replied, setting down my cloth. "This is a surprise."

"A good one, I hope," she said, a small smile playing at the corners of her mouth.

"The best," I assured her, meaning it more than she could know. "What brings you to my humble meat establishment?"

She raised an eyebrow at the phrasing, but her smile widened. "I was in the neighbourhood."

"Liar," I called her out gently. "Your shop is literally across the street. You're always in the neighbourhood."

She laughed, the sound warming something in my chest. "Fine, you caught me. I came to see you specifically."

"I'm flattered," I said, leaning against the counter. "And intrigued. What can I do for you, Genevieve Alden?"

"First, you can stop calling me Genevieve," she said, wrinkling her nose. "Only my grandmother called me that, and only when I was in trouble."

"Were you often in trouble?" I asked, genuinely curious.

"Constantly," she admitted with a grin. "I once turned all her white linens pink because I was trying to create a love potion in the washing machine."

I laughed at that, the image of a young Genie experimenting with domestic appliances oddly endearing. "Did it work? The love potion, I mean."

"Not even a little," she sighed dramatically. "Though Mrs. Beecham's cat did follow me around for a week afterward, so maybe it had some effect."

"Cats have good taste," I said, enjoying the way her cheeks flushed slightly at the compliment.

"Anyway," she continued, setting the paper bag on the counter, "I brought you something."

"For me?" I asked, surprised and touched. "It's not my birthday."

"Consider it a peace offering," she said. "For all the hexed chalk and oily window."

I opened the bag to find a small jar filled with what looked like a thick, greenish salve. The label, written in Genie's elegant script, read "For Hardworking Hands."

"It's for your hands," she explained unnecessarily, a hint of nervousness in her voice. "I noticed they get dry and cracked from all the… meat handling."

I looked down at my hands—scarred, calloused, bearing the marks of years of work both in and out of butcher shops. No one had ever given me hand cream before. It was such a small thing, but it hit me with unexpected force.

"Thank you," I said, my voice rougher than I'd intended. "That's really thoughtful."

"It's nothing," she shrugged, though she looked pleased by my reaction. "Just herbs and oils. Nothing fancy."

"Still," I insisted, opening the jar and sniffing the contents. It smelled of rosemary and something deeper, earthier. "It's nice. Thank you."

An awkward silence fell between us, neither of us quite sure where to go from here. I wanted to ask her out again, to spend more time with her, to learn everything about her. But the conversation with Fraser and Theo earlier weighed on me, a reminder of the complications between us.

"So," she said finally, breaking the silence. "When is the ad at the bus stop being taken down?"

I grinned, relieved by the change of subject. "Taken down?"

"It's juvenile, inappropriate, and completely unprofessional," she said primly, then added with a small smile, "I do laugh every time I walk past it, though."

"Mission accomplished, then," I said, pleased. "I'm working on the next one. It's even worse."

"I can't wait," she said dryly. "The whole town is riveted by our little… whatever this is."

"War? Flirtation? Foreplay?" I suggested, enjoying the way her cheeks flushed again.

"Mrs. Beecham has started a betting pool on when we'll get together," she informed me, rolling her eyes. "Apparently, half the town thinks we're already sleeping together, and the other half thinks we're engaged in some kind of elaborate mating ritual."

"And what do you think?" I asked, my voice dropping lower.

She met my gaze steadily, something flickering in her green eyes that made my breath catch. "I think I'd like to have dinner with you again. Tonight, if you're free."

It was the last thing I'd expected her to say, and exactly what I'd been hoping to hear. "I'm free," I said quickly, perhaps too quickly. "Very free. Extremely available."

She laughed, the tension between us easing slightly. "Good to know. My place this time? I'm not much of a cook, but I can manage pasta without burning down the house."

"Sounds perfect," I agreed, already looking forward to it more than was probably wise. "What time?"

"Seven?" she suggested. "And don't worry about bringing anything. I've got wine."

"Seven it is," I nodded. "I'll be there."

She smiled, a genuine smile that reached her eyes and made my heart do that ridiculous skip again. "Good. I'll see you then."

As she turned to leave, I called after her, "Genie?"

She looked back; eyebrow raised in question.

"Thank you," I said again, holding up the jar of salve. "Really."

Her expression softened. "You're welcome, Ciarán. See you tonight."

After she left, I stood there for a long moment, the jar still in my hand, my mind racing with conflicting emotions. On one hand, I was elated at the prospect of spending more time with her. On the other, I was increasingly aware of the ticking clock, the deadline looming over us.

Two weeks. That's all the time I had to find a solution, a way to satisfy my employer without sacrificing Genie. Two weeks to find a fall guy, or to come up with an alternative that wouldn't end with someone innocent taking the blame.

Two weeks to decide where my loyalties truly laid—with the job that had defined me for over a decade, or with the woman who was rapidly becoming the centre of my world.

Chapter 13
Dinner with the Dead
Genie

I drew three tarot cards that night while cooking pasta and swatting Bernie's hand away from my sauce for the third time.

"I swear to all that is unholy, Bernie, if you add one more herb to this sauce, I will hex your candles to smell like wet dog for a month," I threatened, brandishing my wooden spoon like a weapon.

She pouted; the sprig of basil still clutched in her hand. "But it needs more depth! Just a little basil won't hurt."

"The last time you said, 'just a little' of anything, my brownies tasted like potpourri," I reminded her. "This is a simple marinara sauce. It doesn't need to be an herbal revelation."

"Fine," she sighed dramatically, setting the basil down. "But don't blame me when your date thinks your culinary skills are basic."

"He's Irish," I pointed out. "His people boil everything. I think pasta with actual flavour will impress him regardless."

Bernie laughed, hopping up to sit on the counter beside

the stove. "Fair point. So, cemetery picnic, huh? Bold choice for a second date."

"Third, technically," I corrected, stirring the sauce. "And it's not bold, it's practical. My grandmother's birthday is today, and I always have dinner with her. No reason I can't multitask."

"Most people would reschedule a date rather than combine it with a cemetery visit," she observed, swinging her legs. "But then, you're not most people."

"Exactly," I agreed. "Besides, if he can't handle my eccentricities, it's better to know now."

"True," she nodded. "Though I think the man who put up 'GRAB THE BALLS' posters around town just to make you laugh can probably handle a little necromancy over dinner."

I smiled at that. "He's working on an even worse one, apparently."

"God help us all," Bernie grinned. "You two are perfect for each other. Both equally committed to public indecency."

I turned my attention back to the tarot cards I'd laid out on the kitchen island. Death, Wheel of Fortune, and The Fool stared back at me, their meanings swirling in my mind.

"Interesting spread," Bernie commented, following my gaze. "Death, transformation. Wheel of Fortune, change, and destiny. The Fool, new beginnings, and taking risks."

"Someone's been studying," I remarked, impressed by her accuracy.

She shrugged, a slight blush colouring her cheeks. "I've been reading that book you lent me. It's fascinating."

I studied the cards again, feeling their energy. Death wasn't literal—usually—but it signified profound change, the end of one cycle and the beginning of another. The Wheel of Fortune suggested that fate was in motion, events turning in ways I couldn't control. And The Fool... well, that was about leaping into the unknown, taking risks without knowing the outcome.

Together, they painted a picture of transformation and change, of standing at a crossroads and choosing a new path. The question was, what was ending? What was beginning? And was I ready for it?

"You're overthinking," Bernie said gently, interrupting my musings. "Sometimes cards are just cards."

But we both knew that wasn't true, not for me. The cards were never just cards. They were messages, warnings, guideposts. And tonight's message was clear: change was coming, ready or not.

"Maybe," I conceded, not wanting to worry her. "Anyway, the sauce is done. Can you help me pack everything up? Ciarán will be here soon."

As we transferred the pasta and sauce into insulated containers and packed them into my picnic basket, I tried to push the cards from my mind. Tonight was about dinner with my grandmother and getting to know Ciarán better. The future, with all its transformations and risks, could wait.

But as I gathered candles and lanterns, preparing for our cemetery picnic, I couldn't shake the feeling that something significant was shifting. The air felt charged, like the moment before lightning strikes. And whether I was ready or not, the storm was coming.

Ciarán arrived precisely at seven, looking unfairly handsome in dark jeans and a navy sweater that made his blue eyes even more striking. He carried a small pot of wildflowers, which he handed to me with a slightly sheepish smile.

"I know you said not to bring anything," he said, "but my mother taught me never to show up empty-handed."

The gesture was unexpectedly sweet, and I felt a warmth spread through my chest. "They're beautiful," I said, taking the pot. "Thank you."

"You're welcome," he replied, his eyes taking in the picnic basket and lanterns by the door. "Going somewhere?"

"We are," I confirmed, placing the flowers on the potted plants stand I had next to the front door, the light always hit this spot well first thing in the morning and the wild flowers would flourish there, I eyed the small pot of rosemary that I placed it next to, if Ciarán kept this up, I would have a house filled with pots. "I hope you don't mind a change of venue. It's my grandmother's birthday, and I always have dinner with her."

His eyebrows rose slightly. "Your grandmother lives nearby?"

"In a manner of speaking," I said vaguely. "She's in the Newchurch Cemetery."

To his credit, Ciarán's expression registered only mild surprise, not the horror or awkwardness most people would display at the prospect of a cemetery date. "Ah," he nodded. "A dinner with the dead."

"Is that a problem?" I asked, suddenly uncertain. Maybe this was too weird, even for someone as seemingly unflappable as Ciarán.

But he just smiled, that crooked smile that did ridiculous things to my insides. "Not at all. I've had dinner with worse company than ghosts."

Relief washed over me. "Good. Because I've already packed everything, and I'd hate to have to eat all this pasta by myself."

"Can't have that," he agreed solemnly. "Lead the way, witch."

I handed him the heavier of the two lanterns and picked

up the picnic basket and the other lantern myself. "It's a short walk," I assured him. "The cemetery's just past the edge of town."

The night was cool and clear, the stars bright overhead as we made our way through Newchurch's quiet streets. Ciarán walked beside me, his stride matching mine, a comfortable silence between us.

"So," he said finally, "is this a regular thing for you? Dining with the departed?"

"On special occasions," I replied. "Birthdays, death days, solstices. My grandmother was the one who taught me every-thing I know about herbs and potions. Keeping her updated on my life seems like the least I can do."

He nodded, as if this made perfect sense. "My mother would approve. She was big on respecting our ancestors, keeping their memory alive."

"I'm sorry," I said, remembering his mum was gone.

He shrugged, the gesture not dismissive but accepting. "It was a long time ago. But I still talk to her sometimes, in my head. Tell her about my day, ask what she thinks of my choices. She usually tells me I'm being an eejit."

I laughed at that, charmed by the image of teenage Ciarán being scolded by his mother's ghost. "Sounds like she and my grandmother would get along. Granny Alden never minced words either."

"Strong women raise strong children," he said, glancing at me with something like admiration. "Your grandmother must have been quite a woman."

"She was," I agreed, warmth filling me at the memory. "Fierce, independent, and utterly unapologetic about who she was. The whole town was terrified of her, which she found endlessly amusing."

"Sounds familiar," Ciarán remarked with a grin.

"Are you saying I'm terrifying?" I asked, raising an eyebrow.

"Terrifying, beautiful, and just a little bit dangerous," he confirmed. "It's a compelling combination."

The compliment, delivered so casually, made my cheeks warm. "Flatterer," I accused.

"Just honest," he shrugged. "You are who you are, Genie Alden. No apologies, no pretences. It's refreshing."

The irony of his words wasn't lost on me. Here I was, a woman who helped other women poison their abusive partners, walking with a man who thought I was refreshingly honest. If he knew the truth about my "consultations," would he still find me compelling? Or would he run as far and as fast as he could?

But then, Ciarán had his own secrets. I could sense them in the careful way he answered questions about his past, in the scars on his hands; that hadn't come from butchering meat, and in the watchfulness that never quite left his eyes. We were both hiding parts of ourselves, playing roles that were true but incomplete.

Maybe that's why we were drawn to each other—two people with darkness inside, recognising a kindred spirit.

We reached the cemetery gates, which stood open as they always did. The Newchurch Cemetery was old, dating back to the 1600s, with weathered headstones and ancient yew trees that cast long shadows in the moonlight. Most people found it creepy, especially at night, but to me, it had always been a place of peace and connection.

"The Alden section is this way," I said, leading Ciarán down a winding path toward the eastern corner of the cemetery. "My family's been in Newchurch for generations, so we have quite a bit of real estate here."

"Morbid but practical," he commented, holding his lantern higher to illuminate the path.

"That could be our family motto," I laughed. "'The Alden's: Morbid but Practical since 1612.'"

We reached the Alden family plot, a section marked by a low stone wall and dominated by a large oak tree. Beneath the tree, a collection of headstones bore the Alden name, dates stretching back centuries. My grandmother's grave was one of the newer ones, a simple but elegant stone with her name—Margaret Alden—and the dates of her birth and death, along with the words "She lived by her own rules."

I set down the picnic basket and began arranging candles on and around her headstone, creating a circle of warm light. Ciarán watched, his expression curious but respectful, as I lit each candle with a whispered word rather than a match.

"Impressive party trick," he remarked, setting down his lantern.

"One of many," I replied with a wink. "Help me spread the blanket?"

Together, we laid out the picnic blanket on the grass beside my grandmother's grave. I unpacked the food—pasta, sauce, bread, a bottle of red wine, and two glasses—while Ciarán arranged the lanterns to provide additional light.

"This is not what I expected for our dinner," he admitted, settling onto the blanket across from me. "But I like it. It's peaceful here."

"It is," I agreed, pouring wine into our glasses. "Most people are afraid of cemeteries, especially at night, but I've always found them comforting. All these lives, all these stories, all this history in one place. It's like being surrounded by the greatest library in the world; only the books are people."

He nodded, accepting the glass I handed him. "I can see

that. Though I imagine some of the stories are better left unread."

"True," I conceded. "But even the darkest tales have something to teach us."

I raised my glass in a toast. "To my grandmother, Margaret Alden. Witch, healer, and the most stubborn woman who ever lived. Happy birthday, Granny."

Ciarán clinked his glass against mine. "To Margaret. May her memory continue to inspire."

We both drank, and I felt a familiar presence settle beside us, warm and watchful. Granny was here, drawn by our remembrance and the candles' light. I could see her clearly— a tall, slender woman with silver hair and my same green eyes, wearing the flowing dresses she'd favoured in life. She looked younger than she had when she died; more like the vibrant woman of my childhood memories, rather than the frail figure she'd become at the end.

"Hello, Granny," I said aloud, smiling at her ghostly form. "I brought someone to meet you."

Ciarán's eyes widened slightly, his gaze following mine but seeing nothing. "She's here?" he asked, his voice hushed.

"Right beside you," I confirmed. "She's wearing her favourite purple dress and looking at you very critically."

He straightened unconsciously, as if preparing for inspection. "I hope I pass muster."

I listened as my grandmother spoke, her voice clear to me, though inaudible to Ciarán. "He's handsome enough," she observed. "But there's blood on his hands. Old blood and new. Be careful, Genevieve."

"What's she saying?" Ciarán asked, noticing my expression change.

I hesitated, then decided on a partial truth. "She says

you're handsome enough, but she's reserving judgement on your character."

He laughed, the sound rich and genuine. "Smart woman. I wouldn't trust me with her granddaughter either, at least not right away."

"She's protective," I agreed, serving pasta onto our plates. "Always has been."

"Tell her I have only the best intentions," he said, his blue eyes meeting mine with an intensity that made my breath catch.

I relayed the message, and Granny snorted. "Men always say that," she replied. "But his eyes are honest, at least when he looks at you. That's something."

"She says your eyes are honest," I told Ciarán. "Which, from her, is high praise."

He looked pleased, though slightly uncomfortable with the idea of being observed by someone he couldn't see. "Thank you, Margaret," he said, addressing the empty space beside him. "I promise to treat your granddaughter with the respect she deserves."

Granny laughed at that. "Bold promise. Ask him if that includes respecting her decision to poison abusive men."

I nearly choked on my wine. "Granny!" I hissed, forgetting momentarily that Ciarán couldn't hear her.

"Everything okay?" he asked, concern crossing his face.

"Fine," I assured him quickly. "She just… made an inappropriate joke. She has a wicked sense of humour."

"Another family trait, it seems," he observed with a grin.

We ate our pasta, the conversation flowing easily between us. I told Ciarán stories about my grandmother—how she'd taught me to identify herbs in the wild, how she'd stood up to the town council when they tried to force her to sell her land to developers, how she'd once hexed the mayor's toupee to fly off his head during a particularly boring speech.

He laughed at all the right places, asked thoughtful questions, and seemed genuinely interested in learning about the woman who had shaped so much of who I was. All the while, Granny watched us, her expression softening as the evening progressed.

"He's good for you," she said finally. "Makes you laugh. You don't laugh enough, Genevieve."

Before I could respond, a movement at the edge of the cemetery caught my eye. A tall figure was walking along the path, his silhouette unmistakable even in the dim light. It was the same man I'd seen watching my shop, the one with the cold eyes and predator's grace.

Ciarán noticed my sudden tension and followed my gaze. His expression changed subtly, a hardness entering his eyes that I hadn't seen before. "Friend of yours?" he asked quietly.

"Definitely not," I replied, watching as the man approached. "He was watching my shop yesterday. Gave me the creeps."

Ciarán's posture shifted, becoming more alert, more dangerous. It was a subtle change, but unmistakable. This wasn't the relaxed butcher I'd been having dinner with; this was someone else entirely, someone prepared for violence.

The man stopped a few yards away, his eyes taking in our picnic setup with clinical detachment. "Evening," he said, his accent American but with something else underneath it. "Unusual place for a date."

"Not if you're dating a witch," Ciarán replied, his tone casual but with an edge of warning. "Evening, Jack. Taking a shortcut?"

So Ciarán did know him. The realisation sent a chill down

my spine. Who was this man, and what was his connection to Ciarán?

"Something like that," Jack replied, his gaze shifting to me. "Ms. Alden, right? The skincare shop owner?"

"That's right," I confirmed, keeping my voice steady despite the alarm bells ringing in my head. "Can I help you with something?"

He smiled, a cold expression that didn't reach his eyes. "Just curious about your business. Heard good things. Might stop by sometime."

"We're open nine to five, Tuesday through to Sunday," I said, the standard response feeling absurd in this context. "First consultation is free."

"Generous," he remarked. "What kind of… consultations do you offer?"

The question was loaded, his emphasis making it clear he wasn't asking about face creams. Beside me, I felt Granny's presence intensify, a protective energy radiating from her ghostly form.

"Skincare assessments," I replied evenly. "Product recommendations. The usual."

"The usual," he repeated, his tone suggesting he didn't believe me for a second. "And do you make all your products yourself?"

"I do," I confirmed. "Old family recipes, mostly. Natural ingredients, locally sourced when possible."

"Fascinating," he said, though he looked anything but fascinated. "Must take a lot of knowledge. Chemistry, botany…"

"Basic science and a good memory," I shrugged, trying to appear nonchalant while my heart raced. "Nothing special."

"Don't sell yourself short," Ciarán interjected, his eyes

never leaving Jack. "Genie's products are exceptional. You should try her hand salve. Works wonders for rough hands."

There was something in the way he said it, a subtle emphasis that seemed to carry additional meaning. Jack's eyes narrowed slightly, a silent communication passing between the two men that I couldn't decipher.

"I might do that," Jack said finally. "If I need skincare advice, I'll stop by," he added to me. "Sounds like you're the expert."

"Any time," I replied, the words tasting false on my tongue. "Always happy to help."

He nodded, his gaze lingering on our picnic setup one last time before he turned to leave. "Enjoy your… dinner," he said, the pause making it clear what he thought of our cemetery date. "Nice seeing you, Butcher."

"Jack," Ciarán acknowledged with a nod.

We watched in silence as he walked away, his figure disappearing into the darkness beyond the cemetery gates. Only when he was completely out of sight did I release the breath I'd been holding.

"Who the hell was that?" I demanded, turning to Ciarán. "And don't say 'just a guy I know,' because that was not a normal interaction."

Ciarán's expression was guarded, the openness of earlier replaced by something more calculated. "His name is Jack. He came into the shop yesterday, asking questions about the town. About your shop, specifically."

"Why?" I pressed. "What's his interest in me?"

"I don't know," Ciarán said, though something in his tone made me doubt his sincerity. "Could be nothing. Could be he's just new in town, getting the lay of the land."

"Bullshit," I said flatly.

"I can promise you, I won't let him hurt you." Ciarán sighed, running a hand through his hair.

The statement, meant to be reassuring, only heightened my alarm. "Why would he want to hurt me? What have I done to him?"

"Nothing," Ciarán said quickly. "But I suspect it might have something to do with your work."

"And what's that?" I demanded. "What does skin care mean to someone like that?"

Ciarán was silent for a long moment, his expression troubled. "I can't say more right now," he said finally. "But I need you to trust me when I say I won't let anything happen to you. I'll handle Jack."

"Handle him?" I repeated incredulously. "Who are you, Ciarán? Really?"

He met my gaze steadily, his blue eyes serious. "Someone who cares about you. Someone who wants to protect you. That's all you need to know right now."

I wanted to argue, to demand more answers, but the determination in his expression told me it would be futile. Whatever secrets Ciarán was keeping, he wasn't ready to share them. Not yet.

"Fine," I said, my tone making it clear it was anything but. "But this conversation isn't over. I deserve to know if I'm in danger, and why."

"You're not in danger," he insisted. "Not as long as I'm around."

The certainty in his voice was both comforting and unsettling. What kind of man could make such a promise with such confidence? What kind of man knew how to "handle" someone like Jack?

Not a simple butcher, that was for damn sure.

Granny, who had been silent during the entire exchange

with Jack, spoke up. "He's right about one thing," she said. "He won't let that man hurt you. The Irish one would kill for you, Genevieve. It's written all over him."

The observation sent a chill down my spine, not because it frightened me, but because I knew it was true. There was something in Ciarán's eyes when he looked at Jack, a cold calculation that spoke of violence held in check. And more disturbing still was my own reaction to it—not fear or revulsion, but a sense of recognition; of kinship.

Because I understood that capacity for violence. I carried it within me, too, I'd acted on it once, and would again if necessary. The darkness in Ciarán called to my own, a recognition of shared shadows.

"Let's finish our dinner," I said finally, deciding to set aside the mystery of Jack for now. "The pasta's getting cold, and Granny hates waste."

Ciarán looked relieved at the change of subject. "Can't disappoint Granny," he agreed, picking up his fork again. "Especially on her birthday."

We resumed eating, the conversation gradually returning to lighter topics, though an undercurrent of tension remained. Granny watched us with knowing eyes, occasionally offering commentary that I chose not to translate for Ciarán's benefit.

"He's dangerous," she observed at one point. "But then, so are you. Maybe that's why you fit."

Maybe it was. Or maybe we were both playing with fire, drawn to each other's darkness without understanding the consequences. Either way, I couldn't deny the pull I felt toward Ciarán, the sense that our paths were meant to cross, for better or worse.

Chapter 14
Falling
Ciarán

I walked her home after our dinner, carrying the picnic basket for her while she held the folded blanket. The night was cool and clear; stars scattered across the sky like diamonds on black velvet. We moved in comfortable silence, our shoulders occasionally brushing, each point of contact sending electricity through my body.

I'd never had a cemetery picnic before. Never had dinner with a ghost I couldn't see. Never fallen for a witch who could light candles with a whisper. But here I was, doing all three, and enjoying every moment of it.

In fact, I'd dance naked under the full moon for this woman if she asked. And that thought terrified me more than any job I'd ever taken, any danger I'd ever faced. I'd crossed the water to find a killer, only to fall for a witch with poison-green eyes and secrets as dark as my own.

Gods, my mother would have loved her. Strong, fierce, unapologetically herself—everything my mother had valued, everything she'd taught me to look for in a partner. The thought brought a bittersweet ache to my chest. If my mother were still alive, I'd have brought Genie home to meet her, watched them bond over herbs and old traditions, listened to them exchange stories while pretending not to be completely besotted.

"You're quiet," Genie observed, glancing up at me. "Penny for your thoughts?"

"Just thinking about my mother," I admitted. "She would have liked you."

Her expression softened. "Would she? Even with all my… eccentricities?"

"Because of them," I corrected. "She had no patience for ordinary people. Said they were boring as dishwater and half as useful."

Genie laughed, the sound warming me from the inside out. "Your mother sounds like my kind of woman."

"She was," I agreed, the familiar grief muted by time but never truly gone. "Fierce as a storm and twice as beautiful. Taught me everything worth knowing."

"Like what?" she asked, genuine curiosity in her voice.

"How to respect women, to cook a proper Irish stew. How to tell when someone's lying." I paused, then added with a grin. "To throw a punch without breaking my thumb."

Her eyebrows rose at that last one. "Your mother taught you how to fight?"

"She believed everyone should know how to defend themselves," I explained.

Genie nodded, understanding in her eyes. "My grandmother was the same way. Taught me which herbs could heal, and which could harm. Said a woman should always have options."

"Smart woman," I remarked, thinking of the ghost I couldn't see but who had apparently been judging me all evening. "No wonder you turned out the way you did."

"And how's that?" she asked, a hint of challenge in her voice.

"Extraordinary," I said simply.

Her cheeks flushed, visible even in the dim light of the streetlamps. "Flatterer."

"Just honest," I shrugged. "You're unlike anyone I've ever met, Genie Alden. And trust me, I've met a lot of people."

We reached her house, it was a beautiful place, full of history and character, just like its owner. The kind of place where generations had lived and loved; where secrets were kept and traditions passed down.

She unlocked the door and turned to me, her expression suddenly shy. "Would you like to come in?"

I smiled, my heart rate picking up. "I would love to."

Inside, the house smelled of herbs and old wood and something uniquely Genie—a scent I was coming to associate with comfort and desire in equal measure. She took the picnic basket from me and carried it to the kitchen, her movements graceful and assured in her own space.

"Wine?" she offered, setting the basket on the counter.

"No, thank you," I declined. "I've had enough. Want to keep my wits about me."

Her eyebrow arched at that. "Planning on needing them?"

"Around you? Always," I replied, enjoying the way her eyes darkened at my words.

She set down the blanket she'd been carrying and moved closer to me, close enough that I could feel the heat of her body and smell the lavender in her hair. "And what if I don't want you to keep your wits?" she asked, her voice low and teasing. "What if I want you thoroughly witless?"

My body responded instantly to her words, blood rushing south with such speed I felt momentarily lightheaded. "Then

I'd say you're well on your way to getting what you want," I managed, my voice rougher than I'd intended.

She smiled, a slow, seductive curve of her lips that made my cock throb painfully against my zipper. "Good," she murmured, taking my hand. "Come with me."

I followed her up the stairs, my eyes fixed on the sway of her hips, the way her clothes hugged her curves. She led me to her bedroom, where candles stood on various surfaces, with melted wax pooling below them, and she lit them with whispered words, filling the room with warm, flickering light.

"Gods, that is an impressive party trick," I remarked, watching as the last candle ignited at her command.

"One of many," she replied with a wink, turning to face me. "I have other skills you might find more directly beneficial."

"Is that so?" I asked, moving closer to her. "Care to demonstrate?"

In answer, she closed the distance between us, her hands sliding up my chest to link behind my neck. "With pleasure, just don't scream my name too loud, Daisy and Bernie might hear you," she whispered, rising on her toes to press her lips to mine.

The kiss started gentle, a soft exploration, but quickly deepened as hunger took over. I wrapped my arms around her waist, pulling her flush against me, letting her feel exactly what she did to me. She moaned into the kiss, her body melting against me as her tongue tangled with mine in a dance that was half battle, half surrender.

I walked her backward until her legs hit the edge of the bed, then broke the kiss to look at her. Her lips were swollen, her cheeks flushed, her eyes dark with desire. She was the most beautiful thing I'd ever seen.

"You're staring," she murmured, her hands still playing with the hair at the nape of my neck.

"Can't help it," I admitted. "You're fucking gorgeous, Genie."

Her blush deepened, but she held my gaze. "So are you," she replied, her hands moving to the buttons of my shirt. "And you're wearing too many clothes."

I let her undress me, enjoying the way her breath caught as she revealed my chest and abs. Her fingers traced the scars that marked my skin—souvenirs from a life lived danger-ously—with a gentleness that made my heart ache.

"These aren't from butchering," she observed, her finger following a particularly nasty scar that curved around my ribs.

"No," I agreed, seeing no point in lying. "They're not."

She looked up at me, questions in her eyes, but didn't press. Instead, she leaned forward and pressed her lips to the scar, a gesture so tender it made my chest tight with emotion.

"Your turn," I said, my voice rough with feeling. I reached for the zipper of her dress, sliding it down slowly, revealing inch after inch of pale, perfect skin. The dress pooled at her feet, leaving her in nothing but a black lace bra and matching panties.

"Fuck," I breathed, taking in the sight of her. "You're even more beautiful than I remembered."

She smiled, a hint of shyness in her expression despite her boldness earlier. "You say the nicest things."

"Just honest," I repeated, reaching out to trace the curve of her waist, the swell of her hip. "You're a work of art, Genie Alden."

I unhooked her bra, letting it fall away to reveal her full and perfect breasts, with rosy nipples that hardened under my gaze. I cupped them in my hands, my thumbs brushing over the sensitive peaks, drawing a soft gasp from her lips.

"Sensitive," I observed, repeating the motion and watching her reaction with fascination.

"Very," she agreed breathlessly. "Especially when it's you touching them."

The admission sent a surge of possessive pleasure through me. I lowered my head, taking one nipple into my mouth while my hand continued to tease the other. She arched into my touch, a soft moan escaping her lips as I sucked and licked and gently bit until both nipples were hard peaks and she was writhing against me.

"Ciarán," she gasped, her hands clutching at my shoulders. "Please."

"Please, what?" I asked, straightening to look at her. "Tell me what you want, Genie."

Her eyes met mine, dark with desire but clear with certainty. "I want your mouth on me," she said boldly. "And then I want to taste you. And then I want you inside me; fucking me until we both forget our names."

The explicit request, delivered in her sweet voice, nearly undid me on the spot. "Jesus Christ, woman," I groaned. "You can't just say things like that."

"Why not?" she asked innocently, though the wicked gleam in her eye was anything but. "It's what I want. Don't you want it too?"

"More than my next breath," I admitted, pushing her gently back onto the bed. "Lie back. Let me taste you first."

She complied, settling against the pillows, her dark hair spread out like a halo. I knelt between her legs, hooking my fingers into the waistband of her panties and sliding them down her legs. And then she was naked beneath me, all pale skin and the glistening evidence of her arousal.

I started at her ankles, pressing kisses up her calves to the insides of her knees, and then her thighs—taking my time, building her anticipation. By the time I reached the apex of her thighs, she was trembling, her breath coming in short gasps.

"Please," she whispered again, her hands fisting in the sheets. "Don't tease."

"Not teasing," I assured her, my breath hot against her most sensitive flesh. "Savouring."

At the first touch of my tongue against her core, she gasped, her back arching off the bed. I licked her slowly, savouring her taste—sweet and tangy and uniquely Genie. I found her clit with my tongue, circling it lightly before I sucked it into my mouth.

"Ciarán," she moaned, her hands flying to my hair. "God, yes."

I slipped a finger inside her, finding her hot and wet and ready. A second finger joined the first, curling to find that spot that made her back arch off the bed. All the while, my tongue continued its assault on her clit, alternating between gentle licks and firm pressure.

Her breathing quickened, her moans becoming more desperate. I could feel her tightening around my fingers, her body tensing as she approached the edge.

"Let go," I urged, looking up at her from between her thighs. "Come for me, Genie."

And she did, spectacularly. Her back arched, her thighs clamped around my head, and she cried out my name as she shattered. I worked her through it, lightening my touch as the aftershocks rippled through her.

When she finally relaxed, boneless and panting, I moved back up her body, kissing her deeply so she could taste herself on my tongue. She moaned into the kiss, her hands roaming over my back and shoulders.

"Your turn," she said when we broke for air, pushing me onto my back and reversing our positions.

She took her time exploring my body, her hands and mouth mapping every inch of me with the same attention I'd shown her. When she reached the waistband of my jeans, she looked up at me, a question in her eyes. I nodded, lifting my hips to help as she unbuttoned and unzipped, then pulled the denim down my legs.

My cock strained against my boxers, the fabric tented obscenely. Genie's eyes widened slightly, her tongue darting out to wet her lips in a way that made me throb painfully.

"Someone's eager," she teased, her hand hovering just above the bulge.

"You have no idea," I replied, my voice strained with need. "Been thinking about this since our first night together."

"Me too," she admitted, finally touching me through the fabric. "Every night. In the shower. In bed. Thinking about you, about this."

The image of Genie touching herself while thinking of me was almost enough to make me come on the spot. "Fuck," I groaned as she continued to stroke me through my boxers. "You're killing me, witch."

She grinned, clearly enjoying the power she held over me. "Can't have that," she said innocently. "Not when there's so much more I want to do with you."

She pulled my boxers down, freeing my cock, which sprang up against my stomach, hard and aching. Her eyes darkened at the sight, her lips parting slightly.

"You're even bigger than I remembered," she murmured, wrapping her hand around my length.

I hissed at the contact, my hips bucking involuntarily.

"Genie," I warned, my voice tight with restraint. "If you keep that up, this will be over embarrassingly quickly."

She smiled, a predatory curve of her lips that made my cock jump in her hand. "We can't have that," she agreed, lowering her head. "Not when I've been dreaming about tasting you."

Before I could respond, she took me in her mouth, her lips stretching around my girth. The wet heat of her mouth was exquisite, her tongue swirled around the head of my cock in a way that made my toes curl.

"Fuck," I gasped, my hands fisting the sheets to keep from grabbing her hair. "That feels amazing."

She hummed in acknowledgment, the vibration sending shockwaves of pleasure through me. She worked me with her mouth and hand in perfect synchrony, taking me deeper with each bob of her head. When she looked up at me, her green eyes meet mine as she sucked and I nearly lost it right then.

"Stop," I managed, my voice strained. "I'm too close."

She released me with a wet pop, a satisfied smile on her lips. "Can't have that," she agreed.

I reached for her, pulling her up and onto the bed. In one smooth motion I flipped us, so that she was on her hands and knees, her perfect arse in the air. I positioned myself behind her, running my hands over the smooth skin of her back, her hips, her arse.

"Is this okay?" I asked, needing her consent despite the explicit request she'd made earlier.

"More than okay," she assured me, looking back over her shoulder with desire-darkened eyes. "I want you, Ciarán. All of you."

I reached for the condom I'd optimistically replaced in my wallet, rolling it on with hands that weren't quite steady. Then

I positioned myself at her entrance, the head of my cock sliding through her wetness, teasing her.

"Please," she moaned, pushing back against me. "Don't tease."

"Not teasing," I assured her, echoing her earlier words. "Savouring."

But we were both too far gone for much more foreplay. I pushed forward, entering her in one slow, steady thrust until I was fully seated within her. We both groaned at the sensation —she was tight, hot and perfect around me; her body accepted mine like we were made for each other.

"Fuck," I groaned, holding still to let her adjust to my size. "You feel incredible."

"So do you," she breathed, her hands fisting in the sheets. "Now move."

I obeyed, withdrawing almost completely before thrusting back in. We found our rhythm quickly, her hips pushing back to meet each of my thrusts. I gripped her hips, holding her steady as I drove into her, each stroke deeper than the last.

As promised, I reached for her hair, gathering the dark mass in my fist and pulling it gently; just enough to arch her back and change the angle of my thrusts. She cried out as I hit a particularly sensitive spot, her inner muscles clenching around me in a way that made stars explode behind my eyelids.

"There," she gasped. "Right there."

I kept the angle, driving into her with increasing force, my control slipping with each thrust. The room filled with the sounds of our pleasure—moans, gasps, the slap of skin against skin, and the occasional curse as the intensity built.

Just when I thought I couldn't hold back much longer, I pulled out, flipping her onto her back. I wanted to see her face, to watch her come apart beneath me. She looked up at me with surprise and then understanding, her legs spreading to welcome me back.

I entered her again, this time more slowly, savouring the sensation of being joined with her. This position was more intimate, allowing me to see her expressions, to kiss her as we moved together. I set a gentler pace, each thrust deep and deliberate, my eyes never leaving hers.

"Ciarán," she whispered, her hands cupping my face. "I'm close."

"Me too," I admitted, feeling the familiar tightening at the base of my spine. "Come with me, Genie. Let me feel you."

I reached between us, finding her clit with my thumb, circling it in time with my thrusts. Her eyes widened, her inner muscles clenched around me as she approached her second climax.

"Look at me," I urged as she began to come apart. "Stay with me."

Her eyes locked with mine as she fell over the edge, her body convulsing around my cock in waves of pleasure. The sight of her coming undone, combined with the exquisite pressure of her inner walls, was enough to trigger my own release. I thrust deep one final time, groaning her name as I emptied myself inside her.

For a moment, we stayed connected, our bodies slick with sweat, our breathing ragged. I carefully withdrew, disposing of the condom before I collapsed beside her on the bed. She turned to face me, her expression soft and satisfied in the candlelight.

"That was..." she began, trailing off as if words were inadequate.

"Yeah," I agreed, knowing exactly what she meant. "It was."

She smiled, a genuine smile that reached her eyes and

made my heart do that ridiculous skip again. I pulled her closer, wrapping an arm around her as she nestled against my chest, her hair tickled my chin.

We lay in comfortable silence for a while, our breathing synchronising and slowing. I traced patterns on her skin, marvelling at its softness, at the stark contrast between her pale complexion and my tanned, scarred hands.

"I'm falling for you," I said finally, the words escaping before I could think better of them. "Hard and fast and completely against my better judgement."

She stiffened slightly in my arms, then relaxed, tilting her head to look at me. "That's a dangerous admission," she said softly.

"I'm a dangerous man," I replied, holding her gaze. "But not to you. Never to you."

She studied me for a long moment, her green eyes searching mine. "What if I'm dangerous too?"

"I know you are," I said simply. "I've known since the moment we met."

Her eyebrows rose in surprise. "And that doesn't bother you?"

"Why would it?" I asked. "We all have our shadows, Genie. Some are just darker than others."

She was silent for a moment, her fingers tracing one of the scars on my chest. "No matter what happens," I continued, "I will keep you safe. And one day, maybe I'll be good enough for you to tell all your secrets to."

The words were carefully chosen, a hint that I already knew or suspected some of those secrets. Her eyes narrowed slightly, catching the implication.

"But what if they're the reason you leave?" she asked, her voice barely above a whisper. "What if my secrets are too dark, even for you?"

I laughed softly, the sound rumbling in my chest beneath her ear. "Genie, I have the same issue. You might see the real me and run. I just hope you don't, because there is nothing you could do that would make me run from you."

She looked up at me, her expression a mix of hope and scepticism. "You can't know that. You don't know what I've done."

"I know enough," I insisted, thinking of the pattern of deaths associated with women who visited her shop, of the whispers about the Alden family's history of helping women in trouble. "I know you help people who have nowhere else to turn. I know you dispense a kind of justice that the law can't or won't provide."

Her eyes widened, alarm flashing across her face. "How—"

"It doesn't matter," I interrupted gently. "What matters is that I understand. More than you know."

She studied me again, her gaze penetrating, as if trying to see into my soul. "Who are you, Ciarán Ó Duinn? Really?"

It was the perfect opening to tell her everything—about my past as a hired gun, about my mission in Newchurch. But the words stuck in my throat. Not yet. Not until I had a plan to keep her safe, to ensure that my employer's interest in Cameron Smith's death didn't lead back to her.

"Someone with his own dark past," I said instead. "Someone who recognises a kindred spirit when he sees one. Someone who is falling in love with you, secrets and all."

The L-word hung in the air between us, neither of us quite ready to acknowledge it directly but both feeling its weight. Genie's expression softened, a vulnerability in her eyes that made my chest ache with tenderness.

"I'm falling for you, too," she admitted quietly. "And it terrifies me."

"Good things often do," I said, pulling her closer. "We're both used to living in shadows, Genie. Maybe together we can find a little light."

She smiled at that, a small, hopeful curve of her lips. "Maybe we can," she agreed, nestling closer. "But for now, can we just be? No past, no future, just this moment?"

"Nothing I'd like more," I assured her, pressing a kiss to the top of her head.

As she drifted off to sleep in my arms, I stared at the ceiling, my mind racing despite my body's satiated state. I was in deep, deeper than I'd ever been with anyone. And the most terrifying part wasn't the potential danger to my job or my life.

It was the realisation that I would do anything—absolutely anything—to protect Genie Alden.

Chapter 15
Shadows and Suspicions
Genie

The next few weeks passed in a strange, sweet rhythm. I saw Ciarán every few days, sometimes for dinner, sometimes just for a quick coffee, sometimes for nights that left me pleasantly sore and smiling like an idiot the next morning. It was easy, comfortable, and completely terrifying in its intensity.

The only odd thing was that he was hardly ever at the butcher shop anymore. When I asked about it, he'd shrug and say he was handling paperwork at home, ordering supplies, managing the books—all the tedious administrative tasks that came with running a business.

"Theo and Fraser have the shop covered," he explained one evening as we sat on my porch, watching the sunset. "They're more than capable of handling the day-to-day."

It made sense, but something about it nagged at me. Ciarán didn't strike me as the type to willingly sit behind a desk when he could be working with his hands. But then, what did I really know about him? We were still dancing around each other's secrets, sharing our bodies but keeping parts of our souls carefully guarded.

On a crisp Tuesday morning in early October, I was arranging a new display of autumn-themed skincare products when Daisy burst through the door, her face flushed with excitement.

"Have you heard?" she demanded, not bothering with a greeting.

"Heard what?" I asked, setting down the bottle of pumpkin enzyme exfoliant I'd been holding.

"They found a body in the woods," she said, her voice dropping to a dramatic whisper, despite the shop being empty. "A woman. They're saying it might be murder."

My blood ran cold. "Who?" I asked.

"Rebecca Winters," Daisy confirmed, watching my reaction carefully. "You know, the quiet one who came in for a 'consultation' about two weeks ago?"

I nodded, my mind racing. Rebecca had been one of my clients, a soft-spoken woman with haunted eyes and bruises she'd tried to hide beneath long sleeves. She'd come to me after hearing whispers about the special help Alden Alchemy could provide for women in desperate situations. I'd given her a small vial of clear liquid—foxglove and monkshood, primarily—with careful instructions on dosage and timing.

"What happened?" I asked, trying to keep my voice steady.

"They're not saying much," Daisy replied, perching on the stool behind the counter. "Just that a hiker found her body near the old quarry. But here's the thing—" she leaned forward, lowering her voice further, "—they've taken her husband in for questioning. Apparently, they'd been having problems. Neighbours reported hearing fights."

Relief washed over me, followed immediately by guilt. I shouldn't be relieved that a woman was dead, even if it meant my involvement might remain hidden. But if the police were already looking at the husband, maybe they wouldn't dig too deeply into other possibilities.

"That's terrible," I said, meaning it. Rebecca had been desperate, trapped in a marriage that was slowly killing her. I'd given her an option, a way out; but I'd never wanted this. The poisons I provided were meant to be untraceable, to mimic natural causes—heart failure, stroke, organ shutdown. Not something that would lead to a body in the woods and a police investigation.

"Yeah," Daisy agreed, her initial excitement fading as the reality of the situation sank in. "Poor woman. I always thought she seemed… fragile, you know? Like she might break if you spoke too loudly."

I nodded, remembering Rebecca's trembling hands as she'd taken the vial from me, the desperate hope in her eyes when I'd explained what it would do. "Did they say how she died?"

"Not officially," Daisy said, "Mrs. Beecham's nephew works for the coroner, and she's telling everyone it was poison. Something exotic that they're having trouble identifying."

My stomach dropped. That wasn't right. The mixture I'd given Rebecca was potent but composed of common botanical toxins that any decent toxicology screen would identify. Unless…

"Poison?" I repeated, my mind working frantically. "Are they sure?"

"According to Mrs. Beecham, yes," Daisy shrugged. "But you know how she exaggerates. Could be anything, really."

The bell above the door jingled, interrupting our conversation. Ciarán walked in, carrying two coffee cups and wearing a smile that did ridiculous things to my insides, despite my current state of panic.

"Morning, ladies," he greeted, setting one of the cups on the counter in front of me. "Brought you your usual—vanilla latte with an extra shot and a sprinkle of cinnamon."

"My hero," I said, forcing a smile as I accepted the coffee. "How did you know I needed this today?"

"Psychic powers," he replied with a wink. "Or maybe I just know that you're always in need of caffeine before noon."

Daisy watched our exchange with a knowing smirk. "Well, aren't you two adorable? I think I'm getting a cavity just watching."

"Jealousy is an ugly emotion, Daisy," Ciarán teased, handing her the second cup. "But, because I'm a gentleman, I brought you one too. Black with two sugars, right?"

Her eyebrows shot up in surprise as she accepted the coffee. "Okay, I officially approve of him," she declared to me. "Any man who brings me coffee without being asked is a keeper."

"I'll note that in my 'Ways to Win Over Genie's Friends' handbook," Ciarán said dryly. "Chapter One: Bribery via Caffeine."

"It's a solid strategy," I agreed, taking a sip of my latte. It was perfect, exactly how I liked it. The small gesture of remembering my coffee order shouldn't have affected me so deeply, but it did. It was the little things that were making me fall for him—the coffee deliveries, the way he always carried my bags when we were walking, how he'd started keeping a spare toothbrush at my place without making a big deal of it.

"So, what were you two gossiping about when I came in?" he asked, leaning against the counter. "You looked serious."

Daisy and I exchanged a glance. "They found a body in

the woods," she supplied. "A woman named Rebecca Winters. Possible murder."

I watched Ciarán's face carefully, looking for any reaction. His expression remained neutral, but something flickered in his eyes—recognition? concern? —before he masked it.

"That's terrible," he said, his tone appropriately sombre. "Did they say what happened?"

"Not officially," Daisy repeated her earlier statement. "But rumour has it she was poisoned."

Ciarán's eyes flicked to me briefly, so quickly I might have imagined it. "Poisoned? That's… unusual."

"Isn't it?" Daisy agreed, oblivious to the undercurrents. "Very Agatha Christie. Though, I suppose if you wanted to kill someone in a small town like this, poison would be less messy than shooting them."

"Daisy!" I exclaimed, horrified by her casual analysis.

"What?" she defended. "I'm just saying, if I were planning a murder—which I'm not, to be clear—I'd go with poison. Clean, quiet, and you don't have to worry about disposing of a weapon."

"You've given that disturbing amount of thought," Ciarán observed, though he seemed more amused than alarmed.

"I read a lot of crime novels," she shrugged. "And, I may have gone through a true crime podcast phase last year."

"Remind me never to get on your bad side," he said with a laugh.

The conversation moved on to lighter topics, but I couldn't shake the unease that had settled over me. Rebecca Winters was dead, possibly murdered, and the police were investigating. If they found traces of the poison I'd given her; if they somehow connected it back to me…

"Hey," Ciarán said softly, touching my arm. "You okay? You went somewhere else for a minute there."

I forced another smile. "Just tired. Didn't sleep well last night."

His eyes held mine, concern evident in their blue depths. "Anything I can help with?"

"Not unless you can add more hours to the day," I replied lightly. "Just the usual insomnia."

He didn't look convinced, but he didn't press the issue. "Well, I should get back to those thrilling spreadsheets," he said instead. "Just wanted to drop off your coffee and see your face. Both missions accomplished."

"My hero," I repeated, this time with a genuine smile. "Will I see you later?"

"Count on it," he promised, leaning across the counter to press a quick kiss to my lips. "I'll bring dinner. Any requests?"

"Surprise me," I said. "You know what I like."

"That I do," he agreed with a wink that made my cheeks heat. "See you tonight."

After he left, Daisy turned to me with a raised eyebrow. "Well, well, well. Aren't you two just domestic bliss personified?"

"Shut up," I muttered, though there was no heat in it.

"Seriously, though," she continued, her expression softening. "I haven't seen you this happy in… well, ever. It's a good look on you."

"I am happy," I admitted, the realisation both wonderful and terrifying. "He makes me happy."

"But?" Daisy prompted, knowing me too well.

"But I'm waiting for the other shoe to drop," I confessed. "For him to find out about… you know. And run screaming."

"I don't think he'd run," she said thoughtfully. "There's

something about him, something… I don't know, familiar? Like he'd understand."

I'd had the same thought, more than once. There was a darkness in Ciarán, carefully controlled but unmistakable. A capacity for violence that matched my own. It was part of what drew me to him—the recognition of a kindred spirit; someone who wouldn't flinch from the shadows I carried.

"Maybe," I said noncommittally. "But it's a big risk."

"Love usually is," she replied with uncharacteristic seriousness.

I didn't correct her use of the L-word, though it sent a flutter of panic through my chest. Was that what this was? Love? The thought was both exhilarating and terrifying.

Before I could dwell on it further, the bell above the door jingled again. Bernie rushed in, her cheeks flushed and her hair escaping from its usual neat bun.

"Sorry I'm late!" she exclaimed, dropping her bag behind the counter. "The candle delivery was delayed, and then I had to argue with the supplier about the quality of the beeswax, and then my car wouldn't start, so I had to walk, and—"

"Breathe, Bernie," I interrupted her rambling with a fond smile. "It's fine. We've been dead this morning anyway."

"Poor choice of words," Daisy muttered, earning herself a glare from me.

"What?" Bernie asked, looking between us in confusion. "Did I miss something?"

"They found a body in the woods," Daisy explained for the third time that morning. "Rebecca Winters. Possible poisoning."

Bernie's eyes widened, darting to me in alarm. "Poisoning? Are they sure?"

"It's just a rumour," I said quickly. "Nothing official yet."

"But if it's true…" Bernie trailed off, the implication

clear. If the police started investigating poisonings in Newchurch, it could lead them straight to Alden Alchemy.

"Let's not panic until we have more information," I said firmly, as much for my benefit as for theirs. "For now, it's just a tragic death and a lot of gossip."

"Right," Bernie nodded, though she still looked worried. "Of course. No need to panic."

"Exactly," I agreed. "Now, let's focus on work. The new autumn line isn't going to display itself."

We spent the rest of the morning arranging the display, restocking shelves, and helping the few customers who wandered in. I tried to keep my mind on the task at hand, but my thoughts kept returning to Rebecca Winters and the vial of poison I'd given her. Had she used it as instructed? Had something gone wrong? Or was this something else entirely?

Around noon, I stepped outside for a breath of fresh air, needing a moment away from Daisy and Bernie's concerned glances. As I stood on the sidewalk, enjoying the crisp autumn breeze, I noticed him—the tall, dark-haired man who'd been at the cemetery; the one Ciarán had called Jack. He was across the street, leaning against a parked car, his eyes fixed on my shop.

When he saw me looking, he didn't look away or pretend to be doing something else. He just stared, his gaze cold and assessing. Then, with deliberate slowness, he pushed off from the car and walked away, his movements fluid and controlled. Professional.

A chill ran down my spine that had nothing to do with the October air. This was the third time I'd seen him watching my shop in as many weeks. Once could be a coincidence, twice could be curiosity, but three times? That was surveillance.

I went back inside, trying to shake off the feeling of

unease. "Everything okay?" Bernie asked, noticing my expression.

"Fine," I lied. "Just needed some air."

"Well, while you were getting your air, Mrs. Beecham called," Daisy informed me. "She wants to know if we can make an emergency delivery of her night cream. Apparently, she's having dinner with the new doctor in town and can't possibly be seen with—and I quote—'crepe paper skin and enough wrinkles to map the London Underground.'"

I laughed despite my dark mood. "Did you tell her that no night cream in the world can work miracles in a single afternoon?"

"I did," Daisy confirmed with a grin. "She said, and again I quote, 'Nonsense, dear. Genie's creams are magic, and we all know it. I'll expect delivery by four.'"

"Of course," I sighed, though I was secretly pleased by Mrs. Beecham's faith in my products. "Bernie, can you handle the delivery? I need to stay and finish the inventory."

"Sure," Bernie agreed easily. "I need to stop by the post office anyway to mail the candle orders."

"You're a lifesaver," I told her gratefully.

"Speaking of lifesavers," Daisy interjected, "your hot Irish boyfriend texted while you were outside; said he's bringing Thai food tonight and, I quote, 'something sweet for dessert,' with a winky face emoji. I'm choosing to believe he means actual dessert and not his dick, but with you two, who knows?"

"Daisy!" I exclaimed, feeling my cheeks heat. "Give me my phone!"

She handed it over with a wicked grin. "The fact that you're blushing tells me everything I need to know. Good for you, honey. Get that Irish cream."

"I hate you," I muttered, checking the message. Sure

enough, Ciarán had texted about dinner and dessert, complete with the suggestive emoji.

"No, you don't," Daisy said confidently. "You love me almost as much as you love Mr. Tall, Dark, and Butchering."

I didn't dignify that with a response; but I couldn't help the smile that tugged at my lips as I typed a reply to Ciarán. *Thai sounds perfect. Looking forward to dessert.* 😉

"See? You're smiling like a teenager who just got asked on a date," Daisy observed. "It's adorable and slightly nauseating."

"Leave her alone," Bernie defended me, though she was smiling too. "It's nice to see Genie happy."

"It is," Daisy agreed. "Even if it means we have to hear about his sexual prowess in excruciating detail during our wine nights."

"I do not go into excruciating detail!" I protested.

"'His dick should be registered as a lethal weapon,'" Daisy quoted, mimicking my voice with disturbing accuracy. "'I swear to god, he made me see through time when he—'"

"Okay, okay!" I interrupted, mortified. "I may have over-shared, a bit."

"A bit?" Bernie laughed. "Genie, I know more about Ciarán's… equipment than I do about my own anatomy at this point."

"Can we please change the subject?" I begged, though I was laughing too. "Before I die of embarrassment?"

"Fine," Daisy conceded. "But only because I love you and want you to live long enough to enjoy more time-bending orgasms."

The rest of the day passed in a blur of customers, inventory, and gentle teasing from my friends. By closing time, I was exhausted, but in better spirits than I had been that morning. The news about Rebecca Winters still weighed on me, as did the sight of Jack watching my shop, but the normalcy of work and the banter with Daisy and Bernie had helped ground me.

As I locked up the shop and headed home, I couldn't shake the feeling that I was being watched. I glanced over my shoulder several times, but the streets of Newchurch were quiet, the early evening shadows empty of lurking figures. Still, the prickling sensation at the back of my neck persisted; a warning.

When I reached my house, I checked all the locks twice, drawn the curtains, and performed a quick protection spell—salt across the thresholds, rosemary and rowan berries in small sachets above the doors and windows. It was probably paranoia, but better safe than sorry.

I was just finishing when there was a knock at the door. I jumped, my heart racing, before remembering that Ciarán was coming over with dinner. Taking a deep breath to calm myself, I checked the peephole before opening the door.

Ciarán stood on my porch, holding a bag of takeout and wearing a smile that made my earlier fears seem distant and ridiculous. "Delivery for the beautiful witch," he announced, holding up the bag. "Thai food, as promised."

"My hero," I said for the third time that day, meaning it more each time. "Come in."

As he stepped inside, his eyes swept the room, taking in the salt lines and sachets with a raised eyebrow. "Expecting trouble?" he asked lightly, though there was an undercurrent of concern in his voice.

I shrugged, aiming for casual. "Just being cautious. It's that time of year—the veil between worlds thins as Samhain approaches. Better to be safe."

He nodded, accepting my explanation without question; though I suspected he didn't entirely believe it. "Well, in that case, I'm glad I brought extra spring rolls. Nothing fights off malevolent spirits like deep-fried vegetables."

I laughed, the tension in my shoulders easing slightly. "Absolutely. It's a little-known fact that ghosts are terrified of peanut sauce."

"See? I knew dating a witch would be educational," he grinned, setting the food on the kitchen counter. "Plates?"

Chapter 16
Connecting Dots
Ciarán

I was watching my computer at home, eyes burning from hours of staring at the screen. I was, in fact, doing bookwork like I'd told Genie—invoices, inventory, payroll for Theo and Fraser—but that was just a cover for my real task. On a separate monitor, I was doing recon for my soon-to-be ex-boss.

Dinner with Genie last night had been perfect. The way she'd looked in the candlelight, the easy conversation, the way she fit against me when I held her—it all felt right in a way nothing in my life ever had before. And that's how I knew I was in trouble. Deep, inescapable trouble.

Because I now knew with certainty that she was the one who had helped to kill Cameron Smith. Sure, she'd just provided the goods—the poison that Melissa Smith had used on her husband—but that was enough for my employer. They wanted the person responsible dead, and that person was Genie.

I couldn't let that happen. Wouldn't let that happen. Not even if it meant betraying everything I'd been for the past decade.

"Fuck," I muttered, rubbing my eyes. The surveillance footage from the hidden cameras I'd placed across the road from Genie's shop played on a loop on one of my screens. Nothing unusual today—just the normal flow of customers, Genie's animated conversations with Daisy and Bernie, and the occasional delivery person.

My phone buzzed with a text from Theo: Facial recognition got a hit. Check your email.

I opened the message he'd sent, scanning the information quickly. Jack Mallum, 42, from London. Former military, dishonourable discharge. Suspected ties to several criminal organisations, but nothing that had ever stuck. Most interestingly, he'd been to Newchurch before—six months ago, on holiday with his wife.

His wife, who was now dead. Heart attack, according to the death certificate. No previous heart issues.

I leaned back in my chair, the pieces clicking into place. Jack's wife dies unexpectedly from a heart attack. Six months later, he shows up in Newchurch, watching Genie's shop. It wasn't hard to connect the dots.

Had Jack's wife visited Alden Alchemy during their holiday? Had she purchased a poison meant for her husband but somehow taken it herself? Or had Jack discovered her plan and turned the tables?

Either way, it explained his presence in Newchurch and his interest in Genie. He wasn't working for my employer—he was conducting his own investigation. That made him unpredictable. Dangerous.

I pulled up another file on my computer, one I'd been compiling secretly, separate from the reports I sent to my employer. This one contained information on a connection I'd discovered, a link that made me very, very happy, but one I wasn't ready to use just yet. It was my insurance policy, my ace in the hole—the thing that might just get Genie and me out of this mess alive.

But timing was everything. Use it too soon, and it will lose its power. Too late, and it might not matter at all.

My phone rang, the screen displaying "Unknown Caller." I knew who it was before I answered.

"Ó Duinn," I said, keeping my voice neutral.

"Progress report," came the clipped response. My employer—or rather, their representative. This one was just his middleman with his cultured accent and cold efficiency.

"Still gathering information," I replied, the lie coming easily after years of practice. "Nothing conclusive yet."

"It's been nearly three months," the voice said, disapproval evident. "Cameron Smith's killer walks free while you… what? Play butcher? Enjoy the countryside?"

I bit back a sharp retort. "These things take time if you want them done right. Rush the job, make mistakes. You know that."

A pause, then: "We're not paying you to be thorough. We're paying you to eliminate a problem." They weren't paying me at all; I was working for my freedom.

"And I will," I assured him, though I had no intention of doing any such thing. "But I needed to be certain. The wrong target helps no one."

Another pause, longer this time. "Two weeks, Ó Duinn. Then we send someone else to finish what you started."

The threat was clear. If I didn't deliver results soon, they'd send another operative, and I'd be considered expendable. A loose end to be tied up.

"Understood," I said, keeping my voice steady. "Two weeks."

The call ended without further comment. I set the phone down, my mind racing. Under two weeks to figure out a solution that kept Genie safe, satisfied my employer, and preferably kept me alive in the process. No pressure.

I turned back to my computer, pulling up the file on Rebecca Winters. Her body had been found in the woods yesterday, and already the local police were focusing on the husband. It was the obvious conclusion—domestic disputes turned violent were sadly common, even in a quiet place like Newchurch.

But I knew better. Rebecca Winters had been one of Genie's clients. I'd seen her enter the shop for a *'consultation'*, her body language screaming fear and desperation. She'd left with a small package that she tucked into her purse as the left, her expression a mix of relief and terror.

Now she was dead, apparently poisoned, and her husband was the prime suspect. It fit the pattern I'd been tracking since arriving in Newchurch—abused women visiting Alden Alchemy, abusive partners dying of seemingly natural causes shortly after.

Except Rebecca's death wasn't natural. Something had gone wrong. Either she'd taken the poison herself, accidentally or deliberately, or someone had discovered her plan and turned it against her.

Either way, it complicated things. If the police identified the poison, if they traced it back to Genie…

I shook my head, pushing the thought away. I wouldn't let that happen. I'd make sure the investigation focused solely on the husband, even if I had to plant evidence myself.

The thought should have troubled me more than it did. A year ago, hell, three months ago, I would never have considered interfering with a police investigation to protect someone. But Genie wasn't just "someone." She was… everything; the centre of a world I hadn't known I wanted, until I found myself orbiting her like a planet around the sun.

My computer pinged with an alert from one of the surveillance cameras. Jack Mallum was across the street from Genie's shop again, watching from the same spot he'd occupied yesterday. His presence was becoming more frequent, more obvious. He wanted her to know she was being watched.

I zoomed in on his face, studying his expression. There was something there beyond professional interest—a personal vendetta. If his wife had died because of a poison meant for him, his obsession with Genie made perfect sense. He blamed her for his wife's death.

And men with vendettas were unpredictable. Dangerous.

I needed to neutralise the threat he posed, but I had to be careful. Jack was no amateur. If he suspected I was onto him, he might accelerate his plans, whatever they were.

I picked up my phone again, dialling Theo's number.

"I need you to keep an eye on our friend," I said when he answered. "He's at the usual spot."

"On it," Theo replied, no questions asked. For all his faults—and there were many—Theo was reliable in a crisis.

"Fraser can handle the shop," I said.

"Understood," he said, and I could hear him moving, preparing to leave. "Be careful, Ciarán," Theo added, his voice uncharacteristically serious. "You're in deep with this one."

"I know," I admitted, seeing no point in denying it. "But I'm handling it."

"Are you?" he challenged. "Because from where I'm standing, it looks like you're compromising a job for a woman who makes poison for a living."

"It's more complicated than that," I insisted.

"It always is," Theo sighed. "Just… watch your back."

"That's the plan," I assured him before ending the call.

I turned back to my computer, pulling up the file on Cameron Smith. Successful businessman, pillar of the community, generous donor to local charities. By all accounts, a model citizen.

Except for what he did behind closed doors. The drugs he smuggled in and out to England for my boss and the bruises his wife carefully concealed with makeup and long sleeves. The "accidents" that sent her to the emergency room with broken bones and concussions. The neighbours who heard screams but looked the other way, because Cameron Smith was an important man in the community.

No wonder Melissa Smith had sought help from Genie. She'd been desperate, trapped in a marriage that was slowly killing her. Genie had given her an option, a way out. And now my employer wanted Genie dead for it.

The irony wasn't lost on me. I'd spent years eliminating people who my employers deemed problematic, never questioning the morality of it because I told myself I only targeted those who deserved it—the corrupt, the cruel, the predators. But now, faced with the prospect of harming someone who was doing essentially the same thing—dispensing justice where the law failed—I couldn't do it.

Chapter 17
Things That Go Bump in the Night
Genie

I felt them before I saw them—that prickling sensation at the back of my neck that told me I was being watched. Again.

It had been happening all week, this feeling of being followed. At first, I'd tried to dismiss it as paranoia, a natural response to the news about Rebecca Winters and the mysterious Jack Mallum, who kept appearing around town. But there was nothing paranoid about the tall figure I glimpsed in shop windows' reflections, always maintaining the same distance behind me, never close enough to confront, but never far enough to lose sight of me.

Today was worse. The shop had been unusually quiet, giving me too much time to think about Rebecca's body in the woods, about the poison I'd given her that was meant for her husband, about the investigation that could lead back to me; if I wasn't careful.

"You look like you're planning a murder," Daisy had observed as she caught me staring blankly at a display of facial toners. "Or remembering one."

I'd forced a laugh, though her joke hit uncomfortably close to home. "Just tired. Didn't sleep well last night."

"Ciarán keeping you up?" she'd asked with a suggestive wiggle of her eyebrows.

"Not last night," I'd admitted. "He was working late."

"On what?" Bernie had chimed in, looking up from the candle display she was arranging. "I thought the butcher shop closed at six."

"Paperwork, apparently," I'd replied, trying to keep my tone casual despite the nagging doubt that had been growing in my mind. "He said he's been doing the books at home."

Daisy and Bernie had exchanged a look I couldn't quite interpret.

"What?" I'd demanded.

"Nothing," Daisy had said quickly. "It's just... Mrs Beecham mentioned that Ciarán's been asking a lot of questions about the town. About people who've died recently."

My blood had run cold. "What kind of questions?"

"Just general stuff," Daisy had hedged, clearly regretting bringing it up. "Mrs Beecham didn't think much of it. Said Ciarán was probably trying to get to know the community better."

"Right," I'd agreed, though my mind was racing. "That makes sense."

But it didn't, not really. Why would Ciarán be asking about recent deaths in Newchurch? And why was he working from home so much? The doubts I'd been trying to ignore came flooding back, along with a new, more terrifying possibility: What if Ciarán wasn't who he claimed to be?

I'd pushed the thought away, unwilling to face it. Ciarán made me happy in a way I hadn't been in years, maybe ever. I didn't want to ruin that with suspicion.

Instead, I'd changed the subject, telling them about the figure I'd seen following me.

"Are you sure it's not just a customer?" Bernie had asked, her brow furrowed with concern. "Someone who recognises you from the shop?"

"Positive," I'd insisted. "I never get a good look, but I get the same feeling from them as I got from Jack."

"The one Ciarán said was asking questions at the butchers?" Daisy questioned, her expression growing serious. "Have you told Ciarán about this?"

I'd shaken my head. "I don't want to worry him."

"Genie," Bernie had said gently, "if someone is following you, Ciarán should know. He cares about you. He'd want to help."

"I know," I'd sighed. "I'll tell him tonight."

Daisy was heading out of town with Fraser for a few hours and Bernie had a date she was being mysteriously tight-lipped about.

"Come on," Daisy had pressed as closing time approached. "Who's the lucky person? Anyone we know?"

Bernie had blushed furiously, busying herself with straightening already-neat shelves. "It's not a big deal. Just dinner."

"With whom?" I'd asked, intrigued by her uncharacteristic secrecy.

"If it goes well, I'll tell you," she promised. "If not, I'd rather pretend it never happened."

We'd let it drop, but not before extracting a promise that she'd text us if she wasn't coming home. Then she'd left early to get ready, and Daisy had departed soon after to meet Fraser, leaving me to close up alone.

Which is how I found myself walking home in the gathering dusk, that familiar prickling sensation on the back of my neck telling me I wasn't alone.

I didn't look back. I didn't need to. I knew they were there, maintaining that same careful distance, watching my every move. Instead, I picked up my pace, my keys clutched in my hand like a weapon, my heart pounding in my chest.

The streets of Newchurch were quiet; most shops already closed for the evening. A few people nodded greetings as I passed, but no one I knew well enough to ask for company on my walk home. I considered calling Ciarán, asking him to meet me, but something held me back. The questions Daisy had raised about his interest in recent deaths, combined with my own growing doubts… I needed time to think.

So, I walked faster, my breath coming in quick bursts, relief washing over me when I finally reached the gates of the Alden estate. I hurried up the path to my front door, fumbling with my keys in my haste to get inside.

Once in, I locked the door—deadbolt, chain, and the old iron bar that had protected Alden women for generations. Then I moved through the house, checking windows, drawing curtains, placing new sachets of herbs on sills and thresholds, and checking the salt lines. Bernie always dragged her feet, and she would break a salt line without realising it.

When I was satisfied that the house was secure, I leaned against the wall, trying to calm my racing heart. "Get a grip, Genie," I muttered to myself. "You're a witch, for fuck's sake. Act like it."

But the truth was, all the magic in the world wouldn't stop a bullet or a knife. And whoever was following me didn't seem like the type to be deterred by a protection spell, the spell really only worked on the dead, not the undead.

I considered calling Ciarán again, asking him to come over. He would, I knew. He'd drop whatever he was doing and be here in minutes. But then I'd have to explain why I was so frightened, and that would mean telling him about the person following me, about the growing sense of danger that had been building since Rebecca's body was found.

And what if Daisy was right? What if Ciarán's interest in recent deaths wasn't innocent? What if he was investigating me?

"Stop it," I told myself firmly. "You're being paranoid."

But was I? Ciarán had appeared in Newchurch just months ago; a stranger with scars that didn't come from butchering meat and a past he was careful not to discuss in detail. It was too much of a coincidence to ignore.

I pushed away from the wall, determined to distract myself from these spiralling thoughts. I was hungry, tired, and on edge. Food and a hot bath would help clear my head, help me think more rationally about Ciarán and the stalker and the growing sense that something was very wrong in Newchurch.

In the kitchen, I found a container of Bernie's homemade lasagna in the fridge with a note taped to it: *For emergencies or laziness. Either way, enjoy! xo B*

I smiled despite my anxiety. Bernie might be mysterious about her date tonight, but she was still looking out for me. I put the lasagna in the oven to heat and poured myself a generous glass of wine, sipping it slowly as I tried to sort through my tangled thoughts.

The facts, as I knew them: Rebecca Winters was dead, possibly murdered. Her body had been found in the woods, not at home where the poison I'd given her should have taken effect.

None of it added up to a coherent picture; but all of it made me uneasy.

By the time the lasagna was hot, I'd finished my wine and

was no closer to understanding what was happening. I ate mechanically, barely tasting Bernie's enthusiastic cooking, my mind still churning with possibilities, none of them good.

After dinner, I decided a bath might help. Hot water, essential oils, candles—the works. A proper self-care ritual to calm my nerves and clear my head.

In the bathroom, I lit candles, added lavender and rosemary oil to the running water, and set my tarot deck on the edge of the tub. Maybe the cards would offer some clarity where my thoughts couldn't.

As I reached for the deck, my elbow knocked it, sending cards scattering across the bathroom floor. "Shit," I muttered, kneeling to gather them up.

That's when I saw it—the Death card, standing upright among the fallen cards, as if it had been deliberately placed there. The skeletal figure stared up at me, its message clear: transformation, endings, change.

A chill ran down my spine, despite the steam filling the bathroom. Death wasn't necessarily a bad card—it often signified necessary endings, transformations, the clearing away of the old to make room for the new. But seeing it like this, isolated and upright when all the other cards had fallen flat, felt ominous.

"It's just a coincidence," I told myself, gathering the cards quickly and setting the deck aside. "Cards are just cards."

But I didn't believe it, not really. The cards were never just cards.

I sank into the hot water, trying to let the heat and the scented steam soothe my frayed nerves. I closed my eyes, focusing on my breathing, on the sensation of water against my skin; on anything other than the Death card and what it might mean.

Gradually, the tension began to leave my body. The water

cradled me, warm and comforting, and my thoughts slowed from their frantic pace to a more manageable flow. I thought about the upcoming Samhain ritual I was planning—the candles I'd need to gather, the herbs to dry, the incantations to practice. It was my favourite time of year, when the veil between worlds was thinnest, when I could feel my ancestors the closest to me.

This year's ritual would be particularly important. With everything that was happening—Rebecca's death, the mysterious stalker, my growing relationship with Ciarán—I needed guidance more than ever. The ritual would help me connect with my grandmother and all the Alden women who had come before me, who had faced their own challenges and survived.

The thought was comforting, and I felt myself drifting, not quite asleep but not fully awake either, floating in that liminal space, where intuition was at its strongest and conscious barrier at its weakest.

That's when I heard it—a soft thud from somewhere in the house, like a door closing or a book falling.

My eyelids snapped open, my body instantly alert. I held my breath, listening intently, telling myself it was just the old house settling, the wind against the windows, anything but what it sounded like—someone moving around downstairs.

Then I heard it again, clearer this time. Footsteps. Slow, deliberate, moving across the wooden floor of the entryway.

My heart began to race, adrenaline flooding my system. I stood up quickly, water sloshing over the edge of the tub.

"Bernie?" I called out, my voice sounding thin and frightened even to my own ears. "Daisy? Is that you?"

No response, just another soft thud, closer now. Someone was coming up the stairs.

I looked around frantically for a weapon, cursing myself

for not keeping something—anything—in the bathroom that could be used for defence. The best I could find was a heavy ceramic soap dish, which I gripped tightly as I moved toward the door.

"Hello?" I called again, hating the tremor in my voice. "Who's there?"

Still no answer, but the footsteps continued, slow and steady, approaching the bathroom.

I pressed myself against the wall beside the door, the soap dish raised, my heart pounding so loudly I was sure whoever was out there could hear it. Water dripped from my hair, from my body, pooling at my feet as I waited, every muscle tense, ready to fight or flee.

The footsteps stopped just outside the bathroom door. I could see the shadow of feet in the gap beneath it, could hear breathing on the other side.

Slowly, the doorknob began to turn.

I raised the soap dish higher, preparing to strike as soon as the door opened, my mind raced through possible escape routes, defensive moves; anything that might help me survive whatever was about to happen.

The door began to open, and I held my breath, poised to attack.

Chapter 18
Race Against Time
Ciarán

I had driven fast, faster than the speed limit allowed, the needle pushing well past ninety on narrow country roads not meant for such velocity. My knuckles were white on the steering wheel, every muscle in my body tense as I took the corners so quick, I should have careened into ditches. I was drawing unneeded attention to myself—the kind that got license plates reported and police involved—but I wasn't in the mood to care. Not when every second that passed could mean the difference between Genie alive and Genie dead.

The surveillance feed had been routine, mundane even, until it wasn't. I'd been half-watching the monitors while sorting through financial records, looking for the connection I knew existed between Jack Mallum and Cameron Smith. Then movement on one of the screens caught my eye—Genie leaving her shop, locking up for the night. Normal. Expected.

What wasn't normal was the tall figure that emerged from the shadows across the street moments after she started walking. Jack Mallum, moving with the practiced stealth of a predator, maintaining that careful distance that wouldn't alert his prey, but wouldn't lose her either.

I knew that walk. I'd used it myself countless times. This wasn't surveillance. This was a hunt.

"Fuck," I'd spat, my blood running cold as I watched Jack follow Genie down the darkening street. His body language had changed from the previous times I'd seen him watching her shop. There was purpose in his movements now, determination. He wasn't just gathering information anymore. He was making his move.

I'd switched the video feeds to my phone with trembling fingers, already grabbing my jacket and keys, already calculating the fastest route to the Alden estate, already knowing I might be too late.

The drive was a blur of adrenaline and fear, my mind racing even faster than the car. I had a plan, a carefully constructed exit strategy that would keep Genie safe and satisfy my employer. I'd found enough information and identified the perfect scapegoat. But that plan was for later, not now. Jack Mallum had forced my hand, and I was going to have to move my timeline up. Improvise.

And I fucking hated improvising. Improvisation got people killed. Usually, the wrong people.

My tires screeched as I took another turn too fast, the car fishtailing before I regained control. Sweat beaded on my forehead despite the cool evening air blasting through the vents. I couldn't remember the last time I'd felt this kind of fear—not for myself, but for someone else. For Genie.

Images flashed through my mind as I drove—Genie's smile, the way she looked in the morning light, her fierce independence, her gentle hands. Then suddenly, the thought of her hands going still, of her green eyes empty and unseeing, sent a wave of nausea through me so strong, I had to swallow hard against the bile rising in my throat.

I wouldn't let it happen. I couldn't.

As I sped through the quiet streets of Newchurch, my mind catalogued what I knew about Jack Mallum, searching for anything that might help me anticipate his actions. Former military, dishonourable discharge. Suspected ties to several criminal organisations. Most importantly, he had worked with Cameron Smith in land development before Smith's death.

That last bit was the key, the connection I'd been looking for. Jack wasn't just some random grieving widower with a vendetta. He was connected to my employer, to Cameron Smith, to this whole tangled mess. He was the perfect scapegoat for what had happened to Cameron—a business associate with a motive, means, and opportunity.

But none of that would matter if he got to Genie before I did.

I pushed the car harder, the engine screaming in protest as I accelerated down the final stretch of road leading to the Alden estate. The headlights cut through the gathering darkness, illuminating the high stone walls and wrought iron gates that surrounded Genie's ancestral home.

As I screeched to a halt in front of those gates, the car sliding on the gravel, I saw they were closed. Locked. A barrier between me and Genie that I didn't have time to navigate properly.

No time for subtlety.

I grabbed my knife and gun from the glove box, the familiar weight of the weapons both comforting and terrifying in this context. I checked the gun, ensuring it was loaded and the safety was off. Then I jumped from the car, leaving it running in the driveway, engine still ticking, headlights still blazing, and started to climb the gate.

The wrought iron was cold under my hands, biting into my palms as I hauled myself upward. The decorative spikes at the top were a challenge to navigate, designed to keep intruders out. But I'd scaled worse in my time—electrified fences, barbed wire, walls twice this height—and fear for Genie gave me speed and strength I might not otherwise have had.

I was over in seconds, dropping to the ground on the other side with a thud that jarred my knees and sent a shock of pain up my spine. I ignored it, pushing to my feet and breaking into a run.

The path to the house stretched before me, lined with ancient trees that cast long, grotesque shadows in the fading light. The gravel crunched beneath my boots, each step seeming too loud, too slow. My breath came in controlled bursts, my training kicked in despite the panic clawing at my chest—assess the situation, identify threats, neutralise.

The front door was ajar. Not good. Not fucking good at all.

I slowed as I approached, gun drawn, every sense on high alert. The house was quiet, too quiet. The kind of quiet that follows violence, that hangs in the air like a physical presence. I pushed the door open wider, wincing at the creak of hinges that seemed deafening in the stillness.

The entryway was dark, illuminated only by the faint glow of a lamp from a room further inside. But even in that dim light, I could see the salt lines on the threshold had been disturbed. Someone had walked through them, someone who didn't know or care about their significance.

Genie would never cross her own protection spells. Which meant someone else was in the house. Jack was in the house.

My heart rate kicked up another notch, adrenaline flooded my system with such intensity that my vision sharpened, colours became more vivid, details more pronounced. I moved silently through the entryway, checking rooms as I went, gun at the ready.

The kitchen was empty, the remains of a meal still on the table—a half-eaten plate of lasagna, a wine glass with a lipstick mark on the rim. The living room, likewise deserted. No signs of struggle, but the stillness felt wrong, charged with potential energy like the air before a storm.

Upstairs, then.

I took the stairs two at a time, staying close to the wall where the wood was less likely to creak. At the top, I paused, listening again. A soft sound came from down the hall— water dripping, perhaps, or something else. Something that made the hair on the back of my neck stand up.

I moved toward Genie's bedroom first, finding it empty, the bed neatly made, no sign of disturbance. But a soft light shone from under the bathroom door further down the hall. As I approached, I could hear sounds of a sob—a thud, a gasp, the unmistakable sounds of someone moving around.

My blood turned to ice in my veins. I was too late. Jack had found her. He was hurting her. Maybe killing her at this very moment.

I didn't hesitate. I reached for the doorknob, gun raised, ready to put a bullet between Jack Mallum's eyes the moment I had a clear shot.

What I wasn't ready for was the sight that greeted me when I flung the door open.

Genie stood naked, water dripping from her body, her skin glistening in the candlelight, holding what looked to be a large, heavy soap dish raised above her head. At her feet lay Jack Mallum, blood pooling around his head, his eyes open but unseeing. Genie's pale skin was splattered with flecks of red blood, as was the soap dish in her hand.

"Holy shit," I breathed, taking in the scene.

Genie's head snapped up, her eyes wild with fear and adrenaline. For a moment, she didn't seem to recognise me; the soap dish still raised as if she might bring it down on my head next.

"Genie," I said softly, lowering my gun. "It's me. It's Ciarán."

Recognition dawned in her eyes, followed immediately by a complex mix of emotions—relief, confusion, suspicion.

"Ciarán?" she whispered, her voice shaking. "What are you… how did you…"

Her gaze dropped to the gun in my hand, then back to my face, the questions multiplying in her eyes. Why was I here? How had I known she was in danger? Why was I armed?

All valid questions that I had no good answers for. Not without revealing everything—the surveillance, my real job, the fact that I'd been sent to investigate the very deaths she'd helped cause.

But those revelations would have to wait. Right now, we had a more immediate problem: the dead man on the bathroom floor.

Chapter 19
Aftermath
Genie

I couldn't move. Couldn't breathe. Couldn't process what had just happened. I stood frozen, the soap dish still clutched in my trembling hand, staring down at the body on my bathroom floor. Jack's eyes were open, unseeing, a pool of blood spreading from where his head had connected with the edge of the tub when I'd hit him.

The moment kept replaying in my mind; a horrific loop I couldn't escape. The door opening. The tall figure silhouetted against the hallway light. The surge of terror as I realised someone was in my house, in my bathroom, while I was naked and vulnerable. The soap dish. The swing, harder than I'd intended, driven by pure fear and adrenaline. The sickening crack as it connected with his skull. The way he'd stumbled, eyes wide with surprise, before falling against the tub and then to the floor.

I'd killed him.

It wasn't like with James. That had been a knee jerk reaction. This was violent, immediate, and bloody. This was my hands directly causing death, no buffer of time or distance to soften the reality.

I was vaguely aware of someone saying my name, but it seemed to come from far away, underwater, or through thick glass. Then Ciarán was there, his face swimming into focus as he stepped into the bathroom, gun in hand.

"Genie," he said softly, lowering his gun. "It's me. It's Ciarán."

"Ciarán?" I whispered, my voice shaking. "What are you… how did you…"

"Genie," he said softly, setting the gun down on the counter and moving toward me slowly, hands visible. "Genie, look at me. Not at him. At me."

I tried to focus on his face, to anchor myself in the familiar blue of his eyes, but my gaze kept being pulled back to the body on the floor. "Ciarán?" I whispered, my voice sounding strange and distant to my own ears. "He… he was in my house. In my bathroom. I was in the bath and I heard… and then he…"

"I know," Ciarán soothed, gently taking the soap dish from my hand and setting it aside. "You're safe now. I'm here."

I blinked, looking down at Jack's body again, then back at Ciarán. "I killed him," I said, the words feeling hollow, unreal. "I hit him with the soap dish when he came through the door. He reached for me and I just… reacted."

"You defended yourself," Ciarán corrected, kneeling to check Jack's pulse. "He broke into your home. He was going to hurt you."

A question formed through the fog in my mind, a spark of clarity in the shock. "How did you know?" I asked, suspicion cutting through the numbness. "How did you know he was here? How did you know I was in danger?"

"Later," Ciarán promised, his expression shifting to one of determination. "Right now, we need to handle this."

Before I could process what was happening, he pulled a knife and, in one swift, practiced motion, slit Jack's throat. The blade cut deep, blood lightly welling up from the new wound to join the pool already on my bathroom floor.

I gasped, stumbling back against the wall. "What are you doing?" I cried, my voice rising in panic.

"Shh," he soothed, wiping the blade clean on Jack's shirt with a casualness that was more terrifying than the act itself. "It's okay. I have a plan. Trust me."

I stared at him, this man I thought I knew, as he calmly cleaned his knife after slitting a man's throat on my bathroom floor. "You… you just…"

"Made it look like a professional hit done by me," he finished for me. "Which is what it needs to be. The soap dish was too… amateur. Too messy."

"Amateur?" I repeated, incredulous. "I didn't exactly have time to plan the perfect murder! He was in my bathroom!"

A small smile tugged at Ciarán's lips, incongruous in the grim setting. "I know," he said, standing and moving toward me. "You did what you had to do. And now I'm doing what I have to do to protect you."

I flinched as he reached for me, a reflexive response to the violence I'd just witnessed. Something flickered in his eyes—hurt, maybe, or understanding—but he didn't comment on it.

"Let's get you cleaned up," he said gently, guiding me toward the shower. "Can you stand on your own?"

I nodded, still dazed but becoming more aware of my surroundings, of the blood on my skin, of my nakedness. Ciarán turned on the water, adjusting the temperature before helping me step under the spray. The warm water washed over me, carrying away the blood in pale pink rivulets that swirled down the drain.

"I'll be right back," he said. "Just going to get you some clothes."

As he left, I stood under the water, letting it wash over my face, trying to clear my head. What had just happened? How had my quiet evening turned into this nightmare? And who was Ciarán, really? The casual way he'd slit Jack's throat, the gun he'd carried, his unexplained arrival just when I needed help—none of it fit with the butcher I thought I knew.

He returned with my slip dress and dressing gown, helping me out of the shower and wrapping a towel around me. I let him dry me off, dress me, and then guide me to my bedroom. Some distant part of me was alarmed at my passivity, but I couldn't seem to break through the fog that had settled over my mind.

He sat me on the edge of the bed, then knelt in front of me, looking up into my face with concern. "Genie," he said, his voice gentle but firm. "I need you to come back to me now. I need you here, present. Can you do that?"

I blinked, focusing on him with effort. "I'm here," I said, my voice stronger than before. "I'm just… processing."

"I know," he said, taking my hands in his. They were warm against my cold fingers. "It's a lot. But we don't have much time, and there are things you need to know. Things I should have told you before now."

That caught my attention, pulling me further out of the shock. "Like, why you have a gun?" I asked. "Or how you knew I was in danger? Or why you just slit a man's throat in my bathroom like it was nothing?"

He winced at my last question. "It wasn't nothing," he corrected quietly. "But yes, all of that. And more."

He took a deep breath, his expression serious. "My name is Ciarán Ó Duinn," he began, holding my gaze. "That much is true. I was born in Dublin. I was a butcher's apprentice as a teenager, learned the trade from my uncle."

"But?" I prompted, sensing the shift coming.

"But I haven't been just a butcher for a very long time," he admitted. "For the past decade, I've worked as what you might call a problem solver. A fixer. Someone who... eliminates issues for people wealthy enough to afford my services."

The pieces clicked into place. "You're a hitman," I said flatly.

"I prefer the term 'independent contractor,'" he replied with a weak smile. "But yes, essentially."

I didn't pull my hands away, though part of me felt I should. This man had just killed someone in my bathroom— or rather, ensured someone I'd already fatally injured was definitely dead. I should be terrified. But strangely, I wasn't. "And you're in Newchurch because...?"

"Because someone hired me to find out who killed Cameron Smith," he said, watching my reaction carefully. "To eliminate the person responsible, and once I did, I was being let out of a contract and would be allowed to be a butcher again."

Now I did pull away, fear and betrayal washing over me in a cold wave. "You were sent to kill me," I whispered.

"No," he said quickly, reaching for my hands again but stopping when I flinched. "I was sent to investigate, to find the person responsible. I didn't know it was you when I took the job."

"But you figured it out," I said, my voice hardening as I stood, needing to move, to put distance between us. "How long have you known?"

He hesitated, then admitted, "A while. The pattern was clear once I started looking— women visiting your shop for *'consultations'*, abusive partners dying of seemingly natural causes shortly after."

I paced the room, trying to process this new information. "So, all of this—us—was what? Part of your investigation? Get close to the suspect, gather evidence?"

"No," he insisted, rising to his feet. "God, no, Genie. What happened between us… that was real. Is real. I never expected to feel this way about you. About anyone."

I stopped pacing, turning to face him, fighting back tears I refused to shed. "Then why are you still here? If you know what I've done, if you've known for 'a while,' why haven't you… completed your job?"

The question hung in the air between us, heavy with implication.

"Because I don't want to," he said simply. "Because what you do… it's not wrong. Not to me. You help women who have nowhere else to turn, who are trapped in situations where the law can't or won't help them. You dispense a kind of justice that's technically illegal but morally right."

I studied him, searching for deception, for the lie I expected to find. But his eyes were clear, honest. "And your employer? What do they think about your moral epiphany?"

"They don't know," he admitted. "As far as they're concerned, I'm still investigating, gathering evidence before I make my move."

"But they'll expect results eventually," I pointed out. "What happens then?"

"I had a plan," he assured me. "One that was coming but is now sort of nil and void…" he added with a small smile.

I didn't return the smile. "What plan?"

He hesitated again. "It's better if you don't know all the specifics," he said carefully. "But it involves providing my employers with a scapegoat for Cameron Smith's death.

Someone with motive, means, and opportunity. Someone who can't defend themselves because they're already dead."

My eyes flickered toward the bathroom, understanding dawning. "Jack," I breathed.

He nodded. "Jack Mallum. Former business partner of Cameron Smith in a land development deal that went south. Recently widowed, to a woman named Hannah Mallum, potentially unstable. Perfect suspect."

"His wife," I said suddenly, a memory surfacing through the fog of shock. "I remember her. She came into the shop during their holiday here. Nervous, jumpy. Said her husband had a terrible temper, that she was afraid of what he might do, was told to come and visit me if she was ever in the area from a friend of hers."

"And you gave her something," Ciarán prompted gently. "A poison meant for him."

I nodded slowly, the consultation coming back to me in vivid detail. "A mixture of foxglove and monkshood. Slow acting, meant to mimic heart failure. She was supposed to add it to his food over several weeks, building up the dose gradually."

"But somehow she ended up taking it instead," Ciarán said. "She died of a heart attack with no previous heart issues."

I frowned, confusion cutting through the remaining shock. "That doesn't make sense. The dosage I gave her was calibrated for a man. It shouldn't have affected her unless she took the whole lot in one go."

"Maybe he discovered her plan," Ciarán suggested. "Turned it back on her."

"Maybe," I agreed, though I wasn't convinced.

"What we do know," he continued, "is that Jack blamed

you for his wife's death. He's been watching your shop, following you. Tonight, he decided to act on that vendetta."

"And I killed him," I said, the reality of it hitting me anew. "I killed someone."

"In self-defence," Ciarán reminded me. "He broke into your home, Genie. He was going to hurt you, maybe kill you."

I nodded, accepting this but still troubled. "And now you're going to use his death to… what? Frame him for Cameron Smith's murder?"

"Essentially, yes," he confirmed. "It's not a perfect plan, but it's the best option we have. My employers want someone to blame, someone to punish. Jack fits the bill, and he can't defend himself."

"Because you slit his throat," I pointed out, a hint of accusation in my voice.

"Because you bashed his head in with a soap dish," he countered, his tone sharper than before. "I just made it look more professional. More like the kind of hit my employers would expect from me."

I flinched at his tone, and his expression immediately softened. "I'm sorry," he said. "That was unfair. You were defending yourself. I'm not judging you for that. I've killed more people than I can count, and for far less justifiable reasons."

The admission hung in the air between us, raw and ugly but honest. "How many?" I asked quietly.

"I don't know," he admitted. "I stopped counting years ago."

I absorbed this, trying to reconcile the man I'd fallen for with this new, darker version. "And did they all deserve it?"

"I told myself they did," he said carefully. "I only took jobs targeting people who had done terrible things—abusers, traffickers, those who hurt the vulnerable. But the truth is, I didn't always verify those claims. I took my employers at their word because it was easier that way. Because it let me sleep at night."

"Until now," I observed. "Until me."

"Until you," he agreed. "You made me question everything, Genie. Made me want to be better. To be worthy of you."

I was silent for a long moment, processing everything he'd told me. My world had been turned upside down twice in one night—first by Jack's attack, then by Ciarán's revelations. Yet strangely, I wasn't as shocked by the latter as I should have been; a part of me had always sensed the darkness in him, always recognised a kindred spirit.

"You know," I said finally, "you're not the only one with secrets. With blood on your hands."

"I know," he said softly. "James."

My eyes widened in surprise. "How did you—"

"I've been investigating deaths in Newchurch for months," he reminded me gently. "Including those that happened before I arrived. It wasn't hard to connect the dots —your ex-boyfriend's sudden, unexplained disappearance, the rumours about his behaviour, the way you flinch sometimes when someone raises their voice or moves too quickly."

I looked away, my hands twisting in my lap. "He deserved it," I said, my voice hard. "He was going to kill me. Would have, if I hadn't acted first."

"I believe you," Ciarán assured me. "And I don't judge you for it. How could I? We're not so different, you and I; we both dispense a kind of justice the law can't or won't provide. The only difference is that you do it to protect others. I did it for money."

"Did?" I caught the past tense. "You're planning to stop? To just be a butcher?"

"No, I plan on having a side hustle, but one where I control who I kill," he reminded me with a small smile. "I'm also rather good at disposal, after all. It could come in handy in your line of work."

A reluctant smile tugged at my lips, the first since this nightmare began. "A match made in hell," I murmured.

"Or somewhere in between," he suggested. "Neither of us is entirely good or entirely evil. We're just human. Doing the best we can, in a world that isn't always fair or just."

I considered this, then asked the question that had been hovering at the edge of my thoughts. "What happens now? With… him? I have no rose gardens left." I nodded toward the bathroom.

"Now," Ciarán said, standing and offering me his hand, "I take care of it. And you try to get some rest. It's been a long night and tomorrow will be longer. You will not need to create a new rose garden."

I looked at his outstretched hand for a moment, then up at his face. The man I'd thought I knew was gone, replaced by someone more complex and dangerous, but also honest. Could I trust him? Should I?

But then, what choice did I have? There was a body in my bathroom, and I was at least partially responsible for putting it there. And despite everything, the lies and the revelations, I still felt safer with Ciarán than without him.

I placed my hand in his, allowing him to help me to my feet.

"I don't think I can sleep," I admitted. "Not with… that… in my bathroom."

"You don't have to," he assured me. "I'll handle everything. You can come with me if you want, but it won't be pretty."

I nodded, then surprised myself by stepping forward and wrapping my arms around his waist, pressing my face against his chest. I needed the contact, the warmth, the reminder that I wasn't alone in this nightmare. He held me carefully, as if afraid I might break.

"Thank you," I whispered against his shirt. "For coming when you did. For telling me the truth. For everything."

He pressed a kiss to the top of my head, his arms tightening around me. "Always," he promised. "I will always come for you, Genie. Always protect you. No matter what."

Chapter 20
Special Cuts
Ciarán

There's a certain irony to disposing of a body in a butcher shop. The tools are perfect, the space is designed for it, and the cleanup is straightforward. It's almost too perfect, which is why most professionals avoid it. Too on the nose. Too obvious. But sometimes, the obvious solution is the best one.

I'd wrapped Jack's body in plastic sheeting from Genie's garden shed before loading it into the back of my car. So here we were, at three in the morning, backing my car up to the rear entrance of the butcher's shop. The streets of Newchurch were deserted, the town sleeping peacefully, unaware of the grim cargo we were delivering.

"Wait here," I told Genie as I cut the engine. "I need to disable the alarm and check that the coast is clear."

She nodded, her face pale in the dim light, but her eyes were alert. The shock was still there, but she was pushing through it, forcing herself to function. I admired her resilience even as I worried about the inevitable crash that would come later.

I slipped out of the car and moved quickly to the back

door, punching in the security code and disabling the cameras I'd installed myself—ostensibly for security, but really to monitor the comings and goings at the shop. The lock clicked open, and I stepped inside, flipping on only the lights in the back room and freezer.

Once I was sure we were alone, I returned to the car and opened the trunk. Jack's body lay wrapped in plastic, looking more like a rolled carpet than a human form. I'd done a decent job cleaning up the bathroom at Genie's house, but there would be forensic evidence if anyone looked hard enough. Which meant this next part was crucial—Jack Mallum needed to disappear completely.

"I've called Fraser and Theo," I told Genie as I prepared to lift the body. "They'll be here soon."

"You told them?" she asked, her voice tight with anxiety.

"They already knew what I am," I explained. "What we do. They're in the same line of work."

"The butcher shop is just a cover," she said, understanding dawning. "For all of you."

"Yes and no, they might be in the same line of work, but we were all looking for a retirement job," I corrected.

She didn't smile at my attempt at humour, but she did help me lift Jack's body from the car. He was heavy; a deadweight in the most literal sense, and awkward to manoeuvre through the narrow back door of the shop. But we managed, working together in grim silence until we had him laid out on the large stainless-steel table in the back room.

"Now what?" Genie asked, her voice small in the cavernous space.

"Now we wait for—"

The front door opened, and Fraser slipped in, followed closely by Theo. Both men took in the scene with professional detachment—the body on the table, Genie standing pale and wide-eyed beside it.

"Well, this is a fine mess," Fraser said, his Scottish accent thick. "Jack Mallum, I presume?"

I nodded. "Broke into Genie's house. Tried to attack her. She defended herself."

"And you slit his throat," Theo observed, noting the precise wound that had nothing to do with a soap dish. "Making it look professional. I assume there's a plan here?"

"There is," I confirmed. "We're going to make Jack the fall guy for Cameron Smith's death. He had motive—the land deal that went south. He had means—his military background and connections to various unsavoury characters. And now he's conveniently dead, unable to defend himself."

"And how do we explain his disappearance?" Fraser asked, already moving to the sink to wash his hands, preparing for the grim work ahead.

"We don't," I said. "We present it a job well done."

"And the body?" Theo asked, eyeing the plastic-wrapped form on the table.

"That's where the butcher shop comes in handy," I said, moving to Jack's corpse. "We're going to make him disappear completely."

Genie made a small sound, somewhere between a gasp and a whimper. I looked up to find her staring at Jack's face, now visible as I pulled back the plastic. The reality of what we were about to do seemed to hit her all at once.

"Genie," I said gently, "you don't have to stay for this part. You can wait in the office."

She shook her head stubbornly. "No. I'm part of this. I need to see it through."

I respected her decision, though I worried about the toll it would take. "Alright. But if it gets to be too much, you go to the office. No heroics."

She nodded, and I turned back to the task at hand. "Fraser, get the hooks ready in the freezer. Theo, I need you on the laptop. We need to create a digital trail for Jack—searches about Cameron Smith, about poisons. Make it look like he was planning this for months."

Theo nodded and moved to retrieve my back up laptop from the office. Fraser headed to the freezer, the heavy door swinging open with a metallic creak.

I turned to the body, assessing it with a butcher's eye rather than a hitmans. Jack was a big man, over six feet and solidly built. It would be a lot of work, but not impossible. I'd broken down larger animals before.

"First," I said, pulling out my phone, "we need documentation. Evidence for my employer that Jack was responsible for Cameron's death and has been eliminated."

I positioned Jack's body, arranging it to show the throat wound clearly, then took several photos from different angles. These would be proof of completion, evidence that the job was done.

"Help me get him to the freezer," I said to Fraser, who had returned from his preparations. Together, we lifted Jack's body and carried it into the walk-in freezer, where heavy hooks hung from the ceiling. With practiced efficiency, we hoisted him up, securing him by his ankles so he hung upside down, ready for processing.

I took more photos, these more graphic, showing Jack suspended from the hooks like the animal he was. These weren't for my employer—these were insurance, leverage if I ever needed it. In my line of work, you could never have too much insurance.

"Right," I said, putting my phone away. "Let's get to work."

The next few hours were a blur of methodical, gruesome labour. We worked in silence; each focused on our tasks. Fraser and I broke down Jack's body with professional efficiency, separating meat from bone, organ from tissue. Theo worked on the laptop, creating the digital evidence we needed, occasionally asking questions about details to make the trail more convincing.

And Genie sat on a stool in the corner, watching with a mixture of horror and fascination, occasionally closing her eyes or turning away when it became too much, but always turning back. Always witnessing.

By dawn, Jack Mallum had been reduced to components —meat that looked like any other, bones that would be ground to meal and disposed of gradually, organs that would go into the waste system designed specifically for butcher shops. Nothing identifiable would remain.

"What do we do with… that?" Fraser asked, gesturing to the tubs of meat we'd produced.

I considered for a moment. "We label it as wild boar. Special order. We'll sell it at the market tomorrow."

Fraser barked a laugh, sharp and surprised. "You're not serious."

"Deadly," I replied. "It's the perfect disposal method. Distributed among dozens of customers, consumed, and digested. No body, no evidence."

"That's…" Fraser shook his head, then grinned. "This is the most ethically sourced meat we've ever had."

The comment hung in the air for a moment, inappropriate and terrible and somehow exactly what we needed to break the tension. I found myself laughing, a release of the stress and horror of the night. Fraser joined in, and even Theo cracked a smile.

Then I heard another sound—Genie, laughing until the laughter turned to tears, her body shaking with the force of it. The shock was finally catching up to her, manifesting as this inappropriate, uncontrollable response to Fraser's dark joke.

I moved to her side immediately, wrapping an arm around her shoulders. "Hey," I said softly. "It's okay. We're almost done."

She nodded, still laughing and crying at the same time, unable to stop. "I'm sorry," she gasped between breaths. "I don't know why I'm—"

"It's shock," Theo said, surprising us all by moving to sit beside her. He was usually the most distant of our trio, the least likely to offer comfort. "Perfectly normal response to trauma. Your brain is trying to process something it was never designed to handle."

He opened my laptop, which he'd brought with him, and set it on the counter beside her. "Focus on this," he suggested. "It might help to have something else to think about. I'm preparing the information for Ciarán's boss—creating the narrative that Jack was obsessed with Cameron Smith, that he killed him, and then fled when he realised he was being investigated."

Genie wiped her eyes, taking deep breaths to control her laughter. "How do you know how to do all this?" she asked, gesturing to the laptop where Theo was creating fake search histories, email drafts, and notes.

"I'm not actually a butcher," Theo said with a small smile. "Before I met Ciarán and Fraser, I worked in intelligence. Digital manipulation, information warfare, that sort of thing."

"Theo's our tech guy," I explained, relieved to see Genie

calming down, focusing on the conversation rather than the horror of what we'd just done. "Fraser's our muscle. I'm the strategist."

"And the actual butcher," Fraser added. "Only Ciarán knew how to butcher."

"And now?" Genie asked.

"Now we're all pretty decent butchers," I said with a shrug. "Turns out the skills are transferable."

She nodded, her eyes moving to the tubs of meat that had once been Jack Mallum. "And you're really going to sell that? To people?"

"Best way to dispose of it," I confirmed. "No one will ever know."

"Except us," she said quietly.

"Except us," I agreed. "Can you live with that?"

She was silent for a long moment, considering. Then she nodded slowly. "Yes. He was going to kill me. Would have killed others. And it's not like we're hurting anyone—they're just… eating him."

"That's one way to look at it," Fraser said with a grim chuckle.

"The digital trail is almost complete," Theo reported, typing rapidly. "I've created searches for Cameron Smith, for poisons similar to what killed him. I've made it look like Jack was researching the area to move here, after his holiday with his now dead wife."

"Good," I said, checking my watch. "We need to finish up here. The sun will be up soon, and we need to be gone before the town wakes up."

We worked quickly to clean the shop, removing any trace of our nighttime activities. The meat was packaged and labelled as wild boar, ready for the market. The bones were ground to meal that would be disposed of gradually over the coming weeks. The tools were sanitised, the floors scrubbed, and every surface wiped down.

By the time we finished, the first light of dawn was creeping through the windows. We looked like ordinary butchers preparing for the day's business, not killers disposing of a body.

"What now?" Genie asked as we gathered our things, preparing to leave.

"Now," I said, "I send my report to my employer. Jack Mallum killed Cameron Smith in revenge for a business deal gone wrong. I tracked him down, eliminated him, and he has been disposed of. Case closed."

"And then?" she pressed.

"And then I'm done," I said, the words feeling strange but right. "One last job, completed. I'll have fulfilled my contract, earned my freedom. After that, I'm just a butcher. With a side hustle," I added with a small smile.

She didn't return the smile. "Will they believe it? Your employer?"

"They'll believe what Theo's created," I said confidently. "The evidence will be convincing. And they want this resolved—they don't care who takes the fall as long as someone does."

"If they don't believe it?" she persisted.

I exchanged a glance with Fraser and Theo, a silent communication born of years working together. "Then we have contingencies," I replied. "But it won't come to that."

She nodded, accepting this without further question. She was learning quickly, adapting to this new reality where bodies were disposed of in butcher shops and digital trails were fabricated to frame the dead.

"Let's get you home," I said gently. "You need rest."

"Will you stay?" she asked, her voice small but determined. "I don't… I don't want to be alone."

"Of course," I promised. "As long as you need."

As we left the shop, the sky was lightening to a pale grey, the stars fading as dawn approached. In a few hours, the town would wake up, people would go about their day, and some would visit the market to buy our special wild boar mince, never knowing what—who—they were really purchasing.

And Jack Mallum would be gone, erased from existence except in our memories and in the carefully crafted digital trail Theo had created. A ghost made of data, a scapegoat for a murder he didn't commit but might well have, if he'd had the chance.

It wasn't justice, not really. But in our world, it was the closest thing to it we could manage. A bad man gone, a good woman protected, and the rest of us somewhere in between, doing what we had to do to survive.

As I drove Genie home through the quiet streets of Newchurch, I found myself hoping that this really would be my last contracted job. That I could leave behind the violence and deception, the constant vigilance and moral compromise. I could be just a butcher, with a side hustle and Genie by my actual side, building something real and good despite the darkness in our pasts.

It was a fool's hope, perhaps. But for the first time in years, I allowed myself to hope anyway.

Chapter 21
The Circle of Life
Genie

I couldn't stop staring at the butcher shop across the street. Every time the door opened, every time a customer walked out with a neatly wrapped package, I felt a twist in my stomach. How many of them had bought the "wild boar mince"? How many of Newchurch's residents were unwittingly participating in the most macabre meal of their lives?

"You're going to burn a hole through that window if you keep staring," Bernie said, appearing at my elbow with a steaming mug of coffee.

I jumped, nearly knocking over the display of facial toners I'd been absently rearranging for the past twenty minutes. "Jesus, Bernie! Wear a bell or something."

She grinned, unrepentant. "Sorry. You were in another world." She followed my gaze across the street. "Still thinking about last night?"

Last night. Such a simple phrase for what had been the most surreal, horrifying experience of my life. Killing a man in my bathroom. Watching Ciarán slit his throat with practiced ease. Helping transport the body to the butcher shop. Witnessing three men break down a human being like it was just another day at work.

And in a way, for them, it had been.

"I'm officially becoming a vegetarian after this," I declared, accepting the coffee from Bernie with a grateful nod. "I mean, I know the logic of the disposal method is sound, but cannibalism for the whole town? That's just gross."

Bernie laughed, the sound bright and incongruous against the darkness of our conversation. "It's the circle of life, Genie. Sure, it's a little on the nose, but come on, you never seen the movie 'Fried Green Tomatoes at the Whistle Stop Cafe'?"

I frowned, confused by the reference. "No? Should I have?"

"Well, let's just say it's worth the watch," she said cryptically, then wandered off to help a customer who'd just entered the shop.

I sipped my coffee, trying to focus on the familiar comfort of the bitter liquid rather than the parade of potential cannibals across the street. It wasn't working. Every time the butcher shop door opened, I found myself cataloguing who entered and who left, wondering if Mrs. Beecham would be serving Jack Mallum to her bridge club, or if the vicar would be having him for Sunday dinner.

The bell above my own shop door jingled as the customer left and, Daisy entered with Fraser in tow. They made an odd pair—Daisy all bright colours and flowing fabrics, Fraser built like a brick wall in his butcher's apron, still spattered with what I desperately hoped was animal blood.

"Morning, sunshine," Daisy chirped, far too cheerful for someone who'd been woken up when I had gotten home, to listen to me tell her about Jack Mallum. She handed me another coffee cup. "This is from Ciarán. He said to tell you he'll stop by later."

I stood there with two coffees in hand, feeling slightly ridiculous. "Thanks," I managed, setting one cup down to accept the other. "How is he?"

"Busy," Fraser said, as he leaned in close to my ear. "The mince is nearly sold out. Turns out this town is just as twisted as you."

I eyed Fraser, taking in his amused expression, the casual way he referenced what we'd done. "There is something wrong with you," I said flatly.

He grinned, unrepentant, then leaned in and quietly said. "Aye, probably. But I'm not the one who bashed a man's head in with a soap dish, am I?"

"Fraser!" Daisy hissed, smacking his arm. "Not funny."

"It's a little funny," he argued, then caught my expression and sobered. "Sorry, Genie. Dark humour is how we cope in this business. Didn't mean to upset you."

I sighed, some of the tension leaving my shoulders. "It's fine. I'm just… processing. It's not every day you kill someone and then help turn them into mince for the town market."

"First time for everything," Fraser said with a shrug. "And hopefully the last, yeah?"

"Definitely the last," I agreed fervently. "I prefer my murders to be nice and clean. Poison in a cup, not whatever last night was."

"Improvisation," Daisy supplied, perching on the stool behind the counter. "And from what Ciarán said, you handled it like a pro."

I snorted. "I was in shock for most of it. I still am, I think." I gestured to the two coffee cups. "Case in point."

"Shock's normal," Fraser assured me. "It'll pass. And then you'll just have the nightmares to look forward to."

"Fraser!" Daisy smacked him again, harder this time.

"What? I'm being honest. Better she's prepared."

I appreciated his bluntness, actually. Everyone else had been treating me like I might shatter at any moment. Fraser's matter-of-fact approach was refreshing, if a bit callous.

"So," I said, changing the subject, "What exactly are you two?"

Daisy blushed, a rare sight. "We're not... I mean, we're just..."

"Fucking," Fraser supplied helpfully, earning himself another smack from Daisy. "Ow! What? We are."

"There's more to it than that," Daisy insisted, then caught my raised eyebrow and amended, "Okay, not much more. But we're having fun."

"And that's all it is?" I pressed, genuinely curious. Daisy wasn't usually shy about her conquests, but something about her reaction to Frasers comment suggested this might be different.

"That's all it can be," Fraser said, his tone suddenly serious. "Given what I used to do, what I am... attachments are dangerous."

"Tell that to Ciarán," Daisy countered. "He seems pretty attached to our resident witch."

I felt heat rise to my cheeks. "We're not... I mean, it's complicated."

"It always is," Fraser agreed. "But for what it's worth, I've never seen him like this. Not in all the years I've known him."

"Like what?" I couldn't help asking.

"Happy," Fraser said. "Or as close to it as someone like him gets."

I didn't know how to respond to that. The Ciarán I knew

—or thought I knew—was charming, funny, intense. But happy? I wasn't sure that was the right word for a man who killed people for a living and disposed of bodies in his butcher shop.

"Anyway," Daisy said, clearly sensing my discomfort, "we just stopped by to check on you. And to let you know that Theo's finished setting up the digital trail. As far as anyone can tell, Jack Mallum killed Cameron Smith, then fled when he realised he was being investigated."

"Will they believe it?" I asked.

Fraser and Daisy exchanged a look I couldn't quite interpret. "They'll believe what they're shown," Fraser said carefully. "And what they're being shown is very convincing."

"Theo's good at what he does," Daisy added. "The best, according to Ciarán."

I nodded, trying to take comfort in their confidence. But a nagging worry remained. "And if they don't believe it? If they send someone else to investigate?"

"Then we deal with that when it happens," Fraser said firmly. "But it won't. This isn't Ciarán's first rodeo, Genie. He knows what he's doing."

I wanted to believe that. Needed to believe it. Because the alternative—that we'd killed and disposed of a man for nothing, that danger still loomed on the horizon—was too terrible to contemplate.

"So," Daisy said brightly, clearly trying to change the subject, "what's on the agenda for today? Besides staring at the butcher shop and contemplating the ethical implications of cannibalism?"

I managed a small smile. "Just the usual. Make face creams, sell face creams, try not to think about the fact that I killed a man last night."

"That's the spirit," Bernie chimed in. "Compartmentalisation is key."

"Is that how you all do it?" I asked, genuinely curious. "Just put it in a box and move on?"

The three of them exchanged glances, a silent communication that excluded me. Then Bernie spoke, her voice uncharacteristically serious.

"Everyone copes differently," she said. "Theo works till his fingers bleed. Fraser probably punches things."

"Accurate," Fraser confirmed with a nod.

"And Ciarán?" I couldn't help asking.

Another exchange of glances. "Ciarán doesn't cope," Fraser said finally. "He just… accepts. It's what makes him so good at what he does. And so dangerous."

A chill ran down my spine at his words. I'd seen that quality in Ciarán last night—the calm acceptance as he slit Jack's throat, the methodical way he'd broken down the body. No hesitation, no visible remorse. Just acceptance that this was what needed to be done.

"But he's different with you," Fraser added quickly, perhaps seeing my expression. "Softer. More human."

"Great," I muttered. "I'm dating a robot who occasionally malfunctions around me."

That got a laugh from all three of them, breaking the tension that had settled over our little group.

"Speaking of your homicidal boyfriend," Bernie said, "he's heading this way."

I turned to look out the window and saw Ciarán crossing the street, his butcher's apron gone, replaced by a simple black t-shirt and jeans. He moved with that predator's grace I'd always admired, now understanding its true origin. Not a butcher's practiced efficiency, but a killer's constant readiness.

Yet despite everything I now knew about him, despite the

horrors of the previous night, my heart still skipped a beat at the sight of him. What did that say about me?

"And that's our cue to make ourselves scarce," Daisy announced, grabbing Fraser's arm. "Come on, big guy. Let's go see if anyone's keeled over from eating the special mince yet."

"Daisy!" I hissed, glancing around to make sure no customers had overheard.

She just laughed, pulling Fraser toward the door. "Relax, Genie. Dark humour, remember? It's how you cope."

As they left, passing Ciarán on his way in, I saw them exchange nods—a silent communication between colleagues; between people who shared secrets I was only beginning to understand.

Bernie, too, made herself scarce, mumbling something about inventory in the back room. And then it was just me and Ciarán, standing among the shelves of skincare products that suddenly seemed absurdly normal, absurdly innocent, given what we'd done.

"Hey," he said, his blue eyes searching my face. "How are you holding up?"

I considered lying, saying I was fine. But what was the point? He'd seen me at my worst, at my most vulnerable. He knew exactly what I was capable of, just as I now knew what he could do.

"I keep watching people leave your shop," I admitted. "Wondering if they bought the… special mince."

He nodded, understanding without judgement. "Most did. It sold out within an hour of opening. People love a novelty."

"That's… disturbing," I said, though I couldn't help the small, inappropriate laugh that escaped me. "This whole town is eating a man who tried to kill me."

"Poetic justice," Ciarán suggested with a small smile. "He

came to hurt you, and instead, he's nourishing the community you protect."

I stared at him, caught between horror and amusement at his twisted logic. "There is definitely something wrong with you," I said, echoing my earlier words to Fraser.

"Undoubtedly," he agreed without hesitation. "But you like me anyway."

And that was the crux of it, wasn't it? Despite everything —the lies, the violence, the darkness I now knew he carried —I did like him. I more than liked him. I was falling in love with him; had been since that first night together.

What did that say about me?

"I do," I admitted softly. "God help me, I do."

His expression softened, the hardness that seemed to be his default setting melted away. "Then we're both a little broken," he said, reaching out to tuck a strand of hair behind my ear. "But maybe that's why we fit."

I leaned into his touch, craving the comfort of it despite everything. "Is it over?" I asked. "Really over?"

He knew what I was asking—not just about Jack, but about his job, his life before Newchurch, the danger that had brought him here in the first place.

"Almost," he promised. "I sent my report this morning. Jack Mallum killed Cameron Smith in a dispute over a land deal, gone wrong. I tracked him down and eliminated him. Case closed."

"And they believed it?" I pressed.

"They have no reason not to," he assured me. "The evidence Theo created is convincing. And they want this resolved as much as we do."

I nodded, wanting to believe him, needing to. "So, what happens now?"

"Now," he said, his hand moving to cup my cheek, "we

try to be normal. Or as normal as a hitman-turned-butcher and a witch who poisons abusive men can be."

I laughed despite myself, the sound surprising me with its genuineness. "That's not very normal at all."

It wasn't normal. It wasn't safe. But as his lips met mine, I couldn't bring myself to care.

Chapter 22
Freedom and Futures
Ciarán

It had been two days since we'd sold out of the "wild boar" mince, and I was still hearing about it from customers. Mrs. Beecham had come in this morning specifically to tell me it was the best she'd ever tasted; her bridge club raved about her meatballs. She hoped we'd get more of that "special breed" soon.

The irony wasn't lost on me. Jack Mallum had come to Newchurch to kill Genie, and instead, he'd become dinner for the very community she protected. There was a certain poetic justice to it, though I kept that particular observation to myself. Mrs. Beecham might be the town gossip, but I doubted even she was ready for that level of macabre truth.

I was wiping down the counter, preparing to close for the day, when my phone pinged with an email notification. I recognised the sender immediately—my now former employer. With slightly damp hands, I opened it, scanning the brief message:

Contract fulfilled. Consider our business concluded.

Six words. That's all it took to end a decade of service, of blood and death and moral compromise. Six words, and I was free.

I must have been staring at my phone for longer than I realised, because suddenly Fraser was there, peering over my shoulder, with a fresh beer in his hand.

"Good news?" he asked, though the knowing look in his eyes suggested he'd already guessed.

I handed him the phone wordlessly, watching as he read the message, a slow grin spreading across his face. When he finished, he slapped me on the back hard enough to make me stumble.

"Well, well," he said, "butcher it is now."

"It feels strange," I admitted, taking the phone back and tucking it into my pocket. "To be free. Like, what am I meant to do now? I know I have the shop, but I still feel like I'm missing something."

Fraser's grin softened to a knowing smile. "Aye, I get that. My fingers have been itching for action for days."

I studied him, this man who'd been my partner and friend for years. He'd followed me into this cover without hesitation, had adapted to life as a butcher with surprising ease. But I knew he missed the adrenaline rush of our former life, the danger and power that came with it.

"Speaking of itching," I said, changing the subject, "what's going on with you and Daisy? I thought you didn't do attachments."

Fraser's smile faltered slightly. "I don't. Usually."

"And yet it's been what, months? And you're still seeing her. Exclusively, from what I can tell."

He shrugged, trying for nonchalance, but not quite achieving it. "She's different."

"Different how?"

"She knows what I am," he said. "What we are. And she

doesn't care. She's not afraid, not disgusted. She just accepts it."

I nodded, understanding completely. It was the same with Genie. The relief of being known, truly known, and still wanted—it was intoxicating.

"Do you reckon someone like us can have both?" Fraser asked suddenly, his voice uncharacteristically serious. "The normal life and the other part?"

"I'm going to have both," I said with a certainty that surprised even me. "No matter what."

Fraser raised an eyebrow. "Really? You're gonna keep her?"

"Yes, I am," I confirmed, the words feeling right as they left my mouth. "I actually plan to marry her."

Fraser choked on the beer he'd just taken a swig of, coughing and sputtering. "You're kidding me," he managed between coughs.

"He's not," Theo's voice came from the doorway to the back room. He stepped into the shop, wiping his hands on a towel. "Called his dad this morning and asked to have his mother's ring shipped over."

I shot Theo an annoyed look. "Been eavesdropping, have you?"

"Difficult not to when you're discussing life-altering decisions in the middle of the shop," Theo replied dryly. "And for the record, I think you're making a mistake."

"No one asked you," I retorted, though without heat. Theo's caution was part of what made him valuable as a partner. He saw risks where Fraser and I saw opportunities.

"Do you think this is wise?" Fraser asked, recovering from his shock. "We know that enemies will always take what we care about."

It was a valid concern; one I'd wrestled with myself. In

our line of work—former line of work, I reminded myself—attachments were vulnerabilities. People we cared about became targets, leverage to be used against us. It was why most of us avoided lasting relationships, why we kept people at arm's length.

"I know," I acknowledged. "But I just don't want to be alone anymore. As long as I take jobs that aren't too bad, I should be fine." I paused, then added with a small smile, "Plus, it's not like I'm trying to marry a nun. I mean, she is a serial killer, too."

"That is true," Theo conceded. "That she is."

Fraser looked thoughtful, absently wiping at the beer he'd spilled on his shirt. "Daisy does help her, all the time, and is technically an accessory to murder daily. So is Bernie." He glanced up at me. "They know what we do, and Daisy hasn't cared at all since Genie told her everything two days ago."

A slow smile spread across his face, a realisation dawning. "Maybe we can have it all."

The thought hung in the air between us, tantalising and dangerous. Maybe we could have it all—the normal life and the darker one, the shop and the side jobs, the relationships and the freedom. Maybe we didn't have to choose.

"It won't be easy," Theo warned, ever the voice of caution. "There will always be risks. People from our past who might come looking. Jobs that go wrong."

"Nothing worth having comes easy," I countered. "And we're good at what we do. All of us." I looked between my two friends, my partners in both legitimate business and darker ventures. "We've survived this long. We'll adapt."

Fraser nodded slowly, his expression thoughtful. "So, marriage, huh? Never thought I'd see the day."

"Neither did I," I admitted. "But then, I never thought I'd meet someone like Genie either."

"When are you going to ask her?" Theo inquired, his tone softening slightly. Despite his warnings, I could tell he was happy for me, in his reserved way.

"Soon," I said. "Once the ring arrives. I want to do it properly."

"Properly?" Fraser snorted. "What, down on one knee and all that shite?"

"Yes," I confirmed, ignoring his teasing. "Down on one knee and all that shite. She deserves it."

Fraser's expression sobered. "Aye, she does. After what she's been through, what you've both been through… she deserves something good."

I nodded, grateful for his understanding. "And what about you? Are you going to keep seeing Daisy?"

He shrugged, but there was a new thoughtfulness to his expression. "Maybe. If she'll have me. She's different. Special."

"They both are," Theo agreed. "All three of them, really. Not many women would react to finding out their friends are professional killers by offering to help dispose of the bodies."

"That's Newchurch for you," I said with a small laugh. "Town full of witches and weirdos."

"And now butchers with a side hustle," Fraser added with a grin.

"Speaking of which," Theo interjected, "we should discuss what that side hustle looks like going forward. If we're staying in Newchurch, if we're settling down," he said the words like they were foreign, "then we need rules. Boundaries."

He was right, of course. If we were going to continue taking jobs—and I knew we would, all of us, because it was in our blood—then we needed parameters. Especially now that we had people we cared about, people who could be affected by our choices.

"No jobs that target innocents," I said immediately. "No women, no children. No one who doesn't deserve it."

"Agreed," Fraser nodded. "And no jobs that could lead back to Newchurch. Nothing that puts the shop, or the girls, at risk."

"We vet clients thoroughly," Theo added. "No more taking employers at their word. We verify everything."

"And we work together," I finished. "All three of us, or none of us. No solo jobs."

We looked at each other, these men who had been my brothers in all but blood for years, and I saw the same determination in their eyes that I felt in my heart. We were changing, evolving, but we weren't giving up who we were. Just becoming better versions of ourselves.

"To new beginnings," Fraser said, raising his beer bottle.

"And old skills," Theo added, tapping his own bottle against Fraser's.

I grabbed my water glass from the counter and joined in the toast. "To having it all."

Chapter 23
Questions and Foxglove
Genie

I was rearranging the display of facial toners when the bell above the shop door jingled. Looking up with my practiced customer-service smile, I found myself facing a man I'd never seen before. Tall, with salt-and-pepper hair and the kind of weathered face that suggested he spent more time frowning than smiling. He wore a rumpled suit that had seen better days and carried himself with the unmistakable authority of law enforcement.

My smile didn't falter, but my heart rate kicked up a notch. After the events with Jack Mallum, I was understandably wary of strangers, especially official-looking ones.

"Good morning," I greeted him, setting down the bottle I'd been holding. "Welcome to Alden Alchemy. Can I help you find something?"

He approached the counter, pulling out a badge and ID card. "Detective Inspector Michael Harrow," he introduced himself. "Lancashire Police. I was hoping to ask you a few questions, if you have a moment."

I nodded, keeping my expression neutral despite the alarm

bells ringing in my head. "Of course, Detective. What can I help you with?"

He reached into his jacket pocket and pulled out a photograph, sliding it across the counter toward me. "Do you recognise this woman?"

I looked down at the photo and felt a chill run through me. Rebecca Winters. The woman whose body had been found in the woods. The woman whose husband had been the target of the poison I'd given her.

I didn't lie. There was no point—my shop had security cameras, and she'd paid by card. "Yes, she came into the shop a few weeks ago. Bought some skincare products."

"You remember her specifically?" the detective asked, one eyebrow raised in mild surprise.

"I remember most of my customers," I said with a slight shrug. "But yes, I remember her particularly because…" I hesitated, then decided honesty was the best approach. "Because of the bruises. She had marks on her wrists, and when she reached up to examine a product, her sleeve fell back, and I saw more bruising on her arm. I was concerned her husband might be hurting her."

Detective Harrow nodded, his expression softening slightly. "You're not the first person to mention concerns about her husband. Several neighbours reported hearing arguments, seeing her with unexplained injuries."

"Is he a suspect?" I asked, trying to sound appropriately curious rather than intensely invested in the answer.

"We're exploring all possibilities," he said, the standard non-answer of police everywhere. "Mr. Winters claims his wife began acting strangely after visiting your shop. That she became paranoid, secretive."

I raised my eyebrows, feigning surprise while carefully constructing my response. "More than likely, yes. I mentioned the bruises I'd noticed and suggested that if her husband was hurting her, she should consider leaving him. That kind of conversation can be a wake-up call for women in abusive situations. They often do become more secretive afterward—they're planning their escape."

The detective studied me, his gaze sharp and assessing. "We found a bottle in Mrs. Winters' room," he said after a moment. "A small glass bottle containing traces of a liquid that our lab says contained natural ingredients that could cause harm if ingested. It looks similar to the bottles you use here in your shop."

My heart skipped a beat, but I kept my expression calm as I gestured around the shop. "We use glass bottles for all our products, Detective, on purpose. We encourage all our clients to either drop them back empty so they can be reused or to reuse them themselves. What someone does with an empty bottle of mine is up to them."

He nodded, seemingly satisfied with this answer. Then he smiled, the expression transforming his stern face into something almost friendly. "It's curious, though, isn't it? How many wives who visit this shop seem to have husbands that pass on within a few weeks or years…"

The implication was clear. He knew, or at least suspected, what I was doing. What the Alden women had been doing for generations. My pulse quickened, but I kept my composure, meeting his gaze steadily.

"Please tell me you're not a believer in witches too, Detective," I said with a small laugh, trying to make light of his insinuation.

To my surprise, he laughed as well. "No, in fact, I think all women who were burned at the stake were just women who were miles ahead of the men in that time, and their small dicks were unable to handle it."

The unexpected crudeness from this official-looking man startled a genuine laugh out of me. "Well, that's certainly one theory," I managed, still chuckling.

He turned to leave but paused at the door. "Tell me, Ms. Alden, what does foxglove and monkshood do to a body? Medicinally speaking, of course."

My blood ran cold. Those were exactly the herbs I'd used in the poison I'd given Rebecca. There was no way he could know that unless… unless he'd found more than just the bottle. Unless Rebecca had kept notes, or the lab had somehow identified the specific compounds.

But his expression remained friendly, curious rather than accusatory. I decided to answer truthfully, focusing on the medicinal properties rather than the toxic ones.

"Well, foxglove—or digitalis—is used in heart medications," I explained, keeping my voice steady. "It can regulate heart rhythm when used properly. And monkshood, or aconite, has been used traditionally for pain relief, though it's fallen out of favour in modern medicine due to its potency. Both plants have a long history in herbal medicine; they require careful handling."

He nodded, seemingly satisfied with my answer. "Fascinating. The natural world is full of wonders, isn't it? Substances that can heal or harm, depending on how they're used."

"Exactly," I agreed, relieved that he seemed to be taking my explanation at face value. "It's all about knowledge and respect for the plants."

"Indeed." He smiled again, raising a hand in farewell. "Thank you for your time, Ms. Alden. You've been very helpful."

And with that, he was gone, the bell jingling cheerfully as the door closed behind him.

I waited until I was sure he was out of sight before I let out the breath I'd been holding, sagging against the counter as the tension drained from my body. That had been close. Too close.

The detective knew something—or at least, he suspected. His questions about foxglove and monkshood hadn't been random. He was fishing, trying to get me to incriminate myself.

But why hadn't he pressed harder? Why the friendly demeanour, the almost conspiratorial tone? It was almost as if he…

"Dia duit, mo stór," Ciarán's voice came from the back room, startling me so badly I nearly knocked over a display of facial serums. "Sorry, didn't mean to scare you."

He emerged from the back, wiping his hands on a towel. He must have come in through the rear entrance while I was talking to the detective.

"How long have you been there?" I demanded, my heart still racing from the combination of the detective's visit and Ciarán's sudden appearance.

"Long enough," he said, his expression serious despite the casual tone. "Interesting conversation with our local detective."

"You know him?" I asked, surprised.

Ciarán shrugged. "I make it my business to know all the law enforcement in any area I operate in. Harrow's been with Lancashire Police for fifteen years. Good clearance rate, by-the-book most of the time, but known to look the other way occasionally if he thinks justice is being served."

That explained the detective's odd behaviour—the pointed questions followed by the almost friendly departure. He suspected what I was doing, but he wasn't necessarily opposed to it.

"He knows about the foxglove and monkshood," I said, still shaken. "He specifically asked about them. Those were exactly what I used in Rebecca's poison."

Ciarán's expression darkened. "That's concerning. The lab must have found traces in the bottle."

"But if he has evidence, why didn't he arrest me?" I asked, voicing the question that had been nagging at me.

"Because evidence of the plants isn't evidence of murder," Ciarán explained. "As you said, they have medicinal uses. And even if they found traces in her system, that doesn't prove you gave them to her with the intent to harm. It only proves she ingested them somehow."

"So, I'm safe?" I asked, not entirely convinced.

"For now," he said, moving to stand beside me, his hand finding mine and squeezing gently. "But we should be careful. Harrow might be willing to look the other way to a point, but if more bodies start piling up, he'll have no choice but to act."

I nodded, leaning into him slightly, drawing comfort from his solid presence. "I'll be more careful with the formulations. Use different combinations, make them harder to trace."

"Or," Ciarán suggested, his voice careful, "you could take a break. Just for a while, until this blows over."

I pulled back to look at him, surprised. "A break? From helping women who have nowhere else to turn?"

"Not from helping them," he clarified quickly. "Just from the… pharmaceutical aspect. There are other ways to help— safe houses, legal resources, even just being a listening ear."

I considered his suggestion, understanding the logic behind it, but was reluctant to abandon the methods that had been passed down through generations of Alden women. "I'll think about it," I promised, though we both knew I was unlikely to stop completely.

He nodded, accepting my non-answer with a small smile. "That's all I ask, mo stór."

"What does that mean?" I asked, curious about the Gaelic endearment he had started to use on me lately. "Mo stór?"

"My treasure," he translated, a hint of colour rising to his cheeks. Ciarán Ó Duinn, former hitman and current butcher, was blushing. "It's what my father called my mother."

Something warm unfurled in my chest at his words, at the implication that I held a place in his heart similar to what his mother had held in his father's. "I like it," I said softly.

He smiled, the expression transforming his usually serious face. "Good. Because I plan to call you that for a very long time."

There was something in his tone, something significant that made my heart skip a beat. But before I could question him further, the shop door jingled again, and a group of tourists entered, chattering excitedly about the "natural skin care shop" they'd read about online.

Ciarán stepped back, giving my hand one last squeeze before retreating to the back room. "I'll let you handle this," he said with a wink. "I need to get back to the butcher shop anyway. Fraser's alone, and God knows what trouble he'll get into without supervision."

I laughed, the tension from the detective's visit finally dissipating. "Go. I'll see you tonight?"

"Definitely," he confirmed. "I'll be there."

Chapter 24
Samhain Surprises
Genie

October 31st had always been my favourite day of the year. Most people knew it as Halloween—a night of costumes, candy, and manufactured scares. But for witches like me, it's Samhain (pronounced "sow-in"), the most sacred night in our calendar. The night when the veil between worlds is thinnest, when our ancestors could walk among us, and magic flowed most freely through the earth.

Bernie, Daisy, and I had spent the entire day preparing. The shop had been closed. Samhain was for family, for remembrance, for celebration of the cycle of life and death; not for selling face creams to tourists.

"Pass the sage, would you?" Bernie asked, her hands deep in a bowl of herb-infused butter. We'd taken over my kitchen; every surface covered with food in various stages of preparation.

I handed her the bundle of dried sage from my garden, watching as she crumbled it into the mixture. "Not too much," I cautioned. "Remember what happened last time."

"That was one time," she protested, but measured the herb carefully, nonetheless. "And nobody actually got sick."

"Only because I stopped you before you poisoned us all," I reminded her with a laugh.

"Speaking of poison," Daisy chimed in from where she was arranging sliced apples in a pattern that would become a tarte tatin, "has that detective been back to the shop?"

I shook my head, focusing on the pumpkin soup I was stirring. "No, but I've seen him around town. I think he's keeping an eye on me."

"Creepy," Bernie commented.

"Not really," I said thoughtfully. "I think he's just… waiting. Watching to see if I make a mistake."

"Well, don't," Daisy said firmly. "I'm not visiting you in prison. Grey is not your colour."

I laughed, the tension eased from my shoulders. This was what I needed today—my friends, our traditions, the comforting rhythm of preparing food together, just as women in my family had done for generations on Samhain.

"Do you think the boys will show up?" Bernie asked, changing the subject as she slid her herb butter under the skin of a chicken destined for the oven.

"Ciarán promised they would," I said, though I'd had the same doubt. The butcher boys weren't exactly the type to embrace pagan celebrations in cemeteries.

"Fraser's definitely coming," Daisy confirmed. "He's bringing whiskey."

"Of course he is," Bernie rolled her eyes. "Scottish stereotype much?"

"Hey, don't knock it," Daisy grinned. "That accent gets thicker when he drinks, and it's sexy as hell."

"Too much information," I groaned, though I was smiling.

It was good to see Daisy happy, to see her and Fraser still going strong after several months. It gave me hope for my own relationship with Ciarán.

"What about Theo?" I asked, glancing at Bernie. "Did you invite him?"

A faint blush coloured her cheeks. "I mentioned it. He said he'd think about it."

Daisy and I exchanged knowing looks. There had been something brewing between Bernie and Theo for weeks now —lingering glances, private conversations about books and philosophy, the occasional brush of hands that lasted just a moment too long. Neither would admit to anything, but we had our suspicions.

"Well, I hope he comes," I said neutrally. "It would be nice to have everyone together."

As the afternoon wore on, we finished our cooking and began packing everything into baskets and coolers. The traditional Samhain feast included seasonal foods—apples, nuts, pumpkin, game—as well as dishes that honoured the dead. I'd made my grandmother's favourite pumpkin soup, and Bernie had prepared my mother's herb-roasted chicken. Daisy's contribution was her own specialty—a tarte tatin that would be flambéed at the cemetery; a literal representation of the fire festivals that had once marked this night across the Celtic world.

"Should we explain to the boys what Samhain actually is?" Daisy asked as we loaded the car. "Or just let them think we're weird women who picnic in cemeteries?"

"They already think we're weird," I pointed out. "But yes, I'll give them the abbreviated history lesson."

And I would. Because Samhain wasn't just a night for witches—it was the ancient Celtic festival marking the end of the harvest season and the beginning of winter, the darker half of the year. It was a time when the boundary between this world and the Otherworld thinned, allowing the dead to return to the land of the living. Bonfires were lit, offerings were made, and people wore costumes to confuse malevolent spirits.

Christianity had later co-opted the festival as All Saints' Day (or All Hallows), with the night before becoming All Hallows' Eve—Halloween. But for those of us who followed the old ways, it remained Samhain; a night of remembrance, of honouring our ancestors, of acknowledging the cycle of death and rebirth that governs all life.

By the time we arrived at the Newchurch Cemetery, the sun was setting, painting the sky in shades of orange and purple. We made our way to the Alden section and began setting up our celebration.

Daisy spread thick blankets over the ground while Bernie arranged pillows for comfort. I set out candles—black for remembrance, orange for the harvest, white for protection—and lit them one by one, whispering a small blessing with each flame.

"This is quite the setup," a familiar voice said behind me, and I turned to find Ciarán standing there, a bottle of wine in each hand. Fraser and, to my surprise, Theo flanked him, carrying additional supplies.

"Welcome to Samhain," I greeted them, rising to my feet. "I wasn't sure you'd all come."

"And miss the chance to drink in a cemetery?" Fraser grinned. "Not likely."

"It's an important night for you," Ciarán said more seriously, stepping forward to kiss me softly. "Of course we came."

Something in his tone, in the intensity of his gaze, made my heart flutter. There was a nervous energy about him tonight, a tension I couldn't quite place.

"Well, you're just in time to help set up the food," Daisy declared, directing Fraser to where she wanted the portable camping table placed.

Soon, our Samhain feast was laid out in all its glory—the pumpkin soup kept warm in a thermos, the herb-roasted chicken, roasted vegetables, fresh bread, cheeses, and Daisy's tarte tatin waiting for its dramatic flambé finale. Fraser had indeed brought whiskey, along with the wine Ciarán contributed, and Theo, to everyone's surprise, had brought a traditional Irish soda bread.

"My grandmother's recipe," he explained when I commented on it. "She was from Cork."

"I didn't know you had Irish roots," I said, genuinely surprised. Theo rarely shared personal details.

He shrugged, looking slightly uncomfortable with the attention. "On my mother's side. She used to make this every Halloween—Samhain, I suppose, though she never called it that."

It was a small glimpse into the man behind the reserved exterior, and I found myself warming to him even more.

As we settled onto the blankets and began our meal, I explained the significance of Samhain to the three men, who listened with varying degrees of interest.

"So, the dead can actually walk among us tonight?" Fraser asked, sounding sceptical but intrigued.

"That's the belief," I confirmed. "The veil between worlds is thinnest on Samhain. It's why we set an extra place at our feast—" I gestured to the small plate of food set slightly apart from our circle, "—as an offering to those who have passed."

"And can you see them all?" Ciarán asked quietly. "Your ancestors, or just your grandmother?"

I nodded, meeting his gaze. "Sometimes. Not always. But yes, especially here, where so many of my family are buried. I always see my grandmother, occasionally my mother, and almost always all of them on Samhain."

"That must be... comforting," Theo said, surprising me again. "To know they're still with you in some way."

"It is," I agreed. "Though sometimes they're a bit too opinionated for comfort." That earned a laugh from everyone, easing the solemnity that had settled over our group.

The meal progressed with easy conversation, the six of us forming a strange but harmonious circle in the gathering darkness. Daisy flambéed her tarte tatin with dramatic flair, the blue flames leaping high and drawing appreciative gasps. Fraser told outrageous stories that had us all laughing, while Theo and Bernie engaged in a quiet but intense discussion about Celtic mythology that frequently drew them away from the main conversation.

And Ciarán... Ciarán seemed distracted, his gaze frequently drifting to the centre of the Alden section, where a large oak tree spread its branches over several generations of my family. He was quieter than usual, though he smiled and participated in the conversation. But there was something on his mind, something that kept pulling his attention away.

As we finished the meal and moved on to coffee and whiskey, Ciarán suddenly stood up. "I need some air," he said, which was an odd statement given that we were already outdoors.

"Are you okay?" I asked, concerned.

"Fine," he assured me with a smile that didn't quite reach his eyes. "Just give me a minute."

He walked away from our circle, heading toward the

centre of the Alden section. I watched him go, puzzled by his behaviour.

"What's up with him?" Daisy whispered, leaning close.

"No idea," I replied, my eyes still on Ciarán's retreating form.

Fraser and Theo exchanged a look I couldn't interpret, and Bernie was suddenly very interested in rearranging the dessert plates.

"What's going on?" I demanded, looking between them. "You all know something I don't."

"Just wait," Fraser advised with an uncharacteristically gentle smile. "You'll see."

Before I could press further, Ciarán turned and called out to me. "Genie! Come over here a minute."

I rose to my feet, brushing crumbs from my dress, and made my way toward him, increasingly confused. He was standing in the very centre of the Alden section, beneath the oak tree that my great-great-grandfather had planted. The moonlight filtered through the branches, dappling the ground around him.

As I approached, he took a deep breath, and then, to my complete shock, lowered himself to one knee.

I gasped, my hand flying to my mouth as he reached into his pocket and pulled out a small velvet box.

"Genie Alden," he began, his voice steady despite the vulnerability in his eyes. "I've never been good with words, not the kind that matter. I'm better with actions, with showing rather than telling. But tonight, I want to tell you exactly how I feel."

He opened the box, revealing a ring that caught the moonlight and scattered it like stars. An antique setting, delicate yet substantial, with a central diamond surrounded by smaller stones.

"I love you, mo stór," he continued, his Irish accent thickening with emotion. "In fact, I've loved you for a while now. You fit me like a glove, like a missing piece I never knew was gone until I found you. I've never been happier than I am when I'm with you."

Tears welled in my eyes, blurring my vision. I could hear Bernie squealing somewhere behind me, and Daisy's delighted laugh, but they seemed distant, unimportant compared to the man kneeling before me.

"You know me—all of me—the good and the bad, the light and the dark. And somehow, miraculously, you love me anyway. You've given me a home, a purpose beyond what I ever thought possible. You've shown me that even someone like me can have a future, can build something beautiful."

He took another deep breath, his eyes never leaving mine. "Genie Alden, witch of Newchurch, keeper of my heart, will you marry me?"

For a moment, I couldn't speak, overwhelmed by emotion. And in that moment, I became aware of a presence —no, multiple presences—gathering around us. Turning slightly, I saw them—the ghosts of my family, my ancestors, materialising in the moonlight. My grandmother stood closest, her familiar smile warm and approving. Behind her, my mother and father, holding hands as they always had in life. And others, generations of Alden women stretching back through time, all watching, all present for this moment.

They moved forward as one, surrounding Ciarán, placing their ghostly hands on his shoulders, his head, his back. He shivered, his brow furrowing as he turned his head to the side, clearly sensing something but unable to see what I could.

"My family approves," I said softly, a tear spilling down my cheek.

"Is that a yes?" he asked, hope and love shining in his eyes.

"Yes," I whispered, then louder, "Yes, Ciarán Ó Duinn, I will marry you."

He slid the ring onto my finger—a perfect fit—and rose to his feet, pulling me into his arms. As our lips met in a kiss that sealed our promise; I heard cheers and applause from our friends and felt the blessing of my ancestors surrounding us like a warm embrace.

When we finally broke apart, both breathless and grinning, we turned to find our friends approaching with glasses of whiskey raised in toast.

"About bloody time," Fraser declared, clapping Ciarán on the back. "I thought you were going to chicken out."

"Never," Ciarán replied, his arm tight around my waist.

"It's beautiful," Daisy said, grabbing my hand to examine the ring. "Vintage?"

"It was my mother's," Ciarán explained. "And her mother's before that."

"A family heirloom," Bernie sighed romantically. "That's so perfect."

We celebrated with more whiskey and the last of Daisy's tarte tatin, our Samhain feast becoming an impromptu engagement party. The ghosts of my family lingered, visible only to me, their presence a comforting reminder of the traditions and bonds that had shaped me.

As the night grew later and the temperature dropped, we packed up our celebration. Fraser helped Daisy gather the blankets and pillows, while Theo and Bernie collected the candles and remaining food.

"I'm staying at the shop apartment tonight," Daisy announced as we loaded everything into the cars. "Fraser's going to help me with some… inventory."

The excuse was transparent, but I just smiled and nodded. "Sure. Have fun with that 'inventory.'"

Fraser didn't even bother with a pretence, just grinned and pulled Daisy close. "Congratulations again, you two. We'll celebrate properly at the pub tomorrow."

They left together, Daisy's laughter floating back to us on the night air. I turned to say goodbye to Bernie and Theo, only to find Theo holding out his hand to Bernie with an uncharacteristically open expression.

"Fuck it," he said bluntly. "They're bound to find out sooner or later."

Bernie took his hand with a shy smile, and they walked away together, fingers intertwined.

I stared after them, pointing in disbelief. "Did you see that? Are they…?"

"They've been secretly dating behind all our backs this whole time," Ciarán confirmed, looking amused.

"I had no idea," I said, genuinely shocked. Bernie was terrible at keeping secrets—or so I'd thought. "I mean, I had started to think something was developing but figured nothing had in fact happened."

"Theo is good at hiding shite," Ciarán shrugged. "But that wasn't hidden very well."

We watched them go, both still processing this unexpected development. Then Ciarán turned to me, his expression softening as he took my hand, his thumb brushing over the ring that now adorned it.

"Alone at last, future Mrs. Ó Duinn," he murmured, pulling me close.

"I like the sound of that," I admitted, tilting my face up for his kiss.

The drive back to the Alden estate was charged with anticipation, a current of desire running between us that made the short journey feel endless. By the time we reached the house, the need to touch, to connect, to celebrate our engagement in the most primal way possible was overwhelming.

We barely made it through the front door before Ciarán's hands were on me, his mouth hot and demanding against mine. I responded with equal fervour, my fingers tangling in his hair, pulling him closer as we stumbled toward the stairs.

"Bedroom," I gasped between kisses. "Now."

He lifted me effortlessly, my legs wrapping around his waist as he carried me up the stairs, his lips never leaving mine. I could feel his hardness pressing against me through our clothes, the promise of what was to come made me wet with anticipation. The journey to my bedroom was punctuated by pauses against walls, brief moments where the need to touch and taste overcame the desire to reach our destination.

When we finally tumbled onto my bed, we were both breathing hard, clothes dishevelled, eyes dark with desire. Ciarán braced himself above me, his gaze roaming my face with such tenderness that my heart ached.

"I love you," he said. "More than I ever thought possible."

"Show me," I whispered, reaching for him.

And he did. With reverent hands, he undressed me slowly, his touch worshipful as he revealed my body inch by inch. He started with my blouse, his fingers deftly undoing each button, his lips following the path of exposed skin. When he reached the valley between my breasts, he paused, his hot breath making me shiver as he nuzzled against the lace of my bra.

"So beautiful," he murmured, reaching behind me to unclasp the garment. As it fell away, he cupped my breasts in his hands, his thumbs brushing over my nipples until they hardened into tight peaks. I arched into his touch, a soft moan escaping my lips.

His mouth replaced his hands, his tongue circling one nipple before taking it between his lips, sucking gently at first, then with increased pressure that sent jolts of pleasure straight to my core. I writhed beneath him, my hands clutched at his shoulders, his hair, anything to anchor myself against the tide of sensation.

He lavished the same attention on my other breast, then continued his journey downward, his tongue tracing a wet path across my ribs, my stomach, the sensitive skin just above the waistband of my skirt. With torturous slowness, he slid the skirt down my legs, his fingers trailing fire along my thighs.

When I was left in nothing but my panties, he sat back on his heels, his eyes drinking in the sight of me. "Christ, Genie," he breathed, his accent thicker with desire. "You're a fucking goddess."

I reached for him, tugging at his shirt. "Your turn," I demanded. "I want to see you. All of you."

He complied, stripping off his shirt to reveal the muscled chest, I knew so well. I ran my hands over his skin, tracing the scars that told the story of his violent past, the tattoos that marked significant moments in his life. Each one was familiar to me now, each one part of the man I loved.

His jeans followed, and then his boxers, leaving him gloriously naked before me. His cock stood proud and hard; the tip already glistening with pre-cum. I licked my lips at the sight, and he groaned, his eyes darkening further.

"Come here," I whispered, pulling him down to me.

The feel of his naked skin against mine was electric, the weight of his body pressing me into the mattress a delicious pressure. We kissed deeply, tongues tangling, hands exploring familiar territory with renewed appreciation. This was the man I would marry, the body I would wake up beside for the rest of my life. The thought was both thrilling and humbling.

His hand slid between us, finding the wet heat between my thighs. He stroked me through the thin fabric of my panties, his fingers teased along the edges, never quite giving me what I needed.

"Please," I begged, lifting my hips in silent demand.

He smiled against my lips, then hooked his fingers in the waistband of my panties and slowly, torturously, pulled them down my legs. When they were gone, he settled between my thighs, his breath hot against my most intimate place.

"I want to taste you," he said, his voice rough with desire. "I want to make you come with my mouth, before I fuck you."

The crude words from his usually controlled mouth sent a fresh wave of arousal through me. I spread my legs wider in a silent invitation, and he didn't hesitate.

The first touch of his tongue against my clit made me cry out, my back arching off the bed. He chuckled, the vibration adding to the sensation, then set to work with dedicated precision. He knew exactly how to touch me, how to alternate between broad strokes of his tongue and focused attention on my clit, how to build the tension until I was a writhing, begging mess beneath him.

He slid two fingers inside me and curled them to hit that perfect spot, while his tongue continued its relentless assault on my clit, I shattered. My orgasm crashed over me in waves, my inner walls clenching around his fingers, his name a litany on my lips as pleasure consumed me.

Before I could fully recover, he was moving up my body, positioning himself between my thighs. The blunt head of his cock pressed against my entrance, and he paused, his eyes finding mine.

"Mine," he growled, his accent thick with desire. "Mo chroí, m'anam, mo shaol." My heart, my soul, my life.

"Yours," I agreed, the word a vow as sacred as the one we would make before witnesses. "Always yours."

He pushed into me in one smooth thrust, filling me completely. We both groaned at the sensation, the perfect fit of our bodies together. For a moment, he didn't move, just stayed buried deep inside me, his forehead pressed against mine, our breath mingling.

Then he began to move, slow, deep thrusts that hit every sensitive spot inside me. I wrapped my legs around his waist, changing the angle so he could go even deeper, and he groaned his approval.

"So tight," he murmured against my neck, his teeth grazing the sensitive skin there. "So perfect. So, fucking perfect."

His pace increased, the gentle lovemaking giving way to something more urgent, more primal. His hands gripped my hips, fingers digging into my flesh hard enough to leave marks, and I welcomed it, wanted it, wanted to be marked by him.

I met each thrust with equal fervour, my nails raking down his back, leaving my own marks on his skin. The sound of our bodies coming together, the slick heat of our connection, the gasps and moans filling the room—it was raw, animalistic, and utterly perfect.

"Touch yourself," he commanded, his voice strained with the effort of holding back. "I want to feel you come around my cock."

I slid my hand between us, finding my clit, circling it in

time with his thrusts. The dual stimulation was overwhelming, the tension building rapidly toward another peak.

"That's it," he encouraged, his eyes fixed on my face, watching the pleasure build. "Let go, mo stór. Come for me."

His words pushed me over the edge, and I came with a cry, my inner walls clenching rhythmically around his length. The sensation triggered his own release, and he thrust deep one final time, his cock pulsed inside me as he groaned my name.

For a long moment, we stayed joined, both trembling with aftershocks, his weight a welcome pressure pinning me to the bed. Then he rolled to the side, taking me with him so we lay face to face, still intimately connected.

"I love you," he whispered, brushing a strand of hair from my face with tender fingers.

"I love you too," I replied, my voice hoarse from crying out.

But we weren't done. Not even close. The night was young, and we had an engagement to celebrate.

After a brief rest, his hands began to wander again, reawakening desire with skilled touches. This time, he rolled me onto my stomach, pulling my hips up so I was on my knees before him.

"I want to take you like this," he said, his voice dark with renewed lust. "Is that okay?"

"Yes," I breathed, already wet again at the thought. "Please."

He positioned himself behind me, one hand on my hip, the other guiding his cock to my entrance. He pushed in slowly, the new angle allowing him to go even deeper than before. I gasped at the sensation, my fingers clutching at the sheets.

"Fuck, Genie," he groaned, both hands now gripping my hips. "You feel incredible."

He started to move, his thrusts harder, more demanding in this position. Each one drove me forward, the friction against my sensitive clit building the pleasure rapidly. I pushed back against him, meeting each thrust, wanting more, wanting everything he could give me.

One of his hands slid up my back, then into my hair, gathering it in his fist. He pulled gently, the slight sting adding another layer to the pleasure as he bent over me, his chest against my back.

"Mine," he growled in my ear, punctuating the word with a particularly deep thrust. "Say it."

"Yours," I gasped, the word breaking on a moan as he hit a spot deep inside me that made stars explode behind my eyelids. "I'm yours, Ciarán. Only yours."

His free hand snaked around to find my clit, rubbing in tight circles that had me climbing rapidly toward another peak. "Come with me this time," he demanded, his voice strained. "Together."

His thrusts became erratic, his breathing harsh in my ear, and I knew he was close. So was I, the dual stimulation of his cock inside me and his fingers on my clit pushing me inexorably toward the edge.

"Now," he commanded, and somehow, impossibly, my body obeyed. I came with a scream, my inner walls clamping down on him, milking his release as he thrust deep one final time, his cock pulsed inside me as he groaned my name.

We collapsed together onto the bed, a tangle of sweaty limbs and satisfied sighs. He pulled me close, my back to his chest, his softening cock still inside me, his arm a protective band around my waist.

"Happy?" he asked softly, his lips brushing the sensitive skin behind my ear.

I smiled, turning my head to meet his kiss. "Happier than I ever thought possible."

It was true. Despite the darkness in our pasts, despite the secrets we kept from the world, we had found something real, something worth fighting for. A love that accepted all parts, the good and the bad, the light and the dark.

A witch and a butcher. With side hustles.

It wasn't conventional. It wasn't safe. But as I drifted toward sleep in the arms of my future husband, I knew it was exactly where I was meant to be.

Chapter 25
The Sun and the Storm
Ciarán

I walked into Alden Alchemy carrying Genie's coffee—the same order I'd brought her every day since we'd settled into our routine and would continue to bring her, for as long as she'd let me. The familiar bell jingled above the door, announcing my arrival, but Genie was busy with a customer, discussing the merits of different facial toners with an intensity that made me smile.

My fiancée—Christ, I still couldn't believe I could call her that—took her skincare as seriously as I took my butchery. It was one of the many things I loved about her, that passion for her craft, even the parts of it that didn't involve poisoning abusive husbands.

I slid behind the counter, content to wait and watch her work. She glanced over her shoulder at me, her eyes lighting up in a way that made my heart skip. Even after all these months, she still looked at me like I was something special, something worth having; I'd never get used to that.

"The lavender toner would be perfect for your skin type," she was telling the customer, a middle-aged woman with the weathered complexion of someone who spent a lot of time outdoors. "It's gentle enough for daily use but still effective at balancing oil production."

The woman nodded, clearly sold on Genie's expertise. As they continued their discussion, I noticed movement from the back room. Bernie emerged, her arms laden with candles in various shapes and sizes. She nodded a greeting to me as she passed, heading for an empty display table near the window.

Curious, I wandered over to see what she was setting up. The candles were beautiful in rich, jewel-toned colours. But it was the labels that caught my attention. Each bore a name that would have been more at home in a strip club than a skincare shop.

"'Midnight Mistress'?" I read aloud, picking up a deep purple candle. "'Velvet Vixen'? 'Sultry Siren'?" I couldn't help but laugh. "Why the names?"

Bernie looked up from arranging the display, a mischievous glint in her eye. "These are sex candles," she explained matter-of-factly. "You burn them when making love or fucking, and it makes it better."

I raised an eyebrow, examining the candle in my hand with new interest. "A candle can make it better?"

She smiled, taking the candle from me and placing a different one in my palm with deliberate care. "Ohhhh, my sweet boy," she said, her voice dropped to a conspiratorial whisper. "Give this a try."

With that cryptic advice, she returned to stacking the shelves, leaving me wondering if Bernie was, in fact, a witch too. It wouldn't surprise me. There was something about her —about all three of the women—that hinted at things beyond the ordinary. I was fully onboard with witchcraft now, but I wasn't sure Bernie and Daisy fit into the same category, too.

I was still contemplating the candle when I heard the customer thanking Genie and heading for the door. Returning to the counter, I presented the coffee with a slight bow.

"Your daily offering, mo stór," I said, enjoying the way her eyes crinkled at the corners when she smiled.

"You spoil me," she replied, accepting the cup and taking a grateful sip. "Mmm, perfect. How do you always get it exactly right?"

"Trade secret," I winked. In truth, I'd memorised her order the first time I'd heard her place it, filing away the information as I did with all important details about potential targets. Old habits die hard, even when the target has become the love of my life rather than a mark.

Genie set down her coffee and reached for the deck of tarot cards she kept behind the counter. It was a habit of hers to draw a card each morning, a way of setting the tone for the day. I'd grown fond of the ritual, though I still maintained a healthy scepticism about the cards' predictive powers.

She shuffled the deck with practiced hands, her fingers nimble and sure. As she did, a single card slipped free, landing face-up on the counter between us. The Sun— a bright, golden image of a child on a white horse beneath a radiant sun.

I picked it up carefully, handing it back to her. "Is this a good one?"

Her smile was luminous. "One of the best. The Sun represents success, radiance, and joy. It's about vitality and accomplishment, the warmth of achievement after the darkness of doubt." She took the card from me, her fingers brushing mine in a touch that still sent electricity through my veins. "It's about things coming to fruition, about happiness and truth revealed."

"And that's how you make a killer love story," I said, only half-joking. Our path to each other had been unconventional, to say the least—murder, deception, disposal of bodies—but we'd found our way to happiness, nonetheless.

I leaned across the counter to kiss her, a brief but tender meeting of lips that promised more later. As I pulled back, the bell above the door jingled again, and I turned to see Detective Inspector Harrow entering the shop.

My body tensed automatically, years of training kicked in at the sight of law enforcement. But I kept my expression neutral, my posture relaxed. As far as Harrow knew, I was just a butcher, engaged to the local witch who made excellent skincare products.

"Hello, Detective," Genie greeted him, her voice steady, though I could sense her unease. "What brings you by today?"

Harrow didn't answer immediately. Instead, he stepped aside, allowing three more officers to enter behind him. Their expressions were grim, their postures rigid with official purpose.

"What's this about?" Genie asked, her hand finding mine beneath the counter, squeezing tight.

Harrow's gaze shifted, not to Genie as I'd expected, but to Bernie, who had gone very still by the candle display.

"Bernadette Walsh," he said formally, "you're under arrest for the murder of Mr. John Hunter."

Bernie sighed, a sound of resignation rather than surprise, and held her hands out for the cuffs. "Took you long enough," she muttered.

Genie's confusion was palpable, her grip on my hand tightened to the point of pain. "Bernie? What's going on?"

But Bernie just shook her head slightly, her eyes

conveying a message I couldn't decipher as one of the officers stepped forward to read her the caution.

I watched, mind racing, as they cuffed Bernie and began to lead her toward the door. This made no sense. Bernie, the clumsy, chatty candle-maker with a penchant for adding too many herbs to everything? A murderer? And who the hell was John Hunter?

As they passed us, Bernie paused, looking directly at Genie. "Check the bottom drawer of my desk," she said quietly. "The one with the lock. Key's taped under the third shelf in my room."

Then she was gone, escorted out by the officers, leaving behind a stunned silence and the lingering scent of her candles.

Harrow was the last to leave, pausing at the door to look back at us. His expression was unreadable, but there was something in his eyes—a warning, perhaps, or a question.

"I'll be in touch," he said, and then he too was gone.

Genie turned to me, her face pale with shock. "Did you know?" she whispered. "About Bernie?"

I shook my head, as bewildered as she was. "No idea. I thought I knew everything about everyone in this town, but this..." I trailed off, at a loss for words.

The Sun card still lay on the counter between us, its bright imagery now seeming like a cruel joke. Vitality and accomplishment? Happiness and truth revealed? The only truth revealed today was that we didn't know Bernie as well as we'd thought.

"We need to check that drawer," Genie said, already moving toward the back of the shop.

I caught her arm, stopping her. "Wait. Think about this. If Bernie's involved in something serious enough to get her arrested for murder, do we really want to get tangled up in it?"

She looked at me like I'd grown a second head. "She's our friend, Ciarán. Of course, we're getting tangled up in it."

The End

Want to find out what happens with Bernie?
Turn the page for Chapter One of *Candles Make Great Alibis.*

Candles
make great
Alibis
CASSANDRA DOON
BOOK II

Cinnamon, Cloves & Chemical Warfare

Bernie

The thing about chloroform is that it has this really distinct sweet smell that most people associate with old-timey medical procedures or, you know, kidnapping. This is problematic when trying to create relaxation candles that are intended to help people sleep better. Did you know that chloroform was first used as an anesthetic in 1847? John Snow—not the Game of Thrones guy, the actual doctor—used it on Queen Victoria during childbirth. Fascinating stuff, really.

I'm currently hunched over my workstation in what used to be the conservatory of Genie's family estate, surrounded by wax shavings, essential oil bottles, and what I'm pretty sure is the fourth wick I've accidentally set on fire this morning. The conservatory is absolutely gorgeous—all glass panels and wrought iron, with morning light streaming through like something out of a fairy tale. Genie inherited this whole place when she was nineteen, and honestly, living here feels like being a character in a Gothic romance novel, except instead of brooding men in cravats, we have Daisy's collection of vibrators and my tendency to nearly burn everything down.

The estate is massive—like, genuinely massive. There's

the main house with its six bedrooms, the conservatory where I work, a library that smells of old leather and secrets, and gardens that stretch so far back I'm fairly certain there are parts Genie hasn't even explored yet. The whole place has a lived-in magic to it, as if the walls themselves are holding onto centuries of Alden family spells. Sometimes I catch glimpses of things moving in my peripheral vision, but when I turn to look, there's nothing there. Genie says it's just the house settling, but I'm pretty sure her ancestors are still hanging around, judging my candle-making technique.

I wish I had even a fraction of Genie's magical abilities. She makes it look so effortless—stirring intention into face creams, whispering spells over moisturizers, reading the future in tarot cards like she's checking the weather forecast. Meanwhile, I can barely light a candle without setting something on fire. Though, to be fair, that might be because I keep experimenting with volatile compounds.

The chloroform situation started innocently enough. I was researching natural sleep aids—lavender, chamomile, and valerian root—when I stumbled across some old medical journals discussing the anesthetic properties of various substances. Did you know that chloroform is actually $CHCl_3$? It's a trihalomethane, and while it's incredibly effective at inducing unconsciousness, it's also highly regulated because, well, it can kill you if you use too much. But in tiny amounts, properly diluted and mixed with the right carrier oils, it creates this lovely, drowsy effect that's much more reliable than melatonin.

The problem is the smell. Pure chloroform has this sickly sweet odor that screams "medical emergency" rather than "peaceful slumber." That's where the cinnamon and clove come in. Cinnamon contains cinnamaldehyde, which has this warm, spicy scent that's naturally comforting. Clove oil has eugenol, which not only smells amazing but also has mild anesthetic properties of its own. Together, they should mask the chloroform completely while actually enhancing the overall effect.

I measure out three drops of chloroform—and yes, I'm using proper laboratory pipettes because I'm not completely reckless—into my base wax mixture. The wax itself is a blend of soy and beeswax, because soy burns cleaner but beeswax holds scent better. It's all about the science of molecular bonding and volatility rates. Then I add five drops of cinnamon essential oil and three drops of clove oil, stirring counterclockwise, as Genie once mentioned that counter-clockwise is for banishing negative energy, and insomnia is definitely considered negative energy.

The scent that rises from the mixture is absolutely perfect—warm, spicy, with just a hint of sweetness that could easily be mistaken for vanilla. No trace of the chloroform at all. I'm actually quite proud of this formula. It took me six attempts to get the ratios right, and the first batch nearly knocked me unconscious when I leaned too close to smell it. Did you know that chloroform exposure can cause dizziness, nausea, and in extreme cases, cardiac arrest? It's all about dosage and exposure time.

I pour the mixture into a small mason jar, the kind Genie uses for her face masks. The wick—my fifth attempt this morning—sits perfectly centered, and I resist the urge to immediately light it to test the scent throw. Patience is not my strong suit, but I've learned that hot wax and chloroform don't mix well in enclosed spaces. Last time I tried that, I woke up three hours later with my face pressed against the workbench and a very concerned Daisy shaking my shoulders.

The clock on the conservatory wall—an antique thing with Roman numerals that probably belonged to Genie's great-great-grandmother—shows it's nearly ten-thirty. I promised Genie I'd stop by the shop this morning to help with inventory, and knowing her, she's probably already wondering where I am. She has this way of looking at me when I'm late, like she's trying to decide whether to be worried or exasperated. Usually, it's both.

I cap the chloroform bottle carefully and lock it in the small safe I installed under my workbench. Genie and Daisy think it's where I keep my "expensive essential oils," which isn't technically a lie. Chloroform is definitely expensive, and it is technically an oil-based compound. They don't need to know about my little experiments. They already worry enough about my tendency to set things on fire accidentally; imagine how they'd react if they knew I was working with controlled substances.

The walk from the conservatory to the main house takes me through the kitchen, which is this gorgeous farmhouse-style space with exposed beams and an Aga stove that's older than I am but still works perfectly. Daisy's coffee cup sits abandoned on the counter, lipstick stains around the rim in a shade I'm pretty sure is called "Fuck Me Red" or something equally Daisy-esque. There's a plate of what used to be scones next to it, though they look more like charcoal briquettes now. I may have gotten a bit distracted by my chloroform calculations this morning and forgotten about the oven timer.

I grab my bag—a canvas tote that's seen better days and is currently held together by determination and duct tape—and stuff the new candle inside, wrapped carefully in tissue paper. I also grab a handful of the less-burned scones because Genie never eats enough breakfast, and Bernie's First Law of Friendship states that you should always bring food when visiting someone who's probably surviving on coffee and spite.

The front door of the estate is this massive oak thing with iron hinges that creak like something out of a horror movie. Genie keeps saying she's going to oil them, but I think she secretly likes the dramatic effect. The door opens onto a gravel driveway that curves through gardens that are equal parts beautiful and slightly wild. There are roses everywhere—climbing roses, bush roses, roses in colors I'm pretty sure don't occur naturally. Genie's grandmother was apparently quite the gardener, and the roses have been growing here for decades; some of them have reached heights that seem botanically impossible.

The walk into town takes about fifteen minutes if you stick to the main road, but I prefer the footpath that cuts through the woods behind the estate. It's longer, but it's also more interesting. The path winds between oak trees that are probably centuries old, their branches forming a canopy so thick that even in daylight, it feels like walking through a green cathedral. Sometimes I see things moving in the shadows between the trees—quick flashes of movement that could be rabbits or squirrels, but feel like something else entirely.

Did you know that the area around Pendle Hill has one of the highest concentrations of reported supernatural activity in England? It's been that way since the witch trials in 1612, when ten people were executed for witchcraft. Most historians agree that the trials were probably more about local politics and religious tensions than actual witchcraft, but the legends persist.

The footpath emerges onto the main street just a few doors down from Alden Alchemy, and I can see Genie through the shop window, moving around behind the counter with that efficient grace she has when she's in work mode. The shop itself is gorgeous—all exposed brick and reclaimed wood, with herbs hanging from the ceiling and shelves lined with amber glass jars that catch the light like tiny suns. It smells like lavender and rosemary, with a hint of something else I can never quite identify, but it makes me feel calm and slightly drowsy.

The bell above the door jingles as I push inside, and I immediately trip over the threshold because apparently my coordination hasn't improved since yesterday. The bag of scones goes flying, and I watch in horror as my carefully wrapped candle arcs through the air in what feels like slow motion.

"Genie! The good news is I didn't burn the kitchen down," I announce, trying to inject some enthusiasm into my voice while simultaneously calculating the trajectory of my chloro-form candle and whether it's going to land somewhere that will raise questions.

Genie looks up from whatever she's doing behind the counter, and I can see her already bracing herself for what-ever chaos I'm about to unleash. "That means there's bad news," she says, and honestly, her ability to read me is both impressive and slightly terrifying.

"I tried lighting a candle with my boobs. For Reels." This is technically true—I did try that yesterday, though it was more of a scientific experiment about heat transfer and surface area than actual content creation. The results were... educational.

"That's the sentence that gets me locked up for accessory to idiocy," Genie replies, but I can see the corner of her mouth twitching like she's trying not to smile.

I beam at her because, honestly, making Genie almost smile feels like a major accomplishment. Then I turn to fish a scone out of my bag and immediately knock over a display of night cream with my elbow. The sound of glass clinking fills the shop, and I watch a single jar roll across the floor like it's personally offended by my existence.

"Bernie," Genie sighs, and there's that look again—the perfect blend of worry and exasperation that I've become so familiar with. "This is why we can't have nice things. Or candles. Or Reels."

"Technically," I say, pulling out what I think used to be a scone but now looks more like a geological formation, "this is your fault. You left the good matches next to the cinnamon oil."

It's not really her fault, obviously. The matches were nowhere near the cinnamon oil, and even if they had been, that wouldn't explain why I thought using my cleavage as a candle lighter was a good idea. But deflection is one of my core survival strategies, right up there with random fact-spouting and aggressive optimism.

"Because obviously, the cinnamon oil was going to light itself on fire and give us all warm hugs," Genie says, and I love how she can make sarcasm sound like a form of affection.

I crouch down to help clean up the mess I've made, carefully avoiding the area where my chloroform candle landed. It seems to have rolled under a display case, which is probably for the best. The last thing I need is Genie examining my latest creation too closely. She has this way of looking at things—really looking at them—that makes me think she sees more than she lets on.

"I brought you breakfast," I offer, holding up the charcoal scone. "It's... rustic."

"Bernie, this isn't rustic. This is what happens when carbon and regret have a baby."

I laugh because she's not wrong, but also because there's something so comforting about Genie's particular brand of brutal honesty. Living with her and Daisy has taught me that there are different kinds of families—the ones you're born into, and the ones you choose. And sometimes, if you're really lucky, the ones you choose will let you live in their magical ancestral estate and only judge you a little bit when you accidentally create chemical weapons in their conservatory.

The shop door chimes again, and Daisy walks in looking like she's just stepped off the cover of a magazine dedicated to beautiful women who've had excellent sex. Her hair is perfectly tousled, her makeup is somehow still flawless despite whatever activities she got up to last night, and she's carrying her iced coffee like it's a sacred artifact.

"If I don't get to drink this caffeine and a face mask in the next five minutes, I'm hexing a man," she announces, and I believe her completely.

"Line forms behind me," Genie replies, and I wonder if she's joking or if there's actually a queue of men somewhere waiting to be hexed.

I watch Daisy examine one of Genie's eye serums, and I can't help but feel a little envious of how effortlessly beautiful she is. Not just physically—though she's definitely that—but the way she moves through the world with such confidence, like she knows exactly who she is and what she wants. I've never felt that kind of certainty about anything, except maybe the molecular structure of various compounds and the fact that adding chloroform to candles is probably not something I should mention in casual conversation.

"Is this the new eye serum?" Daisy asks, and Genie explains something about puffiness and poetic justice, which sounds very Genie-esque.

I'm only half-listening because I'm distracted by the way the morning light hits the jars on the shelves, creating little rainbows that dance across the walls. There's something magical about this place—not just because Genie is literally magical, but because it feels like a space where impossible things are possible. Where a clumsy candle-maker can live in a fairy-tale estate with a witch and a sex goddess and somehow fit in, even if she does occasionally knock things over and experiment with controlled substances.

Did you know that the word "serendipity" was coined by Horace Walpole in 1754? He based it on a Persian fairy tale called "The Three Princes of Serendip," about princes who consistently made fortunate discoveries by accident. That's what living here feels like—like I'm constantly stumbling into good fortune, even when I'm literally stumbling into display cases.

The bell jingles again, and Mrs. Beecham shuffles in with her usual air of knowing everyone's business better than they do themselves. She's one of those elderly women who somehow manages to be both sweet and slightly terrifying, like she could either bake you cookies or curse your blood-line, depending on her mood.

I listen as she talks to Genie about hand cream and arthritis, but my attention keeps drifting to the way Genie moves around the shop. There's something so purposeful about everything she does, like every gesture is part of some larger spell. When she hands Mrs. Beecham the jar of cream, her fingers brush against the older woman's hand for just a moment, and I swear I see something pass between them— not visible, exactly, but felt.

Then Mrs. Beecham mentions something about new butchers in town, and I perk up because new people are always interesting. Especially when Daisy immediately starts making innuendos about meat handling, which causes me to snort-laugh so hard that I knock over another jar.

"For fuck's sake, Bernie," Genie sighs, reaching for the broom that I'm starting to think she keeps specifically for my visits. "That's the third one this week."

"Sorry," I mumble, my face heating up. "But Daisy's right. We should check out the new butcher shop. For... meat purposes."

"Meat purposes," Genie repeats in that flat tone that means she's trying not to laugh. "Sure."

And honestly, I am curious about the new butchers. Not for the same reasons as Daisy—my relationship with my own sexuality is complicated at best—but because new people mean new stories, new perspectives, new possibilities. Plus, I've been thinking about expanding my candle business, maybe creating some more masculine scents. If these butchers are as attractive as Mrs. Beecham suggests, they might be willing to provide feedback on my latest creations.

Well, maybe not the chloroform ones. Those are definitely staying between me and my secret nighttime side hustle.

As I help Genie sweep up the glass, I catch a glimpse of my reflection in the shop's antique mirror. I look exactly like what I am—a slightly chaotic woman in her mid-twenties who's probably too enthusiastic about chemistry for her own good. My hair is escaping from its ponytail in about six different directions, there's a smudge of wax on my cheek, and my cardigan has definitely seen better days.

But there's something else in my reflection, something I don't usually see. I look... happy. Genuinely, unselfconsciously happy. Like I belong here, in this magical shop with these incredible women who somehow tolerate my tendency to break things and ask too many questions about molecular structures.

Maybe I don't have Genie's witchy powers or Daisy's supernatural confidence, but I have this—this strange, wonderful life in a fairy-tale house with friends who feel like family. And if I occasionally spike my candles with controlled substances, well, everyone needs a hobby.

The morning sun streams through the shop windows, catching the dust motes in the air and making them dance like tiny spirits. Somewhere in the distance, I can hear the church bells chiming eleven o'clock, and I realize I've been here for over an hour without setting anything on fire or causing any major disasters.

That might be a new personal record.

"So," I say, carefully placing the last piece of broken glass in Genie's dustpan, "when do we go check out these mysterious Irish butchers?"

Genie looks at me with that expression that means she's calculating the probability of me causing an international incident, but then she shrugs. "After lunch. And Bernie?"

"Yeah?"

"Maybe leave the experimental candles at home."

I nod enthusiastically, even though we both know I'm definitely bringing at least one candle with me. After all, what's the point of having a hobby if you can't share it with new people?

Even if they don't know about the chloroform.

Acknowledgments

To my readers—old friends and new faces—thank you for stepping into this wild experiment with me. This isn't my usual genre, but inspiration has a wicked way of grabbing me by the throat and not letting go.

Genie's story started as a one-off, a random spark lit by the real-life lady who handed out poison to unhappy wives with murderous intent (what a muse, eh?). I thought I'd dabble, write the one, and be done. But books are demanding little beasts, and this one refused to stay quiet.

Thank you for trusting me as I strayed off the beaten path —your support means more than poison in a pretty little vial.

About Cassandra Doon

Cassandra Doon hails from New South Wales, Australia, where she was nurtured between the bustling streets of Sydney and the serene snowy mountains of Tumut. Today, she finds inspiration in the breathtaking Scenic Rim of Queensland's Gold Coast. A versatile author with a lifelong passion for storytelling, Cassandra has penned over 26 novels and 5 children's books, exploring a variety of genres. Known for her daydreaming and a head often lost in the clouds, she admits to being more at home in her fictional worlds than on social media. Outside of her literary pursuits, Cassandra is a devoted mother to two boys, dedicating her days to their endless energy as both a soccer mom and Pokémon master.

Also by Cassandra Doon

The 4 Seats Series:

Matteo

Felix

Gabriel

Catcher

Ruhn & Frost

* * *

The 4 Seats Extended World:

Aces

Obsessed Shadows

Adrian Romano

The Moretti Brothers (Coming Soon)

Standalone:

The Kings of Willows Peak

Damaged Goods

Tuesday May

The Devils Cut

The Detectives Mate

Dark Dahlias Rite

A Field of Tulips and Bones

Follow Poppy

To Her

Blood moon

Unit 9

Broken Creek Ranch

Eclipsion (Coming Soon)

The Dead Zone (Coming Soon)

* * *

Oakland Harbour Series:

Missing

Found

Home

* * *

The Boys Series

The Boys Of Hastings House

The Boys of Bittersweet College

The Boys of Nightsbane Academy (Coming Soon)

The Boys of Winchester U (Coming Soon)

* * *

Second Chances Series:

The Waterfall

Wicked Bonds

Writhe (Coming Soon)

The Restaurant (Coming Soon)

* * *

Umbravivus Series:

The Lost Kingdom of Umbravivus (Coming Soon)

The Crowned King of Umbravivus (Coming Soon)

* * *

Butcher and the Witch Series:

Poison is always in the Prettiest Bottle

Candles make Great Alibis

Socials with a Slice of Pie

Also By C.L. Doon

The Rain Dang Detective Series:

Still Waters

Moving Waters

Standalone:

Second Chances at The Riverbend Café 🎧

Lavender (Coming Soon)